jo wilde

Just the Two of Us

FOREVER

New York Boston

Forever
Hachette Book Group
1290 Avenue of the Americas, New York, NY 10104
read-forever.com
twitter.com/readforeverpub

Originally published in Great Britain in 2020 by Piatkus, an imprint of Little, Brown Book Group, Carmelite House, 50 Victoria Embankment, London EC4Y 0DZ

First Forever Trade Edition: April 2022

Forever is an imprint of Grand Central Publishing. The Forever name and logo are trademarks of Hachette Book Group, Inc.

The publisher is not responsible for websites (or their content) that are not owned by the publisher.

The Hachette Speakers Bureau provides a wide range of authors for speaking events. To find out more, go to www.hachettespeakersbureau.com or call (866) 376-6591.

Library of Congress Control Number: 2021945929

ISBNs: 978-1-5387-5506-8 (trade paperback); 978-1-5387-5505-1 (ebook)

Printed in the United States of America

LSC-C

Printing 1, 2022

This book is for Sarah-Jane, Paul, Ella and Joe with love.
Here's to black dust, tropical cocktails, diving boards,
quite a bit of rain and a huge amount of laughter!

Chapter One

Day One

Julie Marshall stepped out of the shiny offices and glanced furtively up and down the busy street. The brown envelope seemed to burn her fingers and she shoved it hastily into her shoulder bag, grateful that she'd thought to bring the big zebra-patterned one she knew Michael hated. It seemed apt. Once she'd handed the papers over, it wouldn't matter what Michael hated. She'd be free to do and live and be however she wished.

"Free!" she said out loud, trying to convince herself. A passing couple looked at her askance. They were young and handsome and their fingers were interlaced with tight confidence. "Don't worry," she threw at them. "I'm not drunk, just getting divorced."

They scurried away, pulling even closer together as if she was some sort of curse they needed to ward off. Maybe she was.

"Free," she said again, quieter this time, but it still didn't sound right. It still didn't fight off the other words struggling to batter their way out of her head: alone, useless, failure.

She shivered and turned determinedly toward the car park. It wasn't a failure to end her marriage. It took strength to admit a relationship wasn't working anymore, or so everyone said. The problem was, she didn't feel strong. She was doing a good impression—walking strong, talking strong, acting strong—but underneath she felt as stable as a vodka jelly.

Earlier, when she'd gone into the estate agent's to pick up details of flats for rent, she'd been so shaky she'd dropped half the leaflets. The young man had looked at her with such concern that she'd blurted out that her daughter had had a nasty break-up. She'd been instantly ashamed of the lie but she was even more ashamed of the truth—that somehow, without noticing, she'd slid from having the sort of marriage she'd smugly known other people envied to the sort that, well, that wasn't really a marriage at all.

She blinked ferociously. She wasn't going to cry. She wasn't going to go back to the dark days. No way. She'd dragged herself out of that mire and she owed it to herself to *stay* out of it. She still had things to do with her life and she wasn't going to let some idea of failure hold her back. People divorced every day and felt better for it. Her own sister had been like a different person when she'd emerged from her marriage ten years ago, hadn't she?

Julie pushed thoughts of Clare aside. Her little sister spent her days lurching from one unsuitable relationship to the next, but that wasn't how Julie was going to do it. She wasn't leaving this man to find another, but to find herself. She groaned at the cliché and fumbled in her bag for the plastic ticket that would let her into the impossibly secure car park. The envelope was in the way and she pushed it impatiently aside as she scrabbled amongst the more usual detritus for the ticket. Her fingers brushed the fluffy ball of a key ring that Adam had given her for Christmas last year—"Let's see you lose this, Mum"—and her heart juddered. She hoped the kids wouldn't be too upset.

They're not kids, Julie, she reminded herself. The girls had long since left home, and, with Adam in his fourth and final year at university, he might as well have done. They were grown-ups

2

with their own lives now and she couldn't stay miserable just for the pretense of a happy home.

Again the tears threatened. Again she pushed them back behind her eyelids. She hated that her marriage had turned to dust, but she no longer had any idea how to hold it together. These days she and Michael shared little more than a front door. They slept in different rooms and managed to keep themselves so busy in their jobs and separate social lives that they could go days without actually seeing each other.

Julie couldn't remember the last time they'd had a proper conversation, one that went beyond informing the other that they'd taken the bins out or that dinner was in the fridge. They cooked for each other but rarely ate together. They took the clothes off the washing line but never off each other's bodies. They didn't even bloody argue any more. She'd tried to fix things over the last few years—she really had—but she'd accepted now that their marriage was beyond repair. And with their thirty-fifth anniversary just a month away, she had to do something. Celebrating a dead marriage would be nothing more than a farce, and it was time to face up to that. Divorce was for the best.

But that didn't mean it wasn't sad.

Her fingers closed gratefully around the plastic ticket and she pressed it to the door pad. Nothing. The big gray door stayed resolutely shut. She turned it over, pressed it again. Still nothing.

"Please let me in," she begged. The door paid no attention. For the third time that afternoon, Julie blinked back tears.

"Pain in the arse, aren't they?" a cheerful voice said, and she turned to see an older woman bustling up behind her. "Just a minute." She dumped handfuls of shopping bags on the floor, gesturing self-consciously to them as she dug for her own ticket. "Supplies. In case we go into whaddyacallit—lockdown."

"Lockdown?" Julie asked. "It won't come to that, surely?"

The woman gave her a sideways look. "Where've you been, dear?"

With a divorce lawyer, Julie wanted to say, but the woman was far too smiley to be hit with that sort of unpleasant detail. She felt foolish suddenly—the world was going mad and she was fretting about one little marriage. But it was *her* marriage, or it had been, and right now it felt all-consuming.

She looked down at the woman's bags, spotting toilet roll, a multipack of custard creams and a large bottle of Baileys.

"That's in case we run out of milk," her new friend said, bending and patting the liqueur as she might a small dog. "It's lovely on cornflakes. Now, here we go!"

She pulled a ticket from her bag and held it up to the pad. The door sprung obligingly open.

"How did you do that?" Julie asked.

"Magic!" The woman smiled and waved Julie ahead of her as she gathered up her shopping. "Did you validate your ticket when you arrived?"

Julie groaned. "Probably not. I'm hopeless at things like that. My husband's always saying…" She stopped. *My husband!* For thirty-four years she'd had a husband. Soon it would just be her.

"Are you OK?" The woman was looking at her in concern, and Julie realized she'd stopped dead halfway up the concrete stairs.

"How will I get out?" she asked, feeling ridiculously shaky again.

"Go to the office, dear; they'll soon sort it."

Julie smiled her thanks and stumbled in the direction indicated, but her thoughts were back at the shiny lawyer's offices, and she clutched her zebra-print bag and its dark contents close against her as she approached the car park attendant.

"I wonder if you could help me?" she asked in her politest voice. "I've messed up, I'm afraid, and I really need to get out."

"Course I can, love," the burly bloke agreed with a grin. "Follow me."

Julie did as she was told, suddenly wondering if she'd actually be better off stuck in this car park than heading for home. It was one thing getting the divorce papers from the lawyers; quite another to hand them over to her husband. How on earth had it come to this?

Half an hour later, Julie pulled off the village high street and onto their quiet cul-de-sac, trepidation rising within her. In the spring sunshine her home looked far too welcoming for comfort. The cherry tree in the middle of the tiny front lawn was just starting to blossom, and the pots either side of the porch were also sending up promising green shoots. She killed the engine and sat on in the car, gazing at the place she'd called home for the last twenty years. It wasn't anything fancy, but it certainly looked good against the blank little flats whose promises of "bijou living" and "cleverly designed spaces" were lurking in her bag alongside the divorce papers.

To get the space they'd needed for their growing family, they'd had to drop their dreams of a cutesy cottage in favor of a 1950s box, but Julie had rapidly grown fond of the smooth white walls and wooden bay windows. When Michael had added a pretty timber-framed porch in an early rush of energy, they'd smugly pronounced it better than any cottage, and it had certainly proved a happy home. Bright curtains hung at every window, and over the side gate you could just catch a glimpse of the large back garden that led out onto the fields beyond. With three energetic kids, all that outdoor space had been the clincher, and they'd made an offer on it twenty minutes after the first viewing. It had been one of the best decisions they'd ever made. But recently her heart had dropped every time she'd pulled onto the drive, and that couldn't go on.

Grasping her bag, she leapt out of the car and let herself in through the front door. It was deathly silent inside; gone were the days when her home reverberated with the happy noises of family life. Michael, however, should be here. Yesterday he'd announced that his engineering company was ordering everyone to work from home, and he was going to set up office in Briony's room. The thought of having him around all the time was what had sent her to collect the papers from the lawyer at last; now all she had to do was hand them over, pick a flat and leave. And with the government bringing in measures in response to the virus and normality starting to shut down, the sooner she did that the better.

She stepped cautiously inside, her heart beating as if she were about to go on some scary fairground ride. There was no sign of her husband in the living room or the kitchen, and it didn't feel quite right to shout a cheery "hello" as a precursor to delivering an affidavit of a goodbye. He must be up in his new office, she thought, and was turning to head for the stairs when a movement outside caught her eye.

Michael was out in the garden, bending down to feed something to Mr. Nibbles, Briony's ancient rabbit. He was chatting unselfconsciously to him and Julie watched, feeling strangely voyeuristic. Her husband was smiling, and she realized that she didn't see that often these days. He mainly nodded or grunted or just shuffled past her. Any words they did exchange were terse and practical; gone were the days when he'd chatted to her as he was doing to the rabbit now.

Sadness pierced her and she clutched at her bag, hearing the envelope crackle under her arm as he rose and came back toward the house. She knew he'd spotted her because his body tensed up. It was sad, but it was also reality; they'd grown apart and it was pointless pretending otherwise.

"You're back," he said gruffly as he came through the door.

"I'm back, yes."

"Nice day?"

"Hmm."

He edged past her, making for the stairs, and she swallowed and forced herself to speak again.

"Actually, no, not that nice. Michael, I need to talk to you."

He stopped, back to her. "Now?"

"Ideally, yes."

She reached into her bag and her fingers closed around the envelope. No point in dragging this out; she just had to get on with it. So why were her hands shaking? "It's important," she stuttered.

He turned toward her with a frown and she braced herself for him to snap.

"Are you OK, Julie?"

To her surprise, his voice was soft, kind. He'd always been kind, actually. She could remember her mum saying that when she'd first brought him home: "Oh, well done, love—you've picked a kind man. They're very much the best sort." She swallowed again.

"I'm OK. Well, actually..."

She tried to take the envelope out of her bag, but it felt impossible, as if there was a *Star Wars*-style force around her, stopping her from delivering it to him. Ridiculous! Taking a deep breath, she pulled it out decisively just as Michael's phone rang and he looked down.

"It's my boss," he said with an apologetic grimace. "I'd better take it."

"But..."

"Can we talk later? After the PM's briefing maybe?"

"The briefing. Of course. Let's talk after."

He lifted the phone and cut off the bleat. "Geoff! How are you?"

Julie stood there, divorce papers behind her back, as he sidled apologetically off down the corridor. The rush of relief was enormous—except, of course, that it meant the deed still had to be done. Ah well. Just having the papers in the house made the decision more real, and a couple of hours to get used to that wouldn't hurt. She slowly drew the little sheaf of property details out of her bag. Perhaps, if she chose a couple, she could set up viewings for next week.

Yes, she decided, as she heard Michael's voice rumbling away up in Briony's room, she'd get changed, make some dinner and settle her nerves a little. Then, after listening to whatever the PM had to say, she and Michael could talk. It was time to find a new, separate path into the future, and hard as that was, it would surely be better for both of them in the long run.

Chapter Two

Julie stared at the television, seeing the word scrolling determinedly across the bottom in shouty red script.

Lockdown.

Above it, the prime minister was speaking into the camera with careful calm about "essential shopping trips" and "key workers," but his words blurred into each other and all she could focus on was that one word.

She shifted on the sofa and glanced at the cushion beneath which the envelope of divorce papers lurked.

"No leaving the house?" she stuttered.

"Except for exercise."

"From when?"

"From now," Michael said. "From right now."

Julie thought of the woman in the car park. She'd be smugly at home with her Baileys now, whilst Julie was stuck here with Michael, the one person she was trying to escape. There was some horrible cosmic irony to this.

"What about the kids?" she cried.

He raised an eyebrow. "What about them?"

"Well, they'll want to come home, surely."

"I doubt that. Sophie will be quite happy snuggled up with Leo in the love nest."

"Don't call it that."

"Why not?"

"It's patronizing."

"It's nice. And they call it that themselves. Leo even made a sign for the door."

"He did? And Sophie let him put it up?"

"Yep. I saw it when I went round last week to mend their loo."

Julie just about managed to stop herself grinding her teeth. Their own downstairs loo had been broken for months; what was he doing mending Sophie's? Leo, her husband of six months, was a potter, for heaven's sake. He had to be good with his hands, didn't he? But then it was nice that Michael was spending time with Soph. Julie would have gone with him if she'd known, if he'd bothered to say. She'd been so busy with spring deliveries at the shop that she'd not seen her elder daughter for weeks, despite her only living twenty minutes away. And now, it seemed, she wouldn't be able to see her for weeks more. Maybe months. It didn't bear thinking about.

"The shop!" she cried.

"You'll have to close it," Michael said.

"I can't."

"The PM says that everyone who can work from home should."

"But *I* can't."

"Why not? You used to."

Julie leapt up. She could feel panic rising and strode across the room to throw open the doors to the conservatory. She'd taken up floristry just after Adam had started school, leaving her with starkly empty days, and had initially done home commissions from a camping table in this sunny room. She'd been so excited at every order back then, but now the thought of working here instead of in the bustling shop with Clare filled her with dread.

Building up her business had got her out of the dark days a few years ago. What if, without it, she returned to that confused, angry mess of a person?

"Did he say shops definitely have to close?" she asked, nodding to the TV.

"I'm afraid so."

"Great!"

She flung herself down on the sofa again. The divorce papers rustled beneath her and her fingers twitched. Perhaps now was the perfect time to present them to him. At least then they'd know where they stood. At least then they could legitimately avoid each other all day instead of pretending it was just their busy lives that forced them apart. And yet somehow it felt wrong to file for divorce on the brink of a global pandemic; not in the Dunkirk spirit the prime minister was urging. There were more pressing concerns than her marriage now, not the least of them being their children.

"Briony's in London, Mike."

"Yes."

"Maybe she should come home? It's bound to be safer in Derbyshire."

He shook his head. "I doubt she'll do that, Julie. She's a—"

"Biochemist, I know."

God, did she know. Michael never stopped going on about it. She could still remember how pleased he'd been when Briony had shown scientific inclinations like his beloved parents, both research chemists. But it wasn't such good news now.

"Surely they'll shut down her lab?" she said.

"Doubt it. They'll need them all for research and she'll be invaluable. She did her dissertation on vaccinology, remember?"

"Of course I remember!" She didn't, not really. She'd never taken the same meticulous interest in the intricacies of Briony's scientific progress as Michael, but she was still very proud of her middle child. And very worried about her. "Even so, she'd be safer here."

"She would," Michael agreed sadly, "but I doubt that'll make much difference to Bri." He glanced at the TV, where *Lockdown* was still scrolling along the bottom in red, then back to Julie. "Is this really happening, Jules?"

Her breath caught at the pet name. He hardly ever called her that these days. Hardly ever called her anything.

"Hard to believe, isn't it?"

"Together we will beat this," the PM was insisting from the TV, but Julie wasn't sure she liked the look of her own personal "together." If she was going to be stuck in the family home, it would be better to have at least some of the family here too. She should speak to Adam. They'd already canceled school exams and now they were saying universities were shutting down. Their youngest child would have nowhere to live but here, thank God.

"I'm going to call Adam," she said. "If they're shutting the universities, he'll have to come home"

Michael nodded, his face softening. "Good. Yes. That would be good. Nice to know one of them is safe."

She gave him a weak smile. At least they had their love for their children to hold them together in these strange days. It was a gossamer web now, but webs were surprisingly strong. She picked up her phone, flicked to her favorites and swiped on her son.

"Mum. Hi."

"Hi, sweetheart. How's things?"

"Mad! They're closing the uni down. It's chaos. No idea what they're going to do about finals. I need those exams to qualify as a surveyor."

"What are they saying?"

"No one's sure yet. I think it might go on our continual assessment marks, so I should be just about OK."

"Just about?"

"Come on, Mum, everyone has a couple of bad assignments."

Julie bit back the obvious response; now was not the time.

"When will you know?"

"No idea. The lecturers are going to have to work on it, I think. Still—no exams, hey? Bonus!"

She could hear him smiling down the phone. He was a sunny child, Adam; always had been. It would be good to have him home.

"When are you coming back, then? Do we need to fetch you? Surely even in a lockdown we're allowed to pick up our own son?"

"Erm…" Something in his voice changed. She heard it as loudly as the crunching of rusty gears.

"Adam?"

"I'm not sure, Mum."

"Not sure if we're allowed?"

He swallowed audibly. "Not sure if I'm coming back."

"What?" She felt Michael staring at her and instinctively turned away. "What do you mean, Adam? Where else will you go?"

"I'm thinking maybe to Chelsea's place."

"Chelsea's?" Julie pictured Adam's girlfriend, a bubbly blonde from somewhere in Kent. "She has a place?"

An awkward pause.

"No. But, er, her parents do."

A chill ran down Julie's spine.

"You're going to her parents' house?"

"Maybe. I don't know yet, Mum. But if we're going to be locked down for ages, I'd like to, you know, be with her."

"Right. Course. Yes. I didn't realize it was that serious."

"Mum, we've been going out for three years."

"Is it that long? Right. Good. Well, how about Chelsea comes here? There's loads of space with just me and Dad.

13

Sophie's got her own place, and Briony will have to stay in London."

"I know. I spoke to her earlier."

"You did?" It always confounded Julie when her children spoke to each other. She loved it, but it was odd too that they had connections that didn't revolve around her. Stupid really. "How is she?"

"Focused on her work. You know Bri—she relishes a challenge."

"She does. I just hope she's safe." Her voice caught and he must have heard it.

"Are you OK, Mum? Is Dad?"

She pulled herself together, forced herself to be cheerful for him.

"We're fine, sweetheart. And as I said, there's loads of space here if you and Chelsea want to come up. It'd be lovely to have you."

Silence. She could hear shuffling sounds and suspected Adam's girlfriend was next to him and that they were exchanging some sort of looks.

"That's very kind, Mum," Adam said eventually. "But Chelsea's parents are all set. Her little sister is lonely."

"*I'm* lonely." It was out before Julie could stop it. She bit furiously at her lip. "Not lonely. I don't mean lonely. Just that I'd like to see you."

"I'm sorry." His voice tightened. "We've made plans. And Chelsea's family are nice. Normal, you know."

"Normal?" The word iced around her heart. "What do you mean? Are we not normal, Adam?"

"Course. Course you are. I didn't mean we're not normal. They're just fun. Not that you're not fun, obviously. It'll just be good to, you know, see somewhere different."

"Different? Right."

He wasn't coming home. Her baby boy wasn't coming home to her; her nest truly was empty. Julie clutched her spare hand into her hair, as if she might hold onto herself that way, but suddenly her whole body seemed to be shaking, the way it had been threatening to do ever since she'd stepped out of the lawyer's offices.

"Mum?" Adam sounded scared now.

"It's fine, Adam," she forced out. "You have fun with Chelsea and her family. That'll be nice for you. They live by the sea, right?"

"Right!" He snatched at this. "At least we can get out on the beach, hey?"

"I guess so. Lovely. That'll be lovely."

"Yes. And we'll come and see you as soon as we can, as soon as all this is over, yeah?"

"Course." She had to end this wretched conversation before she said something she regretted. Or cried. "Great. Give her my love and say thank you to her parents from me, will you? From us."

"I will. And we can FaceTime and stuff, yeah?" He was falling over himself to be nice to her now and she couldn't stand it.

"We can. Got to go, Adam. Take care, sweetheart."

"You too, Mum." And he was gone, doubtless to pour out his relief to blinking Chelsea and her "normal" family.

Julie looked at Michael, sitting straight-backed in his stupid armchair.

"He's not coming?" he asked.

She shook her head.

"So it's…just the two of us, then?"

Julie drew in a deep breath and felt the divorce papers crackle beneath her.

"Just the two of us," she confirmed.

Never had those words sounded more ominous.

Chapter Three

Michael Marshall went into his garage, closed the door behind him and drew in a long, deep breath. Julie was tearing around the house like a whirlwind and he was scared of being caught up in the center of the rush. She'd always had so much energy, his wife. She was like a dynamo, generating it out of seemingly nowhere. When they'd first been together, he'd watched in awe, loving the way she swept him off his utterly grounded feet and into adventures and experiences he'd never known possible. These days, though, she mainly just made him feel tired. And weirdly tearful.

He pushed himself away from the door and whipped the cover off his Moto Guzzi motorcycle, once his dad's pride and joy and now his own. He'd cried when his dad, Ken, had died of a sudden heart attack. He'd cried buckets. And Julie had held him close and wiped his eyes gently and told him to "let it all out." So he had. But that had been different from the strange half-tears that seemed to niggle up out of him at the strangest times these days. That was why the bike was good. You could cry on a bike, because who could distinguish tears from the moisture pushed out of your eyes by good old-fashioned speed?

He patted the Guzzi. She was called Gertie—his dad's choice—and she was a V7 Sport, a classic. He'd love a ride out right now, but he was waiting on a new oil pump from Gary at the garage, and until that came, the poor old girl was grounded. Locked down—like him.

Michael sighed and went over to his spanner set, running his fingers along the perfectly ordered tools to find the right size. He wasn't sure why he was bothering, but the action was reassuring all the same. So many times he'd mended this bike. Italian engineers knew a bit about style but rather less about reliability, and he wasn't sure there was any part of the engine left from when his father had gifted Gertie to him on his eighteenth birthday. That made him sad, but the body was still the same, de-rusted, repainted, but still there. Still beautiful.

"Soon have you sorted, Gertie old girl," he muttered. "Soon have you back on the road."

Except would he? If they were in lockdown, would Gary be able to get him the pump? He'd have to call him, push for it whilst he still could. Then at least he'd be able to head out for a ride if things got too much. If Julie got too much.

He thought of his wife and was hit by the all-too-familiar wave of sadness that seemed to be the only emotion he could usefully call up toward her these days. Things were very, very wrong between them. He might not be the most astute of men, but he wasn't stupid.

Silently he prayed that the florist's wouldn't have to be shut for too many weeks. Julie loved that shop. She'd lavished so much care and attention on it since she'd opened it back in 2006, and it had done very well. She'd won awards, been featured in magazines and, of course, turned quite a profit. But who was going to buy flowers in a lockdown?

"Everyone," he heard Julie's voice say in his head. "If you're shut inside, you'll need beautiful flowers to keep you sane."

They didn't seem like a necessity to Michael, but as she'd pointed out to him on many occasions, he was useless at appreciating beautiful things. Except for the bike, of course. Even Julie had admitted that the bike was beautiful. He could still remember her tumbling out of a café in Budapest on the very street corner where he'd chosen to stop to glug down some water. She'd come bouncing over to admire Gertie in tiny shorts and the most glorious red top, and that evening she'd turned up at his campsite claiming she'd wanted to see the bike again. Hours later, straddling him, she'd admitted that perhaps he'd been the greater draw. He'd not been able to believe his luck. In many ways, he still couldn't.

Julie was a whirlwind, yes, but a warm, colorful, exotic one. She'd brought light to his rather dull life, and if it had sometimes dazzled him, he'd been happy to take that. A studious only child of relatively serious parents, he'd never really experienced the sort of exuberant, impulsive approach Julie took to life, and he'd loved it. They'd all loved it. When his dad had died just two weeks shy of their wedding, Julie had wanted to cancel but Michael and his mum had refused.

"We need happiness," he'd told Julie through tears. "We need it or we'll both go under. *You* are that happiness."

It had been true. Julie had got him through that terrible time with her love and her care and her natural joy. The wedding had been bittersweet but beautiful all the same, and they'd had a wonderful honeymoon on the bike, even if they'd had to cut the trip short to be back for the funeral. They'd never made it to the Greek islands, but it hadn't mattered. They could have gone to Skegness and he'd have been happy as long as she was there.

Suddenly restless, he jumped up and opened the door. The sun was shining across the lawn, lighting up the increasingly shaggy grass. He'd have to mow it.

"Sorry, Nibbles," he apologized to the rabbit, which, true to

18

its name, was nibbling away at the long fronds trapped beneath its cage. How old must the creature be? He grinned at the memory of Briony's war of attrition to secure her beloved pet. That girl knew how to achieve a goal, be it a rabbit or a bio-chemistry degree. She got that from his mother, Bett, who'd always had the same focus and scientific skill as her middle grandchild. He must call her. She'd be all alone in the house, having steadfastly refused to so much as look at another man since his dad's death, and at her age that was a worry.

The sudden slam of a door inside the house made him jump. Julie. She always slammed doors, more teenage than their teenagers.

"Michael?" To his surprise, she shouted out for him. He went back to the bike, crouching instinctively behind it. "Michael, are you there? Clare says we should do online flower deliveries. She wants to paint the logo on her car and I thought you might have some paint we could—" The garage door flew open and there she was, exuberant in a bright yellow jumper. "Michael? What are you doing down there?"

He peered up at her. "Mending Gertie, of course."

"Of course." She peered at the Guzzi and gave a little sigh, then looked up at his shelves. "Paint?"

He put the spanner down on the side and fetched the little pot of metallic red he used to touch up Gertie's glorious body-work. In truth, he was reluctant to hand it over in case he couldn't match her color again, but even he could see that would be churlish.

"Here." He passed it to her.

"Thanks." She took it and tapped on the lid, unusually twitchy. "Got to do what we can to keep the business going, right?"

"Right. So you'll, er, still be going into the shop?"

"If I can."

19

"Is it allowed?"

"If we use it as a workshop rather than a retail unit, yes."

"I see."

"And if it's not, we might do it from here. Like you suggested, remember?"

Had he? What an idiot! He felt suddenly nervous of his wife. She'd always had energy, yes, but she'd never been quite this assertive. When she'd come home earlier and asked to talk, he'd been scared of what she was going to say and he had to admit he still was. He looked around his garage. Perhaps he could move in here permanently? Or perhaps…

"Actually, Julie, I've been wondering if I ought to go and stay with my mum."

"Really?"

Had he imagined it or had her eyes lit up? His chest squeezed.

"I'm worried about her, all on her own. She's eighty-two, you know."

"I know."

"Vulnerable."

"Oh, come on, Michael. Bett's about as vulnerable as a Sherman tank."

"That's not true. She's mentally strong, yes, but she's in the high-risk category. If she caught the virus…"

Julie sucked in a loud breath, looking instantly contrite. "You're right. Sorry. I didn't mean… You know I love your mum." They stood there facing each other, the old clock on the wall ticking loudly between them. "So," Julie said eventually, "have you called her?"

"Not yet. I thought I'd check with you first. See if you, you know…" The words ran out. "Needed me here" he'd been going to say, but it already sounded ridiculous in his head. Julie didn't need him here. If he was honest, she hadn't needed him for years.

"I'm sure she'd be grateful to have you," she said stiffly.

He nodded, picked up his phone. "I'll…"

"Right."

She backed out and the door banged behind her. Trying not to flinch, he found his mum's number, pressing it before he changed his mind. Sitting himself down on the Guzzi, he settled into the perfect curve of the worn leather seat.

"Michael! How lovely. How are you? Isn't this all complete madness?"

Michael blinked at his mother's cheery tone. He'd half convinced himself of the vulnerable thing, but here was Bett Marshall, as formidable as ever.

"It's very strange, Mum, yes. I'm worried about you."

"Me? Heavens, why on earth are you worried about me? Oh, because I'm 'elderly'?"

"Well, yes. I know you're in great health and all that, but this virus can be nasty if you're…" He hesitated, suspecting she'd hate "vulnerable" even more than "elderly."

"A bit knackered anyway?" she offered cheerily. "Thanks, love, but I know that. I'm not stupid. Thirty years as a research chemist has taught me a bit about this sort of thing and I've not lost my faculties yet."

He laughed. "I know that, Mum. You just tend to think you're invincible."

"And tend to prove it too."

"Yes, but…" No point in pursuing this line further. "Look, Mum, I was thinking perhaps I should come and stay with you whilst all this is going on."

"Stay with *me*? Why?"

"To look after you, do your shopping and stuff. It looks as if they're going to stop people over seventy going out altogether, so I thought if I was there then—"

"Stop right there, Michael. I'm ahead of you."

"What?"

"I had a long chat to my mate June, who was an immunologist, and she's explained it all to me. Best to keep us oldies well out of the way so we don't get complications and clog up the hospital beds."

"It's not like that, Mum."

"Course it is. And quite right too."

"But I don't think you should be on your own."

"Me neither, Michael, which is why I'm moving in with Carol and Liz."

"You're what?"

"Moving in with Carol and Liz, my friends from bridge. Carol has the most enormous house and since her husband died she's been rattling around in it, so there's loads of room for Liz and me. We're going to call it the share home. Instead of care home—get it?"

"I get it, Mum."

"All we've got to bring, apparently, is clean undies and three different types of gin. Good or what?"

Michael stared out the window. Mr. Nibbles was hopping gently around his run. Was it Michael's imagination, or were the rabbit's back legs looking a bit creaky? He shivered.

"That's great, Mum. Sounds...fun."

"Doesn't it? She's got a pool, so I can keep fit. And a hot tub. And the most enormous garden I can potter in. And Liz's son is the manager of the local supermarket so he's going to make sure we get loads of food delivered. We won't have to go out for months if that's what it takes. Really, you needn't worry about me at all."

"No. Clearly not."

"Michael? Are you OK?"

"Me? Of course."

"How are things there? Kids OK? Are they coming home?"

"No. They've all got busy lives."

"Indeed. So it'll be just you and Julie then?"

"Looks like it."

"And is that OK?" She sounded suddenly tentative—so unlike her normal self.

"Of course it is, Mum. Why wouldn't it be?"

"Oh, I don't know. It's a funny time of life when the kids first move out. It can be . . . disorientating."

"Can it?"

"Oh, yes. I don't think your father and I ever argued as much as we did when you went to university."

"You argued?"

She laughed softly. "We weren't perfect, Michael. No couple is. Talk to her."

He blinked. "To who?"

"Julie, of course. Your wife."

"Right. Yes. Of course."

"God, I remember you two when you were first dating. I'd never seen you so happy. She wasn't the woman I'd ever have imagined you coming home with, but the moment I saw you together, I knew she was spot on."

"You did?"

Bett tutted. "Will you stop asking anodyne questions, Michael. Of course I did. So talk to her. If nothing else, this lockdown business will mean you have time for that."

"Yes." Michael grimaced. He watched out the window as Julie came out of the house with some carrot peelings for Mr. Nibbles. As was her wont, she simply chucked them in the general direction of the cage, so that only half of them actually went through the bars. They'd get caught up in the mower if he didn't watch out.

"Michael?"

"I will talk to her, Mum. And, er, you have fun with Carol and Liz."

"Oh, I will! I've found the best marmalade gin. They're going to adore it. Take care, love. Speak soon."

"Speak soon," he echoed, but she was already gone, off to pack undies and spirits and head to Carol's mansion.

He watched as Julie paced around the garden and then, to his surprise, turned back to pick up the loose carrot peelings. He saw her bend to say hello to the old rabbit and caught a glimpse of the girl he'd so very happily married nearly thirty-five years ago. He wished he could go back to when it had all been simple, but even the best engineer couldn't build a bridge into the past. Somehow he had to find a way forward. Somehow he had to work out what had gone wrong between them and undo the damage he knew he'd done six months ago at that other, far more tangled wedding, where things had come to a head in such an unforgivably ugly way.

Chapter Four

September 2019

Michael looks at Sophie as Briony fusses around adjusting her tiny train and feels his fatherly heart swell almost more than it did the first time he took this, his eldest child, into his arms twenty-nine years ago. She's a woman now, a bride no less, and stunning in a daisy-lace hippie dress that's so very, very her, but to him she still feels as vulnerable as when she was placed naked into his hands, barely big enough to fill them.

"You look beautiful, darling," he says as she reaches out to take his arm. "I can't believe I'm lucky enough to be accompanying you down the aisle."

"Who else, Dad?" she says simply. "You've got me this far after all. Well, you and Mum."

She gestures to the little gap in the door, and, peering through it, Michael can see Julie at the front, looking stunning in a scarlet dress, as bold as ever.

That's my Julie, he thinks, but almost immediately questions his own assertion. Recently Julie has felt less and less like his. She's buried herself in the shop and hidden behind the wedding as if Sophie's relationship is now the only one that matters.

He watches as she turns to speak to his own mother, sitting in the pew behind her. She laughs softly and looks instantly young. Thirty-four years ago, he thinks, it was Julie who was preparing to walk down the aisle to his side. He wishes he could go back, just for a few minutes, so he could recapture what it felt like to love so totally and utterly that, had the rest of the world fallen away, neither of them would have noticed. He misses that, craves it like an alcoholic craves brandy at breakfast. But at least you can buy brandy if you really need to; the love he and Julie shared so effortlessly seems to have just gone, drained away into a gutter he didn't even know was waiting.

The entrance music strikes up and, shaking off the past, he looks at Sophie again. This is his daughter's day and he's honored to share it with her, so he puts his head up, squeezes her arm in against his own and moves into the church.

At the altar, Leo steps out with a huge smile for his bride, and Michael feels a sudden panic at having to hand his little girl over to him. He tuts at himself for being so patriarchal. He is not losing his daughter, and even if he was, that would have happened two years ago when she moved in with Leo, or nine whole years before that when she left home to live with a gang of mates and make her way as a journalist. She'll be just down the road as she always has been, and until his dying day she will be his little girl.

"Ladies and gentlemen," the vicar says, "we are gathered today to witness the union of this man to this woman."

Michael kisses Sophie on the cheek and she turns to Leo, as she should. It's a joy and a privilege to be a part of this moment and he must make the most of it. But when he steps into the pew next to Julie and feels her stiffen, he fears the show has only just begun.

*

The reception is being held in the most glorious barn, usually home to the innovative local craft center that Leo set up a few years ago with a handful of his arty mates. They worked all yesterday to clear the place of the usual potter's wheels, easels and sewing machines and convert it into the perfect reception venue, complete with home-made bunting and customized fairy lights. Julie was there until late, ostensibly putting the final touches to the long garlands of flowers along the walls, though he suspects she was just avoiding coming home to him. But it was worth it at least. It looks amazing—simple but beautiful, just like Sophie herself.

Almost everything has been provided by friends and family, and it's been a hive of activity. Leo's sister has done the food and his mother the cake. Sophie's best friend has sewn the dresses, three of their gang are providing ceilidh music, and of course Julie has done all the flowers. It's been a real team effort, held together by a hell of a lot of crazy organization, mainly by Michael.

"I haven't a creative bone in my body," he told Sophie back when the venue first went from dream to reality, "but I'm a whiz with a spreadsheet if it helps." And he hopes it has. He's been as meticulous about it as with any work project, and although he knows he's been a pain with his endless reminders and checks, there's no point in doing all the pretty, superficial stuff unless it gets there at the right time and for the right price. But he made sure it did and it all looks amazing. Most importantly of all, Sophie is so happy.

He looks for Julie as the receiving line forms. They have to stand together to shake hands with the guests and show everyone what happy parents they are. They're doing it well. Even Michael's handkerchief coordinates perfectly with Julie's dress. Only they know how much of it is show. Only they know that back home they have slept in separate rooms for well over a year. Michael shakes more hands, smiles more smiles and looks sideways at his wife, noting with a speck of hope in his heart how she meets his eye for the first time in far too long.

The meal goes well. The food is delicious, which is a relief as they are sitting with Leo's parents, who have been proudly telling them all about their daughter's fledgling catering business. Not that Michael can manage to get much of his starter down. The speeches are to be dispersed between the courses, and his is first. He chases his salmon mousse around the plate until it is gut-colored mush, and Julie suddenly puts a hand over his, gently forcing him to release the fork.

"You'll be brilliant, darling."

He stares at her in open surprise. "I'll be glad when it's over."

"At least you're first," Leo's dad offers.

Michael nods tightly and takes a tiny sip of wine, but then Sophie is waving and he's up and at the microphone and it's not so bad. He has his notes, he has all his carefully thought-out anecdotes and jokes. Julie helped him write the speech. To be honest, now that he thinks about it, she virtually wrote it for him, but it's his to deliver and he's determined to do it well.

He catches her eye as he mentions a family camping holiday years back, and she nods keenly and even blows him a little kiss. He's killing it. She's impressed. Perhaps today, with their daughter so happy and echoes of their own wedding inevitably in the confetti-filled air, they can reconnect. Perhaps today they can dance like they used to and talk like they used to and somehow, therefore, love like they used to.

"And I hope," he concludes, trying not to pick up the pace as the end comes into sight, "that Sophie and Leo will be every bit as happy in their married life as Julie and I have been. A toast, ladies and gentlemen—to the bride and groom."

Everyone is on their feet, clapping and cheering. Sophie thanks him with a kiss on his cheek, and as he scuttles back to his seat, Julie caps it with another, full on the lips, drawing their own "aah" of approval.

He blinks and pulls back to look into her eyes, but already Leo's dad is leaning across to clap him on the back and pour him red wine, and there's no time to talk.

The meal is long. Leo's sister is keen to impress, and starters give way to a fish course, a sorbet and a main. Michael drinks hard. Eats little. He applauds all the other speeches with great enthusiasm and cheers loudly when Sophie steps up to make one of her own. She gives him a tiny frown, but that's classic Sophie, so he doesn't fret about it.

Finally it's the turn of the best man, Piers—a handsome chap in a navy uniform who Briony has been eyeing up in a way Michael wishes he hadn't seen. The crowd are well watered and contentedly rowdy. Piers rises to their expectations, providing a few bawdy jokes and some suitably embarrassing memories of Leo, as well as drawing the poor groom into a particularly graphic re-enactment of the famous *Ghost* pottery-wheel scene that attracts approving cheers.

"Of course," he says, beaming round, "I knew Leo was on to a good thing with Sophie the moment I met her gorgeous mother—the scarlet woman!"

A slightly nervous laugh ripples around the room and Michael jumps. What is Piers implying? What does he know? He feels a little stab of humiliation and grabs at his wineglass. It's empty again; thank God they ordered plenty. He reaches for the bottle in the center of the table and, pouring himself more, takes a deep swallow.

"Her dress," Piers says hastily. "Just her dress. She's a happily married woman—sadly!" He winks and the crowd relaxes. "But it's my job this afternoon to thank her for filling this lovely space with all these truly wonderful flowers. It must have taken ages. In fact I know it did, because she was here putting the finishing touches to them as I staggered off to the loo at midnight last night after one too many beers with the groom. That's dedication!"

"To beer?" some wag calls, and everyone laughs.

"To the groom's welfare," Piers says smoothly. "And whilst we're on thank-yous, I'd like to thank Miranda for the amazing food—we've been well and truly spoiled there! Tess for the stunning dresses—don't the girls look amazing? Especially the beautiful bride." There are wild cheers and Sophie blushes happily. Out of the corner of his eye Michael sees Julie beaming, but he can't look away from Piers. It's not that he wants recognition, not at all. He's happy to do the background work in the background, where it belongs. "Thanks to all of Leo's brilliant friends here in the craft barn for helping to transform the place for us. And, of course, Todd, Junket and Little Dave for the fabulous music we're going to enjoy shortly. What a team effort today has been!"

More mad clapping. Michael concentrates on his wine. Julie leans in.

"He should have thanked you," she says loudly.

"Shh."

"I could stand up and—"

"No!" He's horrified. "I'm not a kid, Julie. It's fine. It was just a few spreadsheets."

"It was a lot more than that."

"But invisible."

"As you should be," he thinks she says.

"What?" he demands.

"As it should be. Michael, don't be like this."

"Like what?"

"Belligerent."

"I'm not!"

"OK, OK."

She puts a hand on his arm and gives a little laugh. It looks sweet, but it's hollow and he knows it. All week she has been jumping around trying to act the perfect wife as the guests arrive, and it's really starting to annoy him.

"What's wrong, Julie? Am I not putting on the right show? Not acting the perfect couple? Here, darling one, have more wine."

He pours them both a glass. Some of it sloshes onto the table-cloth. Julie looks nervously at Leo's parents, who have clearly picked up on an undertone and are pointedly looking anywhere but at them. Piers is entertaining the oblivious crowd with a complicated story from the stag do involving a cucumber and a butternut squash, but all Michael can hear is a rush of sound as he stares into Julie's eyes and sees her panicking—not, it seems, because he is upset, but because he might look so. Because the charade of their marriage might crumble.

"Michael, please." She puts a hand on his arm again, but he doesn't want her touch and jerks away. She glares at him, cross now. "It seems to me you *are* being a bit of a kid—a spoiled kid. Sophie really appreciates all you've done, and isn't that what counts?" It used to be endearing the way she'd work to coax him out of a bad mood, but now he wishes she'd just leave it alone. But she won't. "You made a wonderful speech," she tries.

"You wrote it," he shoots back, topping up his glass again.

"I didn't, Michael. I just helped a little."

He glares at her. "You wrote it." He pulls the notes from his pocket and looks at them. "You wrote all of it, including the lies at the end."

"Lies?" she gasps. But what's the point in all this pretense?

Piers is rounding off his speech with some lewd praise for the bridesmaids. Then everyone is on their feet again, glasses raised in yet another toast, and Michael looks around at them all and hates himself for playing along with the farce she's been setting up in their home for far too long. As they retake their seats, he takes a big gulp of wine and gestures for the mike, still standing.

"I wish to make a correction," he announces. Everyone turns to him indulgently, all smiles. Julie tries to grab the mic, but he's too fast for her. "I do not," he says, waving his hand for emphasis, "hope that Sophie and Leo will be as happy as Julie and me. I hope they will be much happier. *Very* much happier."

He sits down to stunned silence. Julie stares at her lap and he looks across at her folded hands, noting the chips already forming in her scarlet nail polish.

"Ceilidh!" Piers cries, and everyone leaps up gratefully, moving tables and chairs to clear a space for the dancing. Leo's parents are amongst the very first to rush off to help, glad to get away from them.

"Thank you very much," Julie fires at him.

He stares at her. "Well, don't you wish them greater happiness?" he asks.

"I do now," she agrees, snatching at a tissue and diving into the crowd.

Michael dances eventually. He dances with Sophie and Briony and Bett and anyone else flung into his path. But not with Julie. Not once with Julie. The next day he wakes up in their beautiful hotel room to find her already gone to start the great clear-up, and he hates himself. He apologizes to Sophie, who brushes it off, perhaps not wanting that particular snapshot in the memory album of her special day. And he tries to apologize to Julie, but she doesn't want to listen, and they go home to a silence even deeper than before.

Chapter Five

Day Two

Julie tied a big bow in the broad red ribbon around the last bouquet of the afternoon—the last, indeed, for who knew how long. The young man had asked for "extravagant"—her favorite sort of request in so many ways—and she hoped that was what she'd provided. Creamy lilies jostled for space with scarlet hyacinths and salvias in an explosion of spring color. She had tentatively told him that red and white traditionally meant blood and bandages, but he'd just laughed and said, "Bollocks to that. To my Cassie they mean Stoke City all the way!" She'd had to admire his style—and his evident love for his girlfriend.

She looked sadly around at her poor shop—her haven, her refuge. In under an hour, she'd have to lock up for the last time. There were almost no flowers in the myriad buckets, giving the place a thin, mean look, but there was nothing else for it. Even she had to accept that flowers weren't going to count as essentials in this harsh new world, and until they could get some sort of online service going, she was desperately trying to run down her stocks so she didn't have to leave them to die, alone and unloved.

"That's a fancy one!" Clare said, coming through from the other side of the shop and looking at the bouquet.

Julie turned to her sister. "Isn't it just? Some Stoke City fan's birthday."

"Nice! Have you got that paint, Jules? Thought I might attack the Fiesta."

Julie reached for the pot of Guzzi-red, then hesitated.

"Are you sure about this, Clare? Perhaps we should test the water before you go defacing your poor car."

Clare laughed. "It can't look much worse than it already does, and if we're going to take this business online, we need a proper delivery vehicle."

"And your Fiesta with my name daubed on it in motorbike paint is 'proper,' is it?"

"Better than nothing."

Julie smiled at her. "That's true. Thank you."

"Hey, thank *you*. Without this business I'd have been jobless for years, not just for a month or two of bloody lockdown. It's the least I can do."

"Rubbish. You had loads of jobs before this one."

"And stuck at none of them, unlike you. You found what you wanted and went for it."

"With the business, maybe."

Julie thought of the brown envelope hidden away in her bedside drawer and cringed. She hadn't even told her sister about the divorce, though Lord knows she'd been tempted. Clare had always been so full of praise for Julie's marriage, and always so reliant on her big sister's even keel as her own bobbed up and down from one man to the next. Ever since their dad had buggered off back when they'd still been in nappies, Julie had tried to help her battling mother by being the steady one for her sister. It was just how their relationship was. No, more than that—how she wanted it. The Julie that Clare saw was the Julie she'd like to be.

Even so, not telling her sister about her intention to leave

Michael had felt wrong. The weight of the secret was like the heaviest boulder on her shoulders, but she owed it to Michael to tell him first. She hated those women who went around slagging off their partners to all and sundry. If nothing else, it showed a hideous lack of self-respect. She was every bit as guilty as Michael here, just quicker to recognize the sadly inevitable and actually do something about it.

Even now, though, it was *their* divorce, and once she'd plucked up the courage to tell him about it, they'd sort it together. Was that warped? If it was, it was no more so than anything else at the moment. But it could wait. It seemed that she and Michael were stuck in the house together for the time being, so presenting the papers would make an already awkward situation far, far worse. And after all, she'd been thinking about this for months, years even, so what difference would a few more weeks make? She had the groundwork in place for when this pandemic loosened its hold on the country and she had her feet under the lawyer's desk. No doubt there'd be a queue for his services after weeks of lockdown. She smiled grimly to herself.

"Julie?"

"Sorry, miles away." She fussed at the bouquet. "This'll be all the red and white the poor Stoke City fans see for a while with the league shut down, hey?"

Clare gave her a sideways look but took pity on her.

"Certainly will. Dharmesh reckons there's no way they'll finish the season now. He's delighted, mind you—his lot were facing relegation."

Julie stared. "Dharmesh? Who the hell is Dharmesh?"

Clare flushed the deep red of the salvias and gave an unconvincing shrug. "Just this bloke I've been out with a couple of times."

"A couple, Clare?"

"Well, maybe three or four. OK, ten—but very close together."

"That's *more* serious, not less. Why haven't I heard about him before?"

Clare gave a shrug. "I didn't want to, you know, curse it."

"Curse it! How would I curse it?"

"Not *you* specifically, Jules. Just anyone. Every blinking time I meet someone I think might be quite nice, I get all excited and tell people and then it instantly fizzles out. They go all elusive on me, or tell me they're only looking for something casual, or I find myself suddenly not fancying them. Stupid, I know, but true. And Dharmesh..." She paused and looked into something suspiciously like the middle distance. "I really like him."

Julie looked more closely at her sister. Her eyes were shining and there was one of those irrepressible smiles on her face, as if happiness was fighting to get out of her. Sickening. But nice, obviously. Julie was glad for her. Clare had been divorced for ten years and had never really met anyone who had stuck. If this Dharmesh was it, then that was wonderful. And it might prove that divorce *was* worthwhile, that the grass really could be greener on the other side of the fence.

"Tell me about him," she urged, but at that moment the bell over the door jangled and someone stepped inside.

"Sophie!" Julie gasped. "What a lovely surprise." She flung herself at her elder daughter, but Sophie stepped back, arms held out to ward her off, and she ground to a halt.

"Sorry, Mum. Social distancing."

Julie blinked. "Right. Of course. Two meters away and all that."

"Exactly."

"But we've not, you know, started yet, have we? Not properly." Sophie gave her a disappointed look and Julie sighed. "So I can't even hug my own kids now?"

"Just for a bit, Mum. I don't like it either."

Julie wasn't so sure. Sophie had always been the spikiest of

36

her three children and it would surely only get worse now. She forced herself to stay calm, to smile.

"Well, I'm glad I've got to see you, Soph. I was worried it would be ages."

"It might be after this, I'm afraid. Leo and I are going to isolate."

"Aren't we all?"

"Totally, I mean. It's, er, it's his asthma."

"Asthma? Leo?" Julie pictured her son-in-law, a burly man with a big beard and warm brown eyes, trying to remember if she'd ever seen him with an inhaler. "It's not that bad, is it?"

"Oh, yes," Sophie shot back, looking anywhere but at Julie. "It's really quite serious. He was in hospital a lot with it as a child and the virus could hit him hard. It's just not worth the risk. I'm already working from home and he can too, so we thought we'd just, you know, get a load of food in and shut ourselves away."

"But vegetables don't keep." It was a stupid thing to say, but it was all she could think of.

"Things are starting to grow in our garden. Leo's polytunnel is working really well, so we've got enough for now if we're happy to live on chard and kohlrabi." She laughed and at least looked at Julie again. Behind her back Clare was pulling a comic face that Julie strove to ignore.

"And are you happy with that?"

"Of course. Why not? We really ought to embrace seasonality in this country and this is the perfect way to be forced into it. It's just spoilt of us to insist on having apples and strawberries flown over to us instead of waiting for them to ripen in our own soil. We'll kill the planet, Mum, just because we can't be a bit creative with our menus."

"True," Julie agreed, turning to try and get out of sight of Clare, who was flapping what Julie could only assume were meant to be invisible angel's wings. Sophie, to be fair, could get a little pious at times. As a feature journalist she was often to be found spouting well-crafted and highly woke statements, but that didn't mean she wasn't right. Julie wasn't actually sure she'd ever tasted kohlrabi, but now was hardly the time to say so. "Sounds excellent, Soph."

"What about milk?" Clare asked mischievously. "Do you, perhaps, have a goat?" Julie shot her a warning glare, but Sophie didn't even flinch.

"D'you know what, Leo suggested that the other day. Any idea where we might get one?"

Wrong-footed, Clare just stared, and Julie felt a sneaking admiration for her daughter. She had no idea if Sophie meant it or not, but she'd certainly shut her aunt up and that was no easy task.

"Farms?" she suggested.

"Maybe. Or maybe we'll just make our own milk from oats."

"Oats?" Clare squeaked.

"Oh, yes. Oat milk is all the rage now. You should try it, Auntie Clare. It tastes good, and it's so much better for the planet."

"But not for the goats."

"How d'you work that out?"

"Because if nobody wants goat's milk any more—or cow's for that matter—then they'll just all get eaten."

Sophie frowned, but then, spotting her aunt's face, shook her head. "You won't get me like that, Clare. This is about macro-biotics, not micro, as well you know."

It was Clare's turn to frown. "I know that little beats a bacon sandwich, Soph, but I'm just a crusty old carnivore so best ignored. Fancy a pot of hyacinths to take home? They'll be no use here once we shut up shop, and they'd look cute in your place."

"Hyacinths would be great, thanks, Clare."

Meat arguments forgotten, or at least suspended, Clare bounced off to the other side of the shop. Julie had added the extension three years ago when the café next door had closed down. It had been the big project she'd needed to get her out of the difficult time after their mum died, and she'd thrown herself into it with every ounce of energy she'd been able to dredge up from her horribly depleted reserves. It had been a big success. Nowadays they sold plants, pots and accessories as well as classic bouquets, and it had proved very popular and very profitable. She was proud of it.

But not fond of it.

The associations were at best complicated, and by and large she was happy to leave Clare to run that part of the business.

"You will take care of yourself, won't you, love?" she asked Sophie once they were alone, stretching up automatically to tuck a strand of her daughter's straw-blonde hair behind one ear. Sophie flinched back.

"Two meters, Mum. Sorry. And of course I will. Or at least Leo will, which amounts to the same thing."

Julie nodded. "He's a good man. Kind."

"He is." Sophie looked at her intently. "And you, Mum, will you be OK?"

"Of course. Why wouldn't I be?"

Sophie shuffled awkwardly. "I don't know. But with this place closed you won't have much to do. And it'll just be you and Dad in the house, and..."

"And what, Soph?"

Sophie scuffed the toe of her trendy boot against the pale green floor of the shop, looking for all the world like a nervous eleven-year-old again.

"Let's just say that I worry about you too, Mum. About whether you're, you know, happy."

"Happy?" The word came out a little too sharply, and Julie

self-consciously plucked a spray of gypsophila out of the nearest bucket and ran her fingers over it, feeling the tiny flowers tickling her skin.

"Mum?" Sophie's voice was low now.

"I'm fine, Soph, honestly. We're both fine."

"OK. It's just, you know, after the wedding…"

Julie's gut twisted at the memory of Michael's cold words and the pressure of the room staring at her as if all her dark secrets were exposed before them. She'd never felt more humiliated, and it had been the very next week, as she'd ferried bin bags full of plastic cups and plates to the recycling, that she'd noted the lawyer's shiny offices and started to quietly build up the courage to pay them a visit.

"Sophie…" she started, but she could find nowhere to take the sentence and thankfully dropped it when Clare came bouncing back.

"Hyacinths!" She held up a pretty terra-cotta bowl full of the blue flowers, then paused, looking from her sister to her niece. "Everything OK?"

"Fine," Julie said. "Everything is totally fine, isn't it, Soph?"

"Oh yeah. The world's about to go into meltdown because of the medical implications of ferociously accelerating globalization, but other than that, everything's fine."

Julie smiled. That was her usual Sophie, back with a woke vengeance.

"Personally," she said, "I'm looking forward to a chance for some quiet time, some stillness in which to, you know, reconnect with myself."

"You are?" Sophie asked, peering at her intently.

"I am," Julie confirmed, though it sounded far more like the sort of thing other people said. For herself, she'd never seen stillness as something aspirational; more something frigging terrifying. But at least Sophie was smiling now.

"That's great, Mum. Really great. Take care, OK. And give Dad my love."

That, at least, Julie could promise with an open heart. She waved Sophie goodbye and turned back to her near-empty buckets, feeling her strength thinning with her precious flowers. Clare was gathering them all up, and she held out a bunch of four large, vibrant sunflowers.

"Fancy taking these home? They match your sofas."

Julie jumped. "God, no!"

Clare frowned at her. "Why on earth not?"

"I just... I just don't like those sofa covers very much."

"Really? I think they're great—lively, vibrant, fun."

Julie grunted. "Yeah, I thought so too when I bought them. I was wrong."

Clare opened her mouth to ask more, but to Julie's huge relief, Stoke City man came bouncing in and she was able to turn to him. As he enthused over how much his girlfriend would love the bouquet, however, she couldn't help but picture the divorce papers lurking in her bedside table and suddenly felt almost overwhelmed by sadness.

"Walk?" she suggested to Clare.

Her sister wrinkled her nose. "You know I don't like walks."

"Yes, but *I* do and I might not be able to see you for weeks after this. Plus, I want to hear more about this lovely new bloke of yours."

"Right. Oh, OK then. For you." Clare flushed again. Goodness, had she actually fallen in love?

Julie fought not to feel jealous as she turned for her coat and keys. It was great if her sister was finally happy, and after all, the longer it took her to describe this Dharmesh bloke, the longer Julie could put off heading home to face being locked down in the mess of her own sorry relationship.

Chapter Six

June 2018

Julie arranges the sunflowers carefully in a vase and carries them through to the living room, bursting with pride to see the newly re-covered furniture. She checks her watch. Michael should be back any time now and she can't wait to see his reaction. It's only sofas, she knows, but she's trying. Things have been rough between them for all sorts of reasons these last couple of years, but it has to stop. Sophie is engaged. She came over and told them last weekend, wrapped around Leo with a beautiful amber ring on her finger and a huge smile across her normally reserved face. Happiness was radiating from them both in infectious waves and Julie is determined to catch it, not just for herself but for her and Michael as a couple.

She feels so much better now; the dark days after her mum's death are definitely behind her, as is all that silly stuff with George. The extended shop has been open over a year now and customers are flooding in, so her worries about the return on her investment are fading. She still doesn't like going into the new side, still feels it's been bought with something like blood money, but she's far enough out of the darkness now to know that's stupid. And Clare loves it. Julie has given her sister autonomy over buying in the plants and bulbs and she's really thrown herself into it. She's often at the shop first these days, and the minute Julie opens the door she can hear her singing. It makes work a very happy place to be—and home a stark contrast.

This is her attempt to change that.

She strokes a hand across the cushions, smoothing out any small wrinkles from her inept sewing. She found a wonderful fabric in a practical dark green with big bold sunflowers all over it, and for the last five days, whilst Michael's been in Dubai, she's been slaving away to transform the bourgeois cream suite he's always disliked into something with a bit more panache. It hasn't been easy on her mum's ancient Singer, but she's persisted with unusual patience, determined to see this through. And she has.

She smiles. Two sofas and an armchair, all perfectly—well, almost perfectly—re-covered for nothing more than the cost of the fabric and a few pricked fingers. She admires the matching sunflowers on the table, then ducks back to the kitchen to fetch two crystal glasses and a bottle of white wine. She even finds the old ice bucket they haven't used for years and puts out some fancy Waitrose canapés. Then she sits herself down to await Michael's reaction.

This is to be the launch of more than just the sofa covers; it's to be the start of the rest of their lives. They vowed to do more for themselves when the kids left home, but ever since that dreadful call from the hospital two years ago, it's been going wrong. That has to stop.

"Hello? Anyone home?"

She jumps at the sound of his voice. The front door has opened as quietly as only Michael can manage; she still doesn't know how he does that. Her nerves flutter like those of some Victorian lady.

"In here!" she calls, sitting up on the edge of the sofa.

"OK," he shouts back. "Just got to nip to the loo. Stick the kettle on, will you?"

"Oh, I think we can do better than that!"

But he's already heading upstairs. Great, she thinks, he needs a blinking poo. He always insists on going upstairs for a poo. And then he'll probably get changed out of his travel clothes, faff around digging out his favorite jumper and his slippers. He could be ages. She fidgets impatiently, trying her very hardest not to hurry him along in case it spoils the surprise. But it's impossible.

"You coming?" she can't stop herself shouting up the stairs.

"Yes, yes. Sorry. You know flying is terrible for my bowels."

"Too much information, Mike! Please come down."

"OK, OK."

She knows as soon as he shuffles into the room that this isn't the right time for a big talk. He's travel-weary and ready to just sink into his armchair and relax. She hopes, though, that she's done enough to revive him, and looks up optimistically as he stands in the doorway.

"Bloody hell," he says, gawping like a moron. "What's gone on in here? It looks like *The Day of the Triffids*."

"I've re-covered the sofas," she says, pretty moronic herself.

"So I see. Why?"

"Why? They were old and dull and worn-out, Mike."

"They were quiet and soft and comfortable."

"They're still bloody comfortable. It's only fabric. You've always said you didn't like them, so I thought I'd surprise you."

"Ah. I didn't mean I didn't *like* them."

"What did you mean then?"

"Just that they weren't that exciting."

"Well, now they are."

"Yes."

"And you don't like it?" Anger bubbles up inside her, as it

so often seems to do these days. "I should have known. You hate change."

"I do not hate change. I'm just not good at surprises."

"You used to be," she throws at him. "Remember when I surprised you at your mum's house—"

"By turning up at the door in nothing but a mac. I do remember that." His eyes darken promisingly.

"And you liked it."

"Well, obviously I liked it."

"Because I was naked?"

He looks sideways at her. "Well, yes, but that was the point, wasn't it?"

"So if I was naked now, you'd like it?"

He shifts. "Is yes the right answer?"

"You tell me."

He looks to the ceiling. "Please, Julie. I'm exhausted. What's this about? Are you saying I'm not adventurous enough, is that it?"

"No, Michael." She sighs. "It's about the sofas, that's all. Just about the sofas."

That's not true, but it's the best place to start. She looks pleadingly at him and he comes slowly forward, leaning over and prodding at the nearest sofa as if the sunflowers might actually be growing up out of it, waiting to . . . to what? Eat him? Tickle him? Make him sneeze?

"It's very . . . vibrant."

"Good."

"Very . . . busy."

"For Christ's sake, Michael, they took me ages."

"I bet." Finally he clocks her face, sees the flowers, the wine, the special nibbles. "It's, er, very good. Very professional. Nice, er, seams."

He plucks at one, still not getting close to it. She wants to

45

scream. Nearly does. Instead, somehow, she reins in her anger and lifts the bottle.

"Glass of wine to celebrate?"

"Celebrate what? The triffids?"

She *does* scream then. Long and hard and loud. That, at least, is one advantage of the kids no longer at being home. No one comes running to see what's wrong and there's no need for awkward lies to cover up the painful truth: that there is now a gaping hole between Julie and Michael. That, indeed, there probably has been a gaping hole for some time; it's just been so filled up with children that they couldn't fall into it before.

Chapter Seven

Gone for a walk with Clare. Home later.

Michael stared uncertainly at the text. Two things were odd about it. The first was that Julie never usually bothered texting him about what time she'd be home. The second was that Clare hated walks. It was a long-running family joke. Runs, yes, cycling, rounders, French cricket, basketball, tennis... any sport at all and she would be right there, but she had a child's aversion to a straightforward, "boring" walk. Was Julie really with her?

He shook the thought away. The truth was that, before lockdown, there was rarely any telling where Julie was. She seemed to have a different club to go to every night of the week—book club, supper club, crochet bloody club. She was useless at crochet. The hat she'd made him last Christmas had looked as if a deranged sheep had shed its wool on his head. But still she persisted.

Mealtimes over the last years had become something of a pass-the-parcel. Whoever got into the kitchen first made food for two, ate their own and left the second portion out to be eaten later or, failing that, for tomorrow's lunch. Occasionally they landed at the table at the same time, but he wouldn't go as far as to call it eating together. The closest they came to that these days was when they went out with other couples and could hide between their friends. That wasn't normal, was it?

He pushed his chair away from his desk—well, Briony's desk—and looked around the room. It was frozen in time, cryogenically preserved at the point at which Briony had left home, as if she might return at any moment, still eighteen, still with pink hair and big DM boots. A rogue tear tickled at the edge of his eye and he brushed it roughly away. This was no good. He couldn't work at home if all he was going to do was cry over children who had perfectly legitimately grown up and headed off to their own lives. He was probably just hungry. Perhaps all he needed was a cup of tea and a biscuit.

Getting up, he strode off down the landing, but then paused, caught by the hodgepodge gallery of family pictures. Julie had never been one for the uniform look, so Sophie's Year 1 class photo sat next to a funky white-framed picture of them all from some studio, and Briony's prom nestled up to a run of clip-frame miniatures of the three kids sledging. They were all great photos, but now that he looked properly, he couldn't find a single one from the last five years. It was almost as if he and Julie had just disappeared once the kids had upped and gone.

Tears threatening, he moved on, away from Briony's room and Sophie's next to it, past Adam's gray-walled den to the far end. Directly opposite each other stood the doors to the big master bedroom and the little spare; or, as they seemed to have become these days, Julie's room and his own. He edged into his and looked around at the blank walls, the anodyne curtains, the wonky wardrobe he'd been meaning to fix for years. He'd only moved in here for a week or two when he'd done his back in two winters ago and Julie's flung-out mode of sleeping and their too-soft mattress had been causing him pain. So why was he still here?

He walked across the landing and opened the door to Julie's bedroom—to *their* bedroom. The contrast couldn't have been more marked. The room oozed Julie. The white floorboards were covered with a multicolored rug that matched the exuberant duvet cover, and plump cushions sat on the bed and spilled over onto the floor. Christ, those cushions had always annoyed the hell out him. What was the point of them? They seemed to exist solely to be moved from bed to floor and back again.

"They're pretty," Julie had always told him when he'd objected, usually batting him over the head with one into the bargain. He supposed they were, if you liked that sort of thing, and if he was honest, he kind of missed them.

He sank down onto the bed—sending a cushion pinging to the floor—and stroked the duvet. Remembering his attempt to return to the marital bed that Christmas, he groaned. He'd given up so easily, crept back to the spare room because it was easier at the time, not realizing that doing so would make it harder and harder ever after.

*

"So, you're back!"

Julie is swaying a little, victim of those sickly colored liqueurs that only ever come out once a year. She tries to sashay across their bedroom and it makes him laugh. He's had a fair bit himself, though not the colored liqueurs—he draws the line at drinks that look like they belong in a sweet shop.

"I'm back." He leans against the headboard and pats the covers. "Come and get me, tiger."

It isn't the sort of thing he'd normally say, but then this doesn't feel normal. Who knows why? They're in *their* bedroom,

49

in *their* house, just as they have been for years—except that for the last month they haven't been, and they're both very aware of that. He's been sleeping in the spare room recently because of his back, but now, with Bett staying for the festive period and all three kids home, there's no choice but to share a room again. And that's suddenly starting to look like a very good thing.

Last night, Christmas Eve, they sat up drinking till far too late before Julie shooed everyone away and insisted on Michael creeping around as Santa. By the time they got to bed, they were both so knackered they just rolled onto their sides and went straight to sleep. And this morning they were woken by Adam—twenty going on twelve—leaping on them with his stocking so had no time to feel awkward. Tonight, though, Christmas night, they are both awake and warmed by their family day, and it seems to Michael the perfect chance to complete his return to Julie's arms.

"I've missed you."

"Oh yeah? Which bits of me?"

"*All* bits." It's true, though he hasn't perhaps realized it until this very moment. It's amazing how damaging a painful back is to the libido. He was even grateful when she went out dancing without him, and back in the day he used to love dancing.

"You're an attractive woman," he says, watching her reach for the zip down the side of her Christmas dress. "*Very* attractive. You've kept well." She shoots him a sideways look and he leaps to correct himself. "Not kept well. I don't mean kept well. Sorry. More, you know, that you've aged well."

She arches an eyebrow. "Like a rump steak?"

He shakes his head. "No. No, much better than a rump steak. And as you know, I love a rump steak."

She giggles, and he leaps up to go and help her with the zip, which has stuck in the velvety fabric under her arm. He tugs at it carefully, and she squirms.

"You're tickling me!"

"Oh yeah?"

He tickles her in earnest, pulling her in against him, and she reaches a hand around his neck. God, it feels good, like the best Christmas present ever—and he got a Guzzi cap from Briony and a new set of spanners from Adam, so that's saying something!

"I've had such a good day," he says, kissing her lightly.

She kisses him back. "Me too. Sophie was so pleased with that composter you found her."

"The one you said was bonkers?" he teases.

"It *is* bonkers, but she likes it and that's what counts."

"She does. And Briony's face when she saw those tickets!"

"Priceless. I got a picture of it, actually. Look."

She wriggles away and reaches for her phone. He bends to kiss her neck as she flicks through to find the right photo, and she gives a soft moan.

"Here."

She passes it to him and starts to undo his shirt buttons, kissing her way down his chest as if they're newlyweds once more, which, after a month in separate beds, they might as well be. She reaches the buttons nearest his waistband and he struggles to focus on the picture of Briony, lovely as it is.

"Oh Julie," he murmurs, but at that moment a text flashes up on her screen, and those words, for some reason, are horribly clear.

Happy Christmas, Julie. I've been thinking a lot and you won't see me again. It's best. But remember—you're beautiful, inside and out.

Michael freezes. Julie has undone the bottom button and is coming back up to push his shirt off his shoulders.

"Michael? Are you OK?"

51

He drops the phone onto the bed. He's not sure what he's read and he doesn't want to think about it. Not now.

"Fine," he says quickly. "I'm fine."

He reaches for her zip and this time it comes free. He draws it down slowly, forcing himself to focus on her lovely body, on the low moan she utters as he eases the dress off her shoulders and dips his head to kiss his way down her collarbone.

Remember—you're beautiful, inside and out.

The text penetrates what should be a surge of luxurious lust. He knows his wife is beautiful, but who else has seen fit to tell her so?

"Julie?"

"Hmm?"

She looks so lovely standing there in her underwear. He should shut up and just enjoy her. But he can't. She grasps his belt buckle, undoes it slowly. "Ready, tiger?" she growls, and he is, he really is. It's just that damn text keeps going round and round in his head.

I've been thinking a lot and you won't see me again.

What does that mean? Does that mean she's been seeing whoever it is before?

Forget it, he tells himself furiously. It could be anything. It could even be a woman. Women say things like that.

But if his mind is listening to his furious logic, his body certainly isn't. Julie releases his trousers and looks up at him.

"Michael? Are you sure you're OK?"

"Course I am. More than OK. I'm great. Just…a bit drunk, you know? And my back's sore."

"Let's get into bed, hey?" Julie suggests, hopeful.

They head for their respective sides. Michael watches her shed her underwear and feels himself stir. Thank God. He reaches eagerly for her, but as she lifts her side of the duvet, her phone falls off and clatters to the floor.

"Don't worry about it," she says, pressing in against him, and he doesn't want to, really he doesn't, but he can still see that message popping up across the top of Briony's smiling face. Is this why Julie's been so distant recently? He thought she was still feeling out of sorts after Linda's death, but maybe that was just him being naïve. His lust droops.

"Michael?"

"It's my back," he stutters.

You won't see me again.

That was what the text said. If it was a something, an anything, it's over. He needs to take Julie into his arms and reclaim her, but he can't get the words out of his head.

"Your back?" She pulls away, stares at him. He arches it with a forced grimace.

"I think it's locked up again. It's painful."

"Oh."

She looks so disappointed, so hurt. But she's not the only one. The Christmas spirit that was chasing so thrillingly around his veins just a few short minutes ago is now churning in his gut, and he feels sick of the whole thing.

"Shall we just go to sleep then?" she asks, her voice small.

"I think we should," he says stiffly.

"Right."

She snaps the light off and they lie there side by side, carefully not touching. Neither of them sleeps for a long, long time.

*

Had she been having an affair? Michael wondered now. So many times since that Christmas he'd thought about bringing the text up, just asking her about it so that he could put his nagging fear to rest, but if he was honest, he was scared of the answer. What if she *had* been seeing someone else? Or still was? What would he do then? He hated thinking there might be secrets between them, but he was also afraid of the truth.

53

His Julie had always been such an open woman, blurting out her feelings at the drop of a hat, embarrassing the kids with impulsive hugs and praise, doing silly dances to her favorite music and weeping loudly at sad films. But in these last years, something had clammed her up. He never knew what she was thinking, what she was feeling.

He pictured her on the very first day he'd seen her in Budapest, laughing so openly at the world, and felt a rush of red-hot fury that that wonderful girl had somehow been taken away. It all went back to that dreadful phone call from the hospital, he was sure of it. Grief was a terrible thing, as he knew so well, and he'd tried to talk to her about her mum, tried to help her as she'd helped him when his dad died, but she just wouldn't let him. She just wouldn't bloody let him.

Grabbing the stupid rainbow cushion off the floor, Michael flung it with all his might at the pillows. It hit with some force, propelling those already there upward. One pinged into the bedside table, sending a pink-covered paperback flying, and he cringed and rushed to pick it up. Putting it back, he noticed the drawer slightly ajar and froze. Julie used to keep a diary when they first met. She'd soon stopped, claiming that having him in her bed gave her far more interesting things to do late at night, but maybe she'd started again. Maybe in there, he'd find the secrets he was sure she was keeping from him.

He reached tentatively for the handle and gave a tiny tug. He could see something brown in there—a notebook? He tugged a little more, but the drawer stuck on one side and suddenly he saw himself sneaking around and hastily pulled away, rushing back to his own room to avoid further temptation. There he sat on the bed, breathing heavily. This was not the mature way to go about things. He and Julie should talk. And if he didn't want to hear what she had to say, then that was just something he was going to have to deal with.

He glanced at his watch. It was a beautiful evening and if she really had gone for a walk she might be a while. What on earth could he do while he waited? Usually he'd head for Gertie, but he'd had a text from Gary saying that supplies of parts were horribly delayed, so there was really nothing he could do for the old girl. Looking round the room, his eyes were drawn to the wonky wardrobe. One of the feet had broken when they'd manhandled it along the landing from Adam's room and it had sat at a drunken angle ever since. Periodically Michael vowed to sort it out, but emptying it had always seemed too daunting a task. Still, he had plenty of time now, so why not?

Delighted to have found a worthwhile task, he opened the door and studied the strange array of cocktail dresses, mock-fur coats and dress suits that were huddled inside like misfits at the edge of a party. Grabbing a handful, he yanked them out and marched along the landing to Sophie's bedroom, dumping them on her bed before returning for more. The activity soothed him and he worked fast, so that before long he was down to the final item.

He drew it out from the far corner of the wardrobe and stopped dead, staring. It was Julie's leather jacket, the one he'd bought her for their two-month anniversary so that she could come out on Gertie with him. He held it out, admiring the assertive black and orange pattern, seeing the creases in the soft leather where her arms had reached out around his waist, spotting the tiny tear where a rogue branch had caught her on a scrubby Italian track. Suddenly the tears were back.

Hurrying down the landing, he flung the jacket onto the pile of lost-memory clothes and slammed Sophie's door on it. The wardrobe, that was what he was meant to be concentrating on—mending the wardrobe. He squared up to it. How best to get it onto its back? He should wait for Julie to come home to help him, but the cheap old thing was surely light enough for one man to shift? He just had to take it slowly, that was all.

Grabbing the front, he began edging it out, one side and then the other, like a reluctant dance partner. Good. Now he just had to take the front edge and tip it and— The pain shot through him as sharply as the crash of the bloody thing against the wall. His back seemed almost to jackknife and he staggered against the bed, nausea welling up into the spaces around the agony and his sight misting so that the muted edges of everything in the room seemed to merge into one.

He tried to ease himself onto the bed, but the upward movement felt impossible, and with a deep moan, he sank to the floor. Curled in on himself, he gritted his teeth and prayed for endurance as the pain kicked him again and again, as merciless as a gang of thugs. Now he had no choice but to wait for Julie and just pray that Clare—or whoever she had gone for a walk with—didn't keep her out all night.

Chapter Eight

Julie turned her key in the lock and pushed open the door, sniffing the air hopefully. She was starving. Clare, it turned out, had had rather a lot to say about the wonderful Dharmesh and they'd walked miles across the fields. It had been quite amusing really, except that the wretched woman had walked so fast, Julie was now exhausted. And starving.

She couldn't detect any nice aromas on the air. Damn. Had Michael not cooked anything? She made for the kitchen. It was quiet in the house but there was nothing unusual about that. Michael had never been a noisy man. He even watched his beloved rugby in near silence, with just a quiet "yes" if his team scored. She'd been in awe of that when they'd first been together. Now she mainly found it irritating. What was wrong with letting your feelings out every once in a while?

The kitchen was empty, clean and tidy with not even a plate or knife on the draining board to suggest any food preparation had gone on at all.

"Michael?"

No answer. He'd be in the garage, of course, tinkering with the damn bike. Julie opened the fridge and peered hopefully inside. There was some chicken marinating promisingly in a dark red paste, but it clearly hadn't made it anywhere near the cooker yet. She glanced at the clock. Gone 7:30. It wasn't like Michael to wait this late for his tea. Unless that motorbike part he'd been waiting for had arrived, of course.

Closing the fridge, she strode across to the door into the garage and pulled it open. Cold air wafted into the kitchen, but there was no Michael there; just Gertie, sitting forlorn and neglected. Next door's patio light was on and a ray was slanting through the garage window and onto the chrome bodywork of the old Guzzi, making it glimmer. Julie smiled. She was a beautiful thing really and it was a miracle that she was still working. Or perhaps a testament to Michael's never-ending care. That bike had carried them down through Europe on honeymoon and it had been, at best, unreliable then. It wasn't its fault they hadn't made it all the way to the Greek islands, mind you, or that she still hadn't been to a single one nearly thirty-five years later.

Uncomfortable at the thought, she turned hastily back into the house.

"Michael?"

Nothing. Was he still working? He had clients all over the world, so perhaps he was talking to someone whose business day was still in full swing. She made for the stairs, remembering to try and mute her usual thunderous tread in case he was on a conference call. There was no sound coming from Briony's room, but she did catch a strange noise from the spare, a sort of dark low moan.

"Michael?" She peered into the room, and there he was, curled up on the floor, white as a royal lily and with dark lines of pain around his eyes. "Oh God, Michael. What happened?" She took in the wardrobe, empty and skewed drunkenly against the wall, and the way her husband was curled awkwardly in on himself. "Back?" He nodded, his teeth visibly gritted. "What can I do?"

He looked at her helplessly and she fought to remember what had worked when he'd hurt it before. It hadn't been like this last time, though. There'd been no dramatic rolling on the ground, just a quiet text from the driveway to say he could do with a little help to get out of the car. She'd thought it was a joke at first, but no, he'd seized up at the wheel after a long day on a cold building site somewhere near Hull.

It had taken ages to ease him out of the car and into the house. Their own bed, with its springy mattress, had proved too soft for him, so they'd moved him into the spare. It had only been meant to be for a week or two but somehow it had stretched out all the way to now. Michael moaned and she shook the thought away.

"Do you think you can move if I help you? If we can get you into bed, you'll be much more comfortable."

"I can try."

She knelt at his side and tried to work out where best to hold him. Bending over, she edged one hand under his lower shoulder and placed the other on his waist. His shirt had rucked up and her hand met his skin, soft and thankfully warm. It felt surprisingly intimate, not least because the position had brought her face to within centimeters of his. His breath was coming in short gasps as he prepared himself to move, and as she felt it waft across her cheek, something deep within her shifted disturbingly. She shook her head. Ridiculous.

"Ready?"

"I don't know, Jules."

His voice shook a little and she tilted her head round to look into his eyes. They'd filled with something like fear, lightening them to the color of cornflowers, and she was reminded uncomfortably of the very first time she'd seen him. He'd been straddling his beloved motorbike on a street corner in Budapest when she'd come out of a café with her

59

mate Susie. Their eyes had met—proper chick-flick met—and she'd been blown away by that blue. So unexpected with his mane of dark hair.

"God, he's hot," she'd said to Susie. "Look at those eyes! And that bike. So cool."

Little did she know then that thirty-five years later she'd be cursing that same damn bike for taking up all the room in the garage while their cars sat out in the rain and the frost. And that she'd spend her days avoiding those blue eyes that had captivated her so completely she'd later trawled every campsite in the city to find them. To find *him*.

She shook the thought away. Those days were gone. There was no harm in acknowledging how lovely they had been, but it wasn't the same now. Time passed. People changed. Bikes rusted and needed endless bloody care. And so did marriages. But that didn't mean she didn't still care. She tightened her grasp on him and felt his own fingers clutch at her.

"You can do this, Michael. I've got you safe, I promise."

She saw him steel himself, then he gave a tight nod and tensed his muscles. Julie braced against the wall and tugged gently.

"Aargh!"

"Sorry. I'm sorry, I—"

"No, keep going. Please."

She screwed her eyes closed against the sheen of sweat that had broken out on his brow and forced herself to pull, dreading the snap of something in his poor bones. Hospital was the last place they wanted to be right now. But at last Michael found his feet and, leaning heavily on her, eased himself onto the bed, breathing heavily.

"OK?"

He gave a grim nod. "Rarely better."

A small laugh escaped her.

"What happened?"

"Bloody DIY, that's what."

Now she did laugh. For such a very practical man, Michael had always been rubbish at DIY. When they'd first moved in together, he'd proudly announced he was going to put up some shelves for her knick-knacks. Several hours and many, many swear words later she'd been faced with three shelves, so askew that her ornaments and photo frames had slid straight off. She hadn't cared back then. He'd looked so gorgeous with his top off, wielding a drill with screws between his lips, that she'd just swept him off to bed without a second thought for the damn shelves.

Later she'd made a feature of them, gluing rainbow bookends onto the lower sections to hold everything in place and quite happily letting her stuff collect up against them. How come what seemed so funny when you were young got irritating as you grew older?

"I'll fetch you some painkillers."

"Thanks."

She brought him a couple of tablets and a glass of water. He looked better now he was on the bed and propped up by pillows. Some of the color was creeping back into his skin and his breathing had evened out. He took the tablets with a grateful smile and swallowed them down.

"Thanks," he said again.

"No problem." She hovered, unsure what to do with herself now. "Are you hungry?"

"D'you know what, I think I am. I left some chicken marinating in the fridge."

"I saw. I can cook it."

"Great."

"Do you want yours up here?"

"I think I'd better. Thanks, Julie."

He sounded so meek and looked so small sitting there

hunched up on the bed. He was dependent on her now and she didn't like that. She didn't like it at all.

Downstairs, she mustered pans and threw chicken and rice at them, adding the first vegetables that came to hand and ignoring the recipe propped neatly on a stand. Michael was a religious follower of instructions and hated it when she cooked like this. She rifled through the pantry cupboard and, turning up a tin of pineapple chunks that looked like it might have been there since the eighties, tossed a few of them into the sauce. She'd call it Hawaiian chicken, perhaps add some banana too. She went back to the fridge, but the only banana they had was far too brown and soft to chop into slices. Typical. She chucked it into the compost in disgust, but the neat little pot was already full and the lid wouldn't go down. Damn.

Michael always emptied the pot into the compost bin down the bottom of the garden. He had some complex scientific system going that she had carefully claimed to misunderstand, cunningly relieving herself of all composting duties, but if his back had gone, he might be out of action for days, weeks even. She rescued the banana and went to throw it in the bin, but then, feeling far too guilty at the eco-crime, returned it to the fridge. The compost lid went down and she sighed in relief. She'd sort it tomorrow, when she wasn't so hungry. She'd have time, after all, far, far too much time.

As the rice came to the boil and the slightly strange-looking sauce around the chicken began to bubble, she turned the rings down and sank onto a chair. She'd not exactly been great at looking after Michael last time he'd been laid up, but it was going to be even worse this time, because now she was living a lie.

Her phone buzzed and she picked it up to see a text from the man himself. She looked at the ceiling. This was typical of him, refusing to just yell down the stairs like everyone else. And OK, so she hated it when the kids did that, but this was just weird.

Sorry for being a pain. Thank you for helping me.

Something in her softened. Why did he have to be so nice just when she'd resolved to start off the parting of ways? Another message pinged in:

Food smells yummy.

She shook her head and typed back:

You mean you're hungry?

I mean the food smells yummy. Sort of fruity.

A pause, then:

And maybe a bit burnt??

"Shit!"

Julie ran to the stove. Sure enough, the sauce, rich with sugary pineapple, was sticking to the edges of the pan. Grabbing a spoon, she scraped off some of the dark line, chucking it into the sink, and then stirred the rest in. Caramelization, wasn't that what they called it?

It's fine. Meant to be like that.

Right. Good. Still smells yummy.

Julie turned the heat off and went to drain the rice. She probably should have used the timer, like Michael was always telling her, but it was too late now. The food smelled, at best, odd, but it was too late to do anything about it. She dished it up, placed Michael's plate on a tray and added a fork and a glass of water, then headed upstairs.

"Here you go."

He took the tray from her and made a visible effort not to peer too closely at the slightly odd-looking food on the plate.

"Is that…"

"Pineapple, yes."

"Was that…"

"In the recipe? No."

"Right."

"Don't you want it?"

"No, no. I mean, yes. I do. I do want it. Thank you." He picked up his fork and took a big mouthful, chewing with steady purpose. "Delicious." She turned to the door. "Are you not eating?"

"Mine's downstairs."

"Right."

"It's just, you know, easier at the table."

"Yes."

She took a couple of steps out of the room, but he looked so frail there, his back hunched and his face still pale.

"Are you OK, Michael?"

"I will be. It just needs rest and it'll ease off."

"I hope so." She looked to the wardrobe, still lolling against the far wall. "What were you trying to do?"

"I wanted to mend the foot. Not exactly difficult."

"It's big, though, to move by yourself. You should have waited for me to come home."

"I had no idea when that would be."

64

"I texted you. I've shut the shop."

He grimaced. "I'm sorry. You love that shop."

She nodded, feeling a sudden, unexpected lump in her throat. She *did* love that shop, for so many reasons.

"I hope it survives, Michael. I'll still have to pay rent, and there's Clare's wages. She needs them to stay afloat, but with no money coming in..."

"We'll figure it out. What about the online deliveries?"

"We're looking into trialing them, but I don't know if people will be able to afford flowers in all this."

"Well, they won't be going out to eat and drink, so perhaps they'll spend their money on other things, hey?"

"Perhaps." She watched as Michael took another bite of his chicken. "I'd better go down or my food will get cold."

"You'd better. Don't want it to go to waste."

"No."

It felt as if there might be more to say but she had no idea what it was. She wanted to talk to him about the shop, to share her worries that her business might not survive and her even greater worries that she might not survive without her business. But he wouldn't get it, not any more. He'd barely even been in the shop since the extension three years ago. So with a little nod, she turned and made for the kitchen.

Once there, she sat down at the table with her own plate, cut off a section of chicken and took a big bite. It was utterly disgusting.

Chapter Nine

February 2017

"Canapés? Veggie? Yes, of course—these ones here."

Julie indicates the little mozzarella and tomato nibbles sitting perkily on the silver plates from their twenty-fifth wedding anniversary party that she'd dug out of the loft. To be honest, most of the canapés are the same as they were then too, but it seemed simpler than reinventing the wheel. It's taken her ages to make them, especially with Michael away in Bodrum, but at least it's been peaceful.

She shivers and glances around the busy shop to see if he's arrived yet, but there's no sign of him. No doubt there'll be a text on her phone about flight delays or traffic jams, but frankly she hasn't got time to look. It's not like he's had much to do with getting the shop ready to open again after the extension anyway, not like when they first opened all those years ago. For a moment she pictures the two of them in here when it was still half the size and just an empty shell, paintbrushes in hand as the sun set outside and the kids slept at home under Linda's care. It seems a long, long time ago. Michael hasn't so much as looked at a paint chart this time round, and as for Linda...

She focuses swiftly on her guests.

"Canapé? More drinks? My son should be bringing the bubbles round shortly, so do grab him."

She glances over for Adam, who is supposedly in charge of the drinks but is rather too busy mooning at Chelsea, the girlfriend he's brought back from university. She's a sweet girl as far as Julie has been able to tell in the five minutes she's had spare to talk to her, but she could do with her son paying less attention to her right now. She fights her way through the gratifying crowd in the little shop to the table she's set up to one side.

"Adam!"

He blinks away from Chelsea's charms and focuses on her.

"Mum! Great, isn't it? Enjoying it?"

"I'd be enjoying it more if everyone had a drink. Can you circulate with the bottles now that most people are here?"

"Sure," he agrees easily, and both he and Chelsea pick up a bottle and head out.

"Thanks, love," she says, and he drops an easy kiss on her head as he passes.

"Pleasure."

She smiles at her sunny boy and watches him bounce over to fill up Briony's glass as she chats away to the lovely old guy who comes every Friday to buy roses for his wife. Her middle child has been home all week, waiting for her new job to start next Monday, and it's been lovely spending some time with her. Michael was gutted he was going to be away when he found out she'd be back, but it was too late to cancel. She knew he should have told work he couldn't make it, because, look, it's almost time for the speeches and he's still not here.

She collars Sophie, who's scribbling away in a notepad, having promised her a stellar write-up in the local paper. She doesn't work for them these days as she's far too busy doing important commissions for the nationals, but they'll take anything she sends.

"Soph, have you heard from your dad?"

She checks her phone. "Oh—yes. He says the flight was delayed but he's on his way now."

"When did he send that?"

She grimaces. "Ten minutes ago."

"The airport's a good forty minutes away. Honestly! I'll just have to do the speech without him."

"We don't know where he was when he sent it. Give it ten minutes at least and I'll check how he's doing."

"Hmm. Oh, Mrs. Jones—how are you? How lovely of you to come. Let me get you a drink." She grabs a glass for the woman who commissioned her for her daughter's enormous wedding last summer. "Canapé? I made them myself."

The shop is so full now that it's getting hard to move around, even with twice the capacity of before. As Mrs. Jones spots some other local worthy to chat to, Julie slides through to the new side and looks around at the freshly painted walls, subtly blue to contrast with the green of the original but with the same varnished wood shelving to house the plants and accessories. They've tidied away the plants today to make room for the guests, but usually they fill the place, making it look and smell as wonderful as Julie imagined when the woman in the café next door first told her that they were going to have to close.

She swallows. How long did she spend looking into that empty little space, imagining it as it looks now?

"Hello there! Those look yummy. May I?"

She looks up, and there is George, their gem of a plant supplier.

"George! Of course. Please, have as many as you want."

"Don't say that, or they'll all be gone." He grins, his brown eyes twinkling as he wolfs down two. "The shop looks fantastic, Julie."

"Thank you."

"You went for the cornflower white in the end then? Good choice."

She nods. George turned up at the shop a few weeks back when she and Clare were poring over the color chart, and was surprisingly informed on the subject. Actually, he's surprisingly informed on pretty much every subject, especially when it comes to plants. With his broad shoulders and his floppy blonde hair, he looks more like a man who'd lecture you on rugby tactics, but he has a passion for all things horticultural that makes him fascinating to talk to. As a fellow professional, of course.

"We wanted to keep it simple, make the plants the stars."

"I like your style!" He grins, looks around again. "Your mum would have loved it, I'm sure."

Julie jumps. "My mum?"

He frowns. "Did you not say you'd bought the lease with your inheritance money?"

"Ah! Yes. Yes, I probably did. I mean, I did. Buy it, that is." She's flustered, stuttering like an idiot.

"You OK, Julie?"

"Yes. I just…"

"You must miss her."

"I do. We, er, we both do."

She looks around for Clare, and is glad to see her coming over, trailing a skinny man in her wake.

"Well," George says easily, "I'm sure she's watching over you today."

"Christ, I hope not!" He blinks and she shakes herself again. "Sorry, George, busy day."

"Of course, of course. I won't hold you up."

"You're not."

"It's fine." He pauses. "We can chat more another time. If you want to, that is?"

She swallows, fights for an answer, but then Clare bounces up.

"Hi, George!"

"Hi, Clare. Lovely this, isn't it?"

"Really lovely," Clare agrees, beaming at him.

The skinny man visibly bristles and tries to insert himself between them. George doesn't even notice.

"Julie and I were just talking about how much your mum would have liked all this."

Clare doesn't even blink. "Oh, she would. Bless her—we couldn't have done it without her."

Julie hears a funny little sound come out of her mouth and isn't surprised when they both look at her askance.

"OK, sis?" Clare asks.

"Fine," she says hastily. "I just, er, reckon we ought to do the speech before people start leaving."

"I'll get out of your way," George says.

"Don't rush off, will you?" Clare trills.

"Oh, I won't," he agrees, although he seems to be looking straight at Julie. It's probably just because the skinny man has now stepped right in front of Clare. No matter. Speech time.

Julie pulls her notes out of her pocket and looks across the happy little crowd to the door. There's still no sign of Michael, but really, so what? This is *her* business, not his, bought with her mum's money—not that she wants to think about that any more than necessary. She can do the speech without him.

She keeps it short, thanking everyone she can think of for helping her out with taking on the building, knocking it through and turning it into the immaculate little space it is now. She remembers, with only a small nudge from Clare, to announce today's ten percent discount.

"Clare and I," she finishes, "are so happy with the way it's turned out and can't wait to get trading again."

She looks at her sister, standing at her side, and forces a smile. This has to be done. They agreed. And it's only fair.

She swallows and gathers herself, and at that moment the door jangles and everyone looks round as Michael sidles in with an apologetic wave. Julie gives him the tiniest of nods. She can't think about him now. She has to finish the speech.

"And so we would like to dedicate the newly extended version of Julie's Flowers to our mother, Linda, may she rest in peace. To Linda!"

"To Linda!" Clare cries heartily at her side, and it's taken up by all their lovely, smiling guests.

Julie glances at the ceiling. I hope you like it, Mum, she thinks. I hope that now that you can see how great it looks, you like it. But she's not sure she does.

"Julie!"

She draws in a breath. "Michael."

"I'm so sorry I was late. The flight was a nightmare and—"

"It doesn't matter."

"But it does. I wanted to be here for you."

"And now you are. Do you have a drink? Collar Adam. He's meant to be doing those. And I think Briony's bringing out more canapés. You must be starving."

"I am actually, but...Ooh, lovely! Are those the little sausage-meat things we made for our twenty-fifth? Remember that—you had me up till three a.m. rolling them out."

"I do remember," she agrees tightly. "Look, I'm sorry, Michael; I really need to, you know, circulate."

"Of course, of course." He's overly hearty, still in work mode perhaps. "And you dedicated it to Linda—that's nice."

"Yes," she agrees, though that's the last thing it is really, and perhaps if he'd been here, making sausage-meat canapés with her, she'd have been able to tell him why.

She takes the tray from Briony and plunges into the crowd.

"Canapé? Veggie? Of course."

Chapter Ten

Day Six

Michael woke and warily opened his eyes. Hallelujah! Sunlight was peeking around the edges of the considerately heavy spare room curtains. He'd made it. For the first time in four long nights his wretched back had eased off enough to let him sleep through.

He felt instantly better. Ridiculous really, but he was buoyed up by the awareness of all those solid hours of sleep working their magic on his body. He'd never really had insomnia before. If he was brutally honest with himself, he'd always slightly looked down on those who did, suspecting it a product of some sort of hysteria, or of insufficient activity during the day. He'd listened to people complaining about being awake in the night and bemoaning the lack of an off switch, and had been smugly certain he'd been sensible enough to have one fitted. Barring the odd bit of jet lag, the only thing that had ever really kept him awake at night had been his children. And even then Julie had picked up most of the slack.

It wasn't that he hadn't wanted to help, just that she'd always heard them first. He'd learned that early on when he'd woken from a very pleasant night's rest to comment to Julie on how lucky they were to have a baby who already slept through. If he concentrated, he could still see her reaction in his mind's eye. Until that point, he'd thought steam only came out of the ears of cartoon characters...

So yes, he was a man with a talent for sleep. Or, as he'd now discovered, a bleeding lucky bastard. Because it turned out that if you woke at three a.m., a little uncomfortable, a little uncertain, a little—dare he say it?—scared, then getting back to sleep was nigh-on impossible. Last night, though, he'd slept through, and the relief was overwhelming.

Slowly he edged off the bed and went to the window. As he pulled the curtains back, sunlight flooded into the room, making him gasp out loud. He drank in the vibrant yellow daffodils at the bottom of the garden, mini suns every bloody one. And if he wasn't mistaken, in the farmer's field beyond...He pressed his nose against the glass. Was that...It was!

"Lambs!" he cried.

"Michael?" Julie's muffled voice came from across the corridor. "Are you OK?"

He clapped a hand over his mouth and hobbled to the door.

"I'm fine. It's just..." He paused on the landing. "Can I come in?"

"Of course."

He nudged open her door and poked his head inside. It was still dark in here, but he could make out Julie lying in the bed, *their* bed. Her bare shoulders stood out, pale and smooth, against the colorful pillows. He stared.

"Michael?"

"Sorry, yes. Miles away. I was just saying...well, lambs!"

"What?"

Even in the semi-darkness, he could see her nose wrinkling as it always did when she was confused. She had a small but very

73

agile nose. He used to tease her about it all the time. He took a couple of steps inside the room.

"There are lambs in the fields at the back. Little tiny newborns all white and bouncy."

He wasn't sure it was the right word to do nature's glorious miracle justice, but Julie sat up anyway. The duvet slipped down her chest, inexorably drawing Michael's gaze before she snatched it close, and he blinked, disorientated.

"Lambs? How gorgeous. I love them when they're new."

He nodded. "At least something in life is getting on as normal. Come and see them."

"Yes. Yes, I will."

She moved to the side of the bed and then stopped, her body suddenly stiff. She was naked, he realized. She was naked and he was standing here in the doorway watching her.

He took a step back and then felt cross with himself. He was her husband. He'd seen her naked more times than he could count, though not—now he came to think about it—for months and months. That was a depressing thought. Over the years, though, he'd explored every damned inch of her. He knew the bits she liked and the bits she hated. He knew the bits *he* liked—which was pretty much all of them. He'd seen her give birth three times. He'd seen her dance and swim and do weird contorted yoga. He'd seen her strip for him. He'd seen her nip to the loo. He'd seen her *on* the loo. He'd caressed her breasts, watched her feed their babies, helped her check for lumps. He knew her inside out, so how come here, on a quiet morning in their own house, she was hesitating to get out of bed in front of him and he was feeling like some sort of perv?

He cleared his throat. "Cup of tea?"

"Lovely."

She smiled gratefully at him and he backed out of the room and made for the stairs, his cheeks flaring. He and Julie had always prided themselves on their natural intimacy. They used to be one of those couples who happily walked around the house naked. Not exhibitionist, not so that the postman was afraid to knock or anything weird like that; just, well, natural. Where had that gone? And how?

His slow progress down the stairs didn't improve his mood. Was this it? All downhill from here? He had so much to do still, so many places to go. They'd had a list once, he and Julie. It had been on the fridge for years, growing steadily longer, their imaginations far fuller than their bank account, so that for every place they knocked off, five more were added—Croatia, Turkey, the Rockies, the Taj Mahal, Paris.

They'd made it to Paris, Turkey too, but nothing further away. And then, at some point, the list of adventures had given way to a list of kids' needs—nappies and pushchairs, tricycles and doll's houses, roller skates and football kits, eyeshadow sets and school trips and driving lessons. No wonder they hadn't been to the Rockies! He loved his children madly and would never be without them. But this morning, bent over like a man with one foot in the frigging grave, he suddenly wondered how much of himself he had given up to them. And how much he and Julie had given up being a couple for being a family, as if, these days, the one could only exist within the other.

The kettle boiled and he carefully made the tea and headed slowly back upstairs. Julie was in his room, safely wrapped up in a big fluffy dressing gown.

"Here you go."

She turned from the window. "Lovely. Thanks, Michael."

She moved over to make room for him at the window and he set his mug on the sill next to hers and looked out. Their garden stretched out below them, not especially well groomed, not especially exciting, but theirs. Adam's abandoned skateboard ramp sat to one side, the old swing still creaked from the apple tree and Mr. Nibbles was out in his run, enjoying a bit of grass in the early sunshine. At the bottom, a little gate led out into the farmer's field, disguised as fence because they weren't really meant to have access. The lambs were close now and he watched as a group of them jostled to get to the top of a small mound, eager to see as much of their new world as they could.

"Ooh, look, they're jumping!" Julie squealed. Sure enough, a couple of the little things were doing that amazing four-footed leap peculiar to new lambs, as if joy was literally propelling them into the air. "They're just so full of life."

"Lucky them." It was out before he could stop it.

"Michael?"

"Lucky them," he repeated, going for a lighter tone and waving a hand in the vague direction of his back.

"Oh. Right. How is it?"

"Getting better, I think. Slowly."

"I hope so."

"Me too. Sorry you've had to do everything."

"Oh, that's fine. Probably as well that you're improving, though. You're a far better cook than me."

"Far duller."

She laughed almost shyly. "With food that might be a good thing. I'm not sure my prawn curry was a culinary triumph."

Michael thought back to last night's meal, which could charitably have been called interesting.

"I wonder if the addition of the baked beans was wise," he said carefully.

She laughed again, louder this time. She'd always been able to take a joke, Julie.

"It was bonkers. Don't know what I was thinking!"

"Well, I'll cook tonight."

"Great."

"You'll be in?"

She sighed. "I'll be in. We're all in, always."

"Course."

She didn't need to sound so glum about it, he thought. She used to love nights in with him. But then he hadn't exactly been great company recently, so perhaps he couldn't blame her. He peered intently at the lambs, willing some of their positivity into himself.

"Can't believe it's nearly April already," he said, and saw her stiffen at the same time as his own body tightened. April—the month of their anniversary. In just three weeks they'd have been married for thirty-five years. But the last few years hadn't been the marriage he'd pictured for them.

Talk to her, Michael, his mum's voice said in his head, and he shivered. She was right, he was sure, but after all this time, he had no idea where to begin.

Chapter Eleven

June 2016

Michael straightens his new shirt and checks his reflection in the unfamiliar mirror. Is it smart enough? Should he wear a tie? A jacket? What's appropriate for a date with your wife of thirty years?

"Beer, mate?" Rob asks, popping his head round the door.

"Please," he says gratefully, accepting the bottle of lager and taking a deep swig. He's more of a real-ale man usually, but anything will do right now. "I feel like I'm going on a bloody first date."

Rob grins at him. "Nice to feel like that after thirty years."

"I guess so."

He daren't tell his mate that this is less the fizz of excitement than a fear of getting it wrong. He thought he'd been so clever with this birthday present. He'd considered it so carefully, keen to spoil her after they'd both been working so hard. Not that he minds that. It was what they agreed, after all. With the kids leaving home, they were going to do things for themselves to stay positive and forward-focused—or something like that—but he has to admit that it seems to have led to rather more time apart than he'd anticipated. But no matter. He bagged his promotion last month, so he'll be under less pressure to say yes to every little trip and can spend more time with Julie. Starting tonight.

He just wishes she seemed more excited about it.

He was so looking forward to presenting the voucher to her on her birthday last month, eager to see her reaction. As an avid *MasterChef* fan for years, she's been going on about eating at a Michelin-starred restaurant, and he was delighted to bag the reservation. He couldn't get it on her birthday itself, which, typically, fell on a Saturday this year, but a Thursday wasn't so bad. Or so he'd thought. Her face when she opened the little envelope, however, was not the picture of delight he'd been eagerly imagining for weeks.

"Oh." That was all she said.

"It's got a Michelin star," Michael told her, "like you've always wanted."

"How lovely," she managed, but it sounded hollow.

She turned the envelope over and over in her hands, as if willing something else to fall out.

"What were you hoping for?" he asked, but her smile was snapping into place and her shoulders were going back and the answer was a bright "Nothing in particular. This is wonderful, Michael. Very thoughtful."

Which was precisely what he'd thought it was, but he seemed to have got it wrong. This last week, however, Julie has seemed more excited, and when she suggested the other day that they meet at the restaurant, like a proper date, he snatched at the idea. It's romantic, something he's never been all that good at, so he's made a real effort.

"Tie?" he asks Rob.

"Nah, mate. Too formal."

"It's a posh place, though."

He tries it on, pictures himself arriving in the restaurant, fiddles with the knot.

"Just the jacket will do. Trust me."

"Why should I trust a man who drinks lager?"

"Oi!" Rob protests, but good-humoredly. Nothing much ever fazes the scruffy old biker.

Michael picks up a little velvet box from the side and checks the necklace is safely snuggled within. The meal was meant to be her main present, but it seems something else might be needed and he agonized for ages over it. He thinks this is perfect—a silver daisy. Very her. Or at least, very much the way she used to be. The way he hopes he can help her be again—if she'll let him.

"Taxi!" Rob says, looking out the window.

Michael downs the last of his beer, tosses the tie decisively aside, puts the jewelry box in his pocket and heads for the door.

"Guessing I won't see you later?" Rob says.

"God, I hope not!"

He fidgets like a teenager all the way. He finds himself day-dreaming about what she'll be wearing, how she'll have her hair, what she'll smell like. And boy, she doesn't disappoint. She's sitting at the bar in a stunning dark orange dress, short enough to reveal her still shapely legs and low enough to expose her luscious cleavage. He stares, drinking her in, before she turns and spots him. The necklace he's chosen will sit just perfectly at the top of the enticing line between her breasts, and he pats the pocket it's nestled in, wondering exactly when to give it to her. And then she's turning and smiling and he's suddenly sure it's all going to be OK.

"Cocktail, my love?" she suggests as he approaches.

She's all twinkly-eyed and it's so lovely to see that he agrees, despite a fairly well-vaunted hatred of fussy drinks. For a moment, he feels a little bit James Bond, though he has the sense not to order a martini. His whisky sour, served in a classy tumbler with no umbrella or gaudy fruit in sight, is surprisingly delicious, and the ambience is wonderfully sophisticated. He's about to draw out his gift when a waiter approaches.

"Your table is ready, sir, madam."

"Brilliant!" Julie blurts.

Michael looks at her askance. "Brilliant, Jules? That's sophisticated!"

She blushes. "Sorry. Got carried away. I'm just, you know, excited about the table. About the food."

"Right." It feels odd suddenly, as if a little of the romance has slipped. "But I was about to give you your present," he protests.

"Oh." She stops, one foot on the floor, one still on the stool. "Sorry. Present?"

"Of course. It's your birthday meal after all."

He gives her what he hopes is a suave smile and the waiter takes a careful step backward. Julie looks awkwardly across the room.

"But our table..."

She's distracted. It isn't the time. He withdraws his hand from his pocket and stands up.

"It'll wait. Shall we?"

"Yes please!"

She beams up at him and takes his arm and all feels well again. It's just the obsequious waiter throwing them. They aren't used to places like this, he thinks, as they're shown through to the muted dining area. Too many of their meals out in the last twenty years have been at McDonald's or, if they're pushing the boat out, Nando's. But now, with the girls in homes of their own and Adam at university, they can get used to dining in style again.

He smiles down at Julie, but they're being led past the intimate tables for two and into the middle of the room. The waiter, for some reason, is ushering them toward a circular table for five, and he's about to tell him there's been some sort of mistake when he sees them—Sophie, Briony and Adam, inexplicably here and now leaping up and shouting: "Surprise!"

"What? How?" He's stuttering like a fool. "Why?" he eventually settles on. "Why are you here?"

"Mum invited us," Adam says.

"To celebrate with you," Briony beams.

Only Sophie sees the look in his eyes.

"Is that OK, Dad?"

Well, what can he say?

"OK? It's wonderful!"

And it is, in its way. He has a lovely evening with his family. The food is delicious, the service impeccable, the chatter long and happy and easy.

But it isn't romantic. And the daisy necklace remains in his pocket, ungiven and unappreciated.

Chapter Twelve

Day Ten

Julie trod her third circle around the kitchen table. April Fool's Day—ha! That was the biggest nonsense ever. This year they were all April fools and life felt like one long practical joke.

Go on, the mop taunted her from the corner behind the fridge, *you know you want to.*

"I do not!" she told it. It sulked. "Or you either," she told the ironing board, cuddled up beside it. "I'm not that desperate."

The truth, however, was that she was getting dangerously close.

Eight days she'd been at home kicking her heels while her poor shop sat gathering dust. Clare had done her best with taking the business online, but it had soon become apparent that people weren't really ordering flowers at the moment, with their priorities being toilet roll and flour. Reluctantly Julie had filled out the government forms to furlough her sister and tried to think of jobs she could usefully do to prep the business for rebirth when this was all over. There weren't many. Her stock books were straight, her accounts up to date, her website as slick as it needed to be. It had been sort of nice to find out that she was actually quite efficient, but it hadn't left her with much to do, and that rankled.

Work had been the religion of her youth: "Idle hands are the devil's tools" her mum had always told her two girls, and they'd both taken it to heart in different ways, Clare with schoolwork and Julie with craft projects. Julie's had been very much the messier approach and she'd often envied Clare the quiet order of her contained desk. Sometimes she'd even tried to put her head down over her own books, but within a week or two she'd see a dressing table tossed into a skip, or find a book on rag rugs, and she'd be off again, creating.

Linda had admired her projects, when she'd had the chance to look. She'd brought them up single-handedly in a time when that had been far from the norm, and had always had at least two jobs on the go, as well as endless necessary DIY projects to keep their house just about holding together. Looking back, Julie couldn't quite remember when her mother's incessant productivity had turned into incessant partying instead. Probably when her purse-lipped parents had died, leaving her with all the funds she'd so badly needed when the girls were small. Credit to her, Linda had thrown herself into spending money with the same gusto she'd shown in earning it.

Julie shuddered. This was the problem with having so much time in the day—memories could creep up on you. Normally she kept them at bay with work and socializing, but without those walls in place they ran amok, and sometimes, especially if she woke at night, she feared a return of the dark days after Linda's death three years ago. She ground her teeth. Yesterday she'd gone to the shop, all set to spring-clean the hell out of it, but the sight of the place so hollow and empty had cut through her bleaching enthusiasm, and in the end she'd abandoned it and come home.

Perhaps she could loan it to someone to live in, she thought now, fighting to be positive. A nurse perhaps, worried about returning to their family, or a youngster whose parents were driving them mad. Her thoughts went to Adam, living it up with blinking Chelsea's family. She'd FaceTimed him last night, seen him sitting on someone else's sofa with someone else's curtains behind him. Funny pattern they'd been. Very geometric. Not her sort of thing at all, but maybe it was Adam's. He was going to be a surveyor after all; he probably liked the sort of quiet order that squares and rectangles offered. Maybe it was all her swirls and flowers that he was running away from.

God, she missed him. It was almost as painful as it had been when he'd gone off traveling in his year out and her house had suddenly been so empty. She should have been used to it by then. She'd hated it when Sophie had left to live down the road with friends, and even more so when Briony had insisted on picking a university three hours away, but when Adam had gone it had felt as if life had almost stopped.

Other mothers talked about how much they loved having daughters to talk to, but for Julie it had always been Adam who'd had time for her. Briony had been too busy studying and Sophie too caught up in chasing the next worthy cause to waste time sitting about the kitchen gossiping. Adam, however, had always had all the time in the world, and it wasn't until he'd gone that she'd realized how much she'd come to rely on that. And now he was sitting chatting to Chelsea's mum instead.

They're normal, he'd said. It stung still. His own family were normal too, surely? Super-normal. Straightforward jobs, ordinary house, straight-down-the-line kids. Sophie marrying a potter was about the most out-there thing that any of them had ever done. So what was it Adam was after at Chelsea's house?

Maybe Chelsea's parents slept in the same room.

The thought popped, unwelcomed, into her head. Michael hadn't slept in her bed since that Christmas a couple of years ago, when all three kids were staying. The Christmas they'd been so close to actually having sex before his back had apparently locked up the moment her dress had come off. It had looked fine playing beer pong with the kids the next day, she'd noticed, but it had been a funny time for her, and when he'd crept back to the harder mattress of the spare room once everyone had gone away again, she'd been quite glad of the space.

She'd try again in another month, she had promised herself, and then in another, and then when she eventually had, it had gone so poorly she'd not bothered again. But when he'd stood there the other morning as she'd gone to get up, it had felt so very weird and she couldn't get it out of her head. Perhaps it had been because of the brown envelope in her bedside drawer. Had he sensed it? Had he *read* it? She could swear the drawer had been open further than usual the other day, so she'd moved the envelope into the next drawer down, beneath all those worthy books she'd always meant to read.

He'd taken to bringing her a cup of tea in bed every morning recently. He was awake early, he said, and routine was good. He'd been reading an article that said they had to find ways to anchor themselves to some form of normality. Julie could see his point, but given that he'd last made her tea in bed five years ago, she wasn't sure it felt in any way normal. Nice, though. She'd started wearing a T-shirt so that she could sit up and take the mug without it feeling awkward. They only managed the odd stilted sentence or two—talk of government advice or new stats or Facebook posts—but it was something to get her going in the morning.

But that still left the rest of the day. She went out for her hour's exercise religiously; twice if she hadn't actually seen anyone the first time. The fields were fuller than she'd ever seen them. If you panned around you could always see one or two people out with delighted (or weary) dogs, or jogging in thrown-together outfits, or just meandering along, grateful to escape the house. But there was space enough to stay at least twenty meters apart from each other, so it seemed safe enough. Every time she traced her way through the green grass, past the lambs, through the hedges full of singing birds and round the trees bursting into blossom, she thought of those poor people stuck in fifth-floor flats and thanked her lucky stars for all she had. But it didn't mean it wasn't hard.

"God, I hate this!" she all but shouted at the mop.

She pushed open the back door and escaped into the garden. The sun was shining and she wandered over to move Mr. Nibbles' cage to a fresh patch of grass. He was lazing in bed but came hopping out as she tugged on the run.

"Morning, Mr. N."

He didn't reply. She sometimes fancied that he talked to Michael, who, after all, had been the one who'd given in to Briony's nagging and who, as far as Julie could see, had taken to the rabbit almost as much as his daughter had. She looked around.

"You could do some gardening," Michael had suggested the other day. "Plant those flower beds you've always wanted."

It had been a good idea, she supposed, but not an especially appealing one, as she wasn't actually that keen on growing flowers. She knew everyone else thought that was really weird for a florist, but she didn't see why. No one expected an artist to make their own paints, did they?

"I could restore some of the furniture," she'd countered. "I've been meaning to distress the dining room table for years."

Michael had closed his eyes. "How do you distress a table, Julie?"

"Oh, you know, sand it down, rough it up a bit, paint it."

"Right. Sounds—"

"Don't say messy."

He bit his lip. "I wasn't going to."

But he had been, and as she'd need him to help her carry the table outside, she'd given up. Oh, this was useless. She missed the shop so much, missed working there with her sister and all her lovely flowers. She hadn't realized until she was robbed of it quite how much she'd come to rely on it not just for work, but for her own sanity.

*

Julie locks up the shop and heads around the back toward the parking area, but pulls up short in front of the café. The ex-café. The business closed last month and the place sits forlornly empty now. Even the tables and chairs have gone, with just one broken chair sitting unhappily in the far corner next to an abandoned broom and a chipped coffee mug. It's as if the owner lost all motivation at the back end of the cleaning process and just put her stuff down and walked out. Julie can't say she blames her. It would break her heart to have to close the flower shop, especially now, when it's all she has to throw her energies into.

Adam has been off traveling the world for six months, after finishing his A levels, and she surely ought to be used to his absence. She *has* to get used to it. He'll be home at the back end of the summer, but only to get ready for university. He has officially left and she has to turn her attention to her own life now, just as she and Michael promised each other they would do. As it is right she should do.

She refuses to be identified simply as a mum. She has a career, friends, hobbies. Yet there is no denying that looking after her kids has been a huge part of her life, and to find herself with none of that to do has been a bit like a professional sportswoman suddenly ceasing to train. She's been failing miserably in all the little projects she lined up for herself to avoid being a cliché of an empty-nester, finding it almost impossible to muster her usual energy for any of them. But the café—the café has finally fired up her imagination.

She presses her face to the glass. Already she can see dust

gathering in the cracks between the wooden floorboards and on the light fittings. The walls are a dark orange, and although it's a color she loves, it makes the space look smaller than it is. If it was hers, she'd be able to knock the connecting wall through and double the space in her own shop. Then she'd paint it something light and bright—and, of course, fill it with flowers. Or maybe plants. Clare thinks plants would be good. She's found a nursery that would be prepared to do them a really good deal on wholesale supplies, and is full of ideas. Not full of money, though, but Julie has a plan for that.

She looks back to her own frontage and smiles at the curling lines of the words above the door: Julie's Flowers. She can hardly believe it's ten whole years since she opened the shop, but it has to be because, even more unbelievably, she turns fifty in two months' time. Fifty! It's best not to think about that too much. And definitely best not to say it out loud. She knows she's meant to be a liberated, sassy, wrinkles-give-you-character type of a woman, but it's a lot easier to appreciate that sort of approach in others than to feel it yourself.

The only good thing about such a big birthday, as far as she can see, is the big present. Michael gave her the first half of her shop for her fortieth, and she's praying that the second might follow now.

She gives a little skip, as if she's approaching five not fifty, and then looks hastily around in case she's been seen. Two small boys are staring at her whilst their mum chats to a friend, but they don't seem to mind her jumping around in front of an empty shop, so she just smiles at them and skips again. She's been dropping all sorts of hints. Michael doesn't really get to the shop much these days, with all the hours he works, but that doesn't matter. She's pinned the estate agent's details up in the kitchen. And she's been talking at dinner about her favorite things in life, about her goals with Adam off to uni, about how good it is that Michael is earning more money now and can invest in her, to grow the business. He's not stupid, Michael; he'll get it.

Half a shop at forty; a whole shop at fifty. She needs it. It will be her new nest now that Adam is gone, and she can't wait.

*

Slowly Julie opened her eyes. She'd been so naïve back then. She'd expected Michael to deliver, and the disappointment had been huge. Unfairly so. That restaurant had been lovely, after all. And she had, in the end, felt a little bit mean inviting the kids along. If he'd just bought her the shop lease, though, she wouldn't have had to look for the money elsewhere, would she?

Enough, Julie!

The sun beat relentlessly down, coaxing her out of her dark thoughts. She wasn't some little woman, reliant on her husband's charity, and it wasn't fair to blame him for all that had followed. It was her own fault and she had to deal with it and move on. It was just the inactivity that was getting to her; that and the loneliness. What she needed was a little company, even if it had to be virtual. She leapt up, newly decisive, pulled out her phone and FaceTimed Clare. Her sister answered on the second ring.

"Julie! How the devil are you?"

"Bored? Fed up? A bit lonely."

Clare pulled a face. "Try being me. I'm not meant to see Dharmesh at all in lockdown. It's hell, Julie. I've finally found a man I actually like being with, and we're kept apart by a bloody worldwide virus. What sort of batshit karma is that?!"

Julie smiled at her sister, feeling instantly better as she watched her pull a silly face.

"You'll just have to move in with him."

"God, no! There is no way that poor man is ready for a full-time me. I'd kill off any hope of a proper relationship instantly. Especially the way I am right now—climbing the frigging walls with boredom. I even did a Zumba class yesterday. Zumba, Julie! You know how I feel about Zumba."

At that, Julie actually laughed, her mood lifting further. She did know; her sister had been most vociferous about it. Zumba, in Clare's book, was even worse than a walk, because it was not only not a sport, it was a dance pretending to be a sport. Not that Clare disliked dancing, as long as it was after midnight and at least a bottle of wine, and, obviously, not pretending to be a sport. Clare had very complex rules.

"Did you enjoy it?"

She shrugged. "It was OK. Nothing like a good game of hockey, but at least it got me moving about a bit. I'm useless at it, mind. I'm not too bad at the leg bits, but as soon as I try and put the arms in as well, I just lose it. How do people do that, Julie?"

"I don't know, sis. Maybe there's more to dancing than you thought?"

Clare stuck her tongue out at her. "Well, anyway, I found myself signing up to do it again this morning. It might be rubbish, but it beats doing absolutely nothing at all."

"Zumba?" Julie said thoughtfully.

"Hey, sis—do it with me. It's a Zoom thing. There's the teacher in a big picture and then all the little participants in tiny squares. They can barely see you at all, which, take it from me, is a very good thing."

"When is it?"

Clare glanced at the clock behind her. "In ten minutes."

"Ten? No way. I'm not ready."

"But you can be."

"No, I—"

"Come on—don't be a bore."

"What?!"

"In normal life you'd whip up a full bouquet in ten minutes."

"But I'd *enjoy* doing that!"

"I know," Clare said sadly. She sighed. "I miss the shop, Julie."

"Me too. So, so much. I wish—"

Clare clicked her fingers.

"No point wishing, sis—shift your ass upstairs and get some kit on. I'll send you the link and I expect to see you prancing away in your little square next to me bang on the hour."

Julie groaned, but there was no arguing with Clare when she got like this; the best thing to do was just to capitulate, so she headed inside to try and find something vaguely Zumba-appropriate in her wardrobe.

She could hear Michael chatting away to his colleagues in Briony's room and envied him his job. All credit to him, he'd thrown himself into it these ten years and had shot up the ladder. First the promotion they'd agreed he should aim for, and then another soon after.

She bit at her relentlessly resurfacing resentment, trying to chase it away. It wasn't Michael's fault he could still work in lockdown, and it wasn't his fault that she couldn't, though he'd done precious little to encourage her recently. It was a miracle she'd made anything of the shop at all. Her mum had thought that, she was sure of it, and perhaps Michael had too.

"Well, if so, they were wrong," she hissed into her wardrobe, digging for a T-shirt big enough to cover her distinctly un-Zumba-like body. "I did it anyway. I did it all myself."

Downstairs, the ancient hallway clock chimed the hour and she jumped. She'd be late; Clare would kill her. Not that Clare *could* kill her, being shut away in her house and all, but even so . . . She pulled on leggings and scrambled downstairs to grab the iPad, already regretting saying she'd do this. She wasn't in the mood. She'd be better digging the stupid flower beds, or maybe pulling her plastic training blooms down from the loft to practice with, or—

"Morning, class!"

The girl was that infuriating combination of petite and buxom that Julie refused to believe was natural. She looked about twelve and had hair as bouncy as her perfect body, and a smile that was so friendly it was hard—despite all the rest of her irritating perfections—to dislike her.

"I'm Shelley, and this is Zuuumba!"

Oh Lord, such a long vowel. Julie glanced anxiously at the door; the last thing she needed was Michael coming down for a cuppa and walking in on her Zuuumba-ing with Shelley.

"Welcome back to all my regulars and lovely to see a couple of new faces. Give us a wave, Brenda!" An older lady gave an enthusiastic wiggle. "And hiya, Julie!"

It took Julie a minute to realize that the other older lady next to Brenda was herself. Reluctantly she waved. A text pinged up on her phone.

Hiya, Julie!!

Piss off, Clare. I'm concentrating.

In her tiny square Clare gave her a covert thumbs-up. Julie stuck her tongue out at her, then realized everyone else could see and focused on Shelley.

"So today we're going round the world!" Shelley cried. "We may all be stuck in our houses, but if we work with our feet, we can travel as far as we want."

Somehow Julie doubted it. She looked down at her own feet, slightly gnarled and misshapen in graying socks, and wished them luck. But Shelley was bouncing around now and she'd just have to take a leap of faith and follow her. She did the warm-up moves as best she could, then suddenly Shelley was calling: "And taaango!"

The girl went up onto the balls of her feet and did some sort of kick-wiggle combination that Julie tried and failed to follow. The wiggle felt quite nice, though, so she decided not to worry too much about the specifics. Her little square was *very* small after all.

"Cha cha cha!" Shelley encouraged, exaggerating her movements for them all to copy. Around her, twelve middle-aged women shuffled about in some sort of parody of her movements. Part of Julie wanted to laugh, but another part was just enjoying the feel of the music.

"And now—arms. Like this, ladies. Loveleeee!"

It was not, as far as Julie could see, in the slightest bit lovely. Arms were waving in all sorts of directions, more like Dutch windmills than Argentinian seductresses. Clare was right, getting four limbs in time with each other was impossible. Still, as long as both her legs and her arms were moving, that had to be burning calories, and burning calories meant she'd be allowed wine later. She threw herself into it with abandon.

Higher, Julie.

She ignored Clare's facetious text. She'd talk to her afterward. For now, Shelley was taking them across to Egypt and a bit of belly-dancing. Ah well—at least she was equipped for that one!

She wasn't sure how long Michael had been standing there when she noticed him. She'd been concentrating so hard on the Bollywood moves that she'd seen nothing but Shelley's snake-like body for ages. She froze.

"Oh, don't stop," he said. "You look great."

"I do not."

She tugged at the T-shirt, trying to get it to cover her saggy arse.

"You do! I'd forgotten what a great dancer you are."

94

Julie felt herself blush like a girl. "Nonsense, Michael. I can't get any of the moves right."

"They look pretty right to me."

"Not compared to her." She gestured to Shelley as the girl danced on to the hypnotic music. Michael came forward a few steps and peered at the screen.

"Oh. I hadn't even noticed her."

"Bollocks!"

"I hadn't. I was enjoying watching you."

"Voyeur," she teased, still feeling rather sultry. Her feet, it turned out, weren't half bad at taking her around the world, though her arms were definitely playing catch-up. "You can join in if you like."

He tipped his head to one side, considering, and then to her astonishment, he nodded.

"OK then. What's next?"

"Erm…" She looked at the screen, where Shelley was announcing a "coooool-down" and dropping into something gentle to match the strains of "The Blue Danube." "Looks a bit like a waltz."

"Perfect. May I?"

"I'm not sure that Shelley…"

But Shelley had spotted Michael's arrival and was clapping delightedly.

"Ooh, look, Julie has a partner for this one. Loveleeee!"

So as Michael held out his hand and bowed, Julie had little chance but to put her own hand into his and allow him to pull her close. She'd never understood before why people had originally thought the waltz such a racy dance, but standing in her living room with her own husband and half a dozen total strangers watching, it felt unbelievably intimate. It was the closest they'd got to each other in a long time.

She let her head drop against his shoulder and felt him lead

95

her gently across the carpet: one-two-three, one-two-three. She glanced at her phone for a sarcastic text from Clare, but none came. One-two-three, one-two-three. The music shifted into Lewis Capaldi, but Michael didn't stop and neither did she. Maybe, if they kept going, her feet could carry her not just around the world, but back in time. One-two-three, one—

"And that's it for today! Well done, ladies—and our guest gent too, of course. Give yourselves a great big clap and I hope to see you all again tomorrow for Shelley's Zuuumba!"

The screen cut to black, the music died and Michael let go of her hands.

"That was nice," he said.

"Yes. Yes, it was. Er, thank you." They looked at each other, unsure what to do next, and when her phone rang out, Julie leapt for it. "Clare!"

Michael looked at her a little sadly, then with a soft smile made for the kitchen. As Julie sank down to listen to her sister's opinion on the class—"Travel with our feet? What crap!"—she heard the kettle click on and wished for a moment that she hadn't bothered to pick up.

Chapter Thirteen

"Michael!" Bett sounded endearingly surprised to see him, despite it having been her who'd placed the FaceTime call. "How are you, sweetheart?"

Michael gladly put down the report on a particularly tricky gorge in the Czech Republic that he'd been failing to make head or tail of for far too long now. His mind seemed to have been scrambled ever since that strange Zumba class earlier.

"Good, Mum, thanks."

"Surviving?"

"So far."

"And the kids?"

"They're fine too. Sophie's in full lockdown with Leo and Adam is safe on the coast with his girlfriend. Briony's in London, though, which is a bit of a worry."

"Isn't it just. How's Julie coping?"

Michael pictured his wife dancing away in the living room earlier and squirmed.

"She's good."

"I'm glad to hear that. Look after her, won't you?"

"Of course." There were some odd noises coming from

downstairs actually; he probably ought to investigate. In a minute. "But how are *you*, Mum?"

"Oh, I'm right as rain, sweetheart. The gin's running a bit low but we've set up our own still."

Michael stared at the screen in horror. "Isn't that a bit dangerous? You can produce methanol, you know, if—"

"Michael, please! I'm a chemist. I know what I'm doing."

"Course you do. Sorry. It'd just be ironic to avoid the virus and poison yourself with dodgy moonshine."

"Moonshine!" Bett chuckled. "I'll tell Liz to call it that. She's doing the labels."

"Labels? Plural? How much of this stuff are you making, Mum?"

"Oh, you know." She waved an airy hand. "Enough."

"For the three of you, or for the whole bridge club?"

She looked shifty. "It's important in these harsh times to help your neighbors."

"With milk and medicine and stuff, yes—not with illegal alcohol."

Bett rolled her eyes. "Honestly, Michael. When did you get so stuffy?"

Michael frowned. Was that what he was? Stuffy? He swallowed.

"I think maybe I was always a bit like that."

Bett laughed. "Nonsense, Michael. You were a serious child, for sure, but to be fair to you, Ken and I were a bit serious back then too. All that work. I wish we'd gone out a bit more, eaten meals in interesting restaurants, traveled to unusual places, gone dancing."

Michael's thoughts leapt straight back to Julie and those sinuous Bollywood moves he'd walked in on.

"You do?" he squeaked.

She nodded. "That was one of the reasons I was glad you found Julie—she's never been afraid of pushing the boundaries."

"No."

"And she released that in you too."

"Well, maybe it's gone back inside these days."

Bett leant forward, so close to the screen that all he could see was her eyes. It was freaky.

"Mum! What are you doing?"

"Getting a good look at you. You've not talked to her yet, have you?"

"We talk."

"Talk? Or *talk*?"

He groaned. "Women! We talk, OK."

She sat back, put her hands up. "OK! Now, would you like some moonshine? I can't get it to you at the moment, obviously, but I can save you a bottle from the second batch."

"Second...?" Michael gave up. "Sounds great, Mum, thanks."

"Fantastic. I'll look forward to sharing a tipple with you and Jules when we're let out again."

"That would be good. I'd better go, Mum. Work, you know."

"Of course. Love to all. Take care. Byeee!"

"Byeee," Michael echoed faintly, but Bett was already gone.

He looked down at his report, but it seemed even less appealing than before. He could hear Julie clattering around downstairs, doing goodness knows what, and felt a strong urge to go and offer to help, but he was feeling strangely shy about facing her after their waltz.

Oh, it had been lovely. She'd felt so very natural in his arms, and yet the moment the music had stopped, they'd pulled apart, both suddenly aware of how long it had been since they'd danced together and unsure of how to behave. These days Julie did all her dancing out with the girls. Michael hated dancing, or so she told everyone, Michael included.

"I don't hate dancing," he'd insisted when she'd first started going out with Clare, after Adam had left home and their evenings had suddenly felt very empty. "I just hate tacky clubs."

But somehow him not liking dancing had become embedded in her head, and she'd gone out with Clare more and more, leaving him at home to watch documentaries on seventies musicians, as if tacitly agreeing that his nights out were in the past. Why had he done that? Why hadn't he just been open to going along? And was it too late to change? He looked again at the door, willing himself to go down to his wife, but at that moment a meeting reminder popped up on his computer. Damn! Ah well, he'd get this out of the way and then perhaps he'd go and find out what the hell Julie was up to down there.

Julie looked at the mass of coats around her feet and wondered if a slightly more methodical approach would have been a good idea. Ah well, too late now! The coat hooks were exposed and that had been her main aim, so she should just get on with the job in hand and worry about tidying up later. She looked for the toolbox but it was the other side of the coat mountain. Damn— why did she never think these things through properly?

She'd been fired up to actually get on and do something, that was the problem. All that silly dancing had left her restless and fidgety. She'd considered going up into the loft for her plastic flowers, but when she'd got upstairs, Michael had been talking away to people and she'd worried about making too much noise. It had been a relief to spot the list of jobs that had taken over the kitchen board:

> *Downstairs loo—flush sticks*
> *Coat hooks by back door bent—coats fall off*
> *Paint football marks off back door*
> *Mend hinge on back door*
> *Get new frigging back door*

Post-Zumba Julie had not found it especially helpful. She was hardly going to knock up a new back door, was she? And there was no point in either mending or painting it if they were going to replace it. The loo was beyond her—she'd tried once before and just succeeded in flooding the hall—so she'd decided to go for it with the coat hooks. She had perhaps, however, gone for it a little too enthusiastically.

She looked at the pile of coats, wondering as she always did why they had so many of the things. There were big anoraks and light walking coats, going-out coats, denim jackets, rain macs and biker jackets. Something snagged in Julie's mind at the last one. Where was *her* biker jacket? It was a beautiful thing, boldly colored in orange and black and made of the softest leather, with all the fancy pads to keep her safe if she fell off. Michael had bought it for her quite soon into their relationship. Some sort of anniversary—one of those month-based ones that seemed important in the days before you were staring a thirty-five-year one in the face.

She'd been stunned. It had been the most expensive thing anyone but her parents had ever bought her. Actually, anyone *including* her parents. He'd bowled her over like that often in the early days—broken out of his straight-bloke persona to do something totally surprising and, as a result, ridiculously romantic. Not that he'd seen it that way.

"You can't come on the bike with me without decent protection," he'd said, shy in the face of her gratitude.

"Decent protection doesn't have to come in flash orange and black," she'd replied, kissing him. "I love it."

And once she'd got on the bike, she'd loved it even more. The whole experience had caught her instantly—to her great surprise. You couldn't talk on a motorbike and she'd thought she'd hate that, but actually she'd found it curiously restful. There was no need to find words, no need to entertain or interest anyone.

101

You could just sit there and take everything in, and for Julie that had been a welcome novelty.

She'd always felt the pressure of silence, had never really understood how people could describe it as "companionable." For her it smacked of disinterest, of social failure, of people not getting along with each other. She'd always been first to fill a conversational gap and the bike had been a revelation—she could just be there on Gertie's leather seat with Michael without having to actually say anything at all. To stay on, to stay still and to watch the road pass beneath them were all that were required of her, and she'd loved it immediately. Better than any fancy meditation, better than any sport, better than any therapy.

Nasty, dangerous things, bikes, she reminded herself with a shudder. She didn't want to go on one, not since the accident, but she couldn't stop a sudden yearning for the sheer glamour of tugging that jacket on and feeling instantly like a more exciting version of herself.

Enough, she told herself. This wasn't going to get the hooks straight. Fighting her way through the coats, she snatched up the toolbox and found some pliers. She placed them carefully around the first hook and pulled gently upward. As if by magic, the metal curved obediently back into place—or somewhere close. Delighted, Julie stood back and admired her handiwork. This DIY lark was easy. It took a matter of moments to complete the run of ten; then, pleased with herself, she took a picture and bent to the far less satisfying task of re-hanging the coats. Replacing just those that belonged to her or Michael, however, took very little time. She stared at the remaining pile. She could put them in the spare room wardrobe, except that it was currently stuck on its side. Where had Michael put its contents?

She glanced up at the ceiling, picturing him above her in Briony's room. Her body stirred again at the memory of the gentle yet assertive way he'd taken her in his arms, and, unnerved, she bent to gather the coats. She'd ask him where to put them, perhaps see if he wanted a cup of tea whilst she was at it, or maybe some lunch. He made dinner most nights now, after all, so she owed him. They weren't the most natural of meals. Once they'd covered whatever had been in the daily briefing and any updates either of them had on the kids, it was hard to find much to talk about. They'd had a happy moment yesterday when he'd shown her a gorgeous video of ducks nesting in the empty canals of Venice, but then they'd both remembered that Venice was another of those places they'd always intended to visit and it had all got awkward again.

Drawing in a deep breath, she headed upstairs to Briony's door. She eased it open and peeped around, but Michael was deep in some conference call, talking very earnestly at four attentive faces on the screen about cantilevers and dead loads. It sounded quite impressive actually, in his low, serious voice, and she could have stood there for ages listening. It was definitely not, however, a good thing to interrupt just to ask about coats, so instead she backed hastily out.

Michael looked longingly at the door as it closed—remarkably gently—behind Julie, then turned reluctantly back to the others in his meeting, willing them to hurry up. It was fantastic that the company were going to back his innovative bridge design, but now he just wanted rid of them. He'd only noticed Julie as she'd turned to go, but as far as he could see, she'd had a pile of coats in her arms. Why?

He made a couple of encouraging noises to the senior executive who was warbling on about government sponsorship and wished he'd looked into that app someone had told him about that made you look like you were paying attention while you actually drifted off to something more interesting.

He thought of the clothing he'd pulled out of the wardrobe

before he'd done his stupid back in and the final item sprang to mind—Julie's biker jacket. When had they last been on holiday together? Not just on the bike, but at all? There'd been a few weekends away with friends, but always in boisterous groups, and with the kids gone, there'd been none of the amazing family holidays they'd enjoyed so much when they were younger. They should have resurrected that list of places to visit. Wasn't that what they'd always planned? He'd crossed Croatia off a few years ago, but that had been with Rob, a fellow biker from the Guzzi enthusiasts club that Julie had bought him membership for after... well, after she'd stopped wanting to come out on Gertie any more.

"Everything OK, Michael?" The senior exec was staring at him curiously.

"Yes, yes. Sorry—some sort of noise outside, that's all. Working from home, hey?"

They all laughed heartily from their various home offices around the world, so very different but drawn together by this global pandemic. At the last meeting, their Chinese consultant's two-year-old daughter had toddled into the middle of a discussion on legal issues and they'd all paused a moment to smile at her, business problems thrown into instant perspective. The barriers between work and home life seemed to have broken down a little, and to Michael it felt like a good thing. He'd never dared talk to his boss about domestic issues when his kids had been little. Perhaps it would have been easier if he had; perhaps he'd have been able to help Julie out more.

He could hear Julie going into Sophie's room and fidgeted as the accountant picked up an ominously large sheet of figures and began addressing the meeting. For the first time in ages, work did not seem the all-involving pleasure it had been for the last ten years, and for the first time too, he questioned what that particular egotistical pleasure had robbed him of.

"How come you get to do that?" Julie's voice came to him out of the past, as he remembered the time he'd been sent on a last-minute trip to Reykjavik. He'd rushed into the house explaining to her that he had to go tomorrow and could she help him pack.

"Do what?" he'd asked.

"Just drop everything and head off."

He'd frowned at her. "It's work, Julie."

"I know it's work, but you still get to just do it." He hadn't understood, had been stupid enough to say so. "What about the kids, Michael? What about me? What about the family? Remember that time I went to the florists' conference in Amsterdam? Days it took me to organize that. Days of finding lifts for the kids to their clubs and sorting their various school and sports bags, days of making sure the fridge was full so that no one would starve and writing lists of things to remember, all just so I could have two poxy days of 'work.' But you—you just get to pack up and head off without a backward glance."

"Right. I get it. Sorry. The thing is, though, I really do need to pack."

It hadn't gone down well. He could still remember her "help-ing" him—flinging shirts at his suitcase like they were grenades. But when he'd called the next day from his lonely hotel room, she'd been apologetic. She understood how it was with his work, she'd insisted, it just felt hard when all she ever seemed to do was make life easier for everyone else. They'd talked for a long time that night, far later than he should have done given the big meetings he'd had the next day, but it had been worth it. As had her nights out with Clare—her reward, if you wanted to call it that, for all she had to put up with. But perhaps, on reflection, it would have been better if they'd gone out together.

He sat forward, suddenly decisive, and cut into the account-ant's list of figures.

105

"I'm terribly sorry but I really am going to have to go. There's a delivery at the door. Do carry on without me and I'll catch up tomorrow."

"Delivery?" he heard one of them echo, but he was already clicking them off and heading for the door.

"Michael!" Julie jumped as Michael entered Sophie's room behind her. "I thought you were on a work call."

"I was. I got bored of it."

She stared at him, struggling to believe her ears. "You got bored? Of work?"

He shrugged. "It happens. I could hear you out here and thought you might, erm, need a hand. What are you doing?"

She looked down at the mound of coats in her arms, then remembered her triumph.

"I fixed the coat hooks, Michael. It was easy. Here, look." She dropped the coats to fish her phone out of her pocket and show him the photo. His eyes went straight to the mess at her feet, but, credit to him, he pulled them away and bent to look at the phone instead. "See—all straight. The coats won't keep falling off any more. And I've streamlined. I've only left the ones belonging to you and me." The words fell between them. She shifted, feeling the weight of the coats on her feet. "So, er, I need to find a home for these ones," she hurried on.

"So I see."

"And I just wondered where you'd put the stuff out of the wardrobe, but you were busy talking so I kind of figured it might be in here and—it is!"

She gestured to the bed and he looked over.

"I did rather just dump them," he admitted, bending to help her pick up the new additions. "Oh, but Julie, you'll never guess what I found in there."

"What?"

He looked at the bed and her eyes followed his and landed on the orange and black jacket. She gasped.

"Is that...?"

"It is."

Stepping over her pile of coats, she advanced and picked it up, memories swirling around her. The styling was so cool, the leather so supple in her hands, the safety pads hard and secure.

"I loved this jacket."

"I know."

"It was the best present I ever had."

"So you said at the time."

"It *was*."

She itched to try it on and, glancing self-consciously at Michael, she slid first her right and then her left arm into the sleeves and drew in a long, deep breath. It felt amazing. The leather was buttery against her bare arms, the padding pushed her shoulders back and her head up. Closing her eyes, she ran her hands across the front and tugged at the zipped sides, automatically jutting her hip and pushing her breasts forward as if she were a different Julie now—a younger, bolder, sassier Julie.

"Gorgeous," Michael's voice said into her reverie.

Her eyes flew open and she caught sight of herself in Sophie's mirror, standing there like a fool in a jacket from the past. Hastily she shrugged it off.

"Don't take it off, Jules. It suits you."

"Yeah, well, I don't need it any more, do I?" Hurt flashed across his eyes and she felt bad. "But I'll, er, take it downstairs anyway. In case." She cast around for a diversion. "Hey—tell you what, if you're done working, we should tackle the loft."

He squinted at her. "The loft?"

It was a bit of a mad idea perhaps, but the restlessness had only increased with Michael at her side, and she might as well do something purposeful with it.

"I want to get my plastic flowers out. Remember, the ones from when I was learning floristry?"

"I remember. They were all over the house. And so were all those Post-its with the Latin flower names on them."

Julie rolled her eyes at the memory. It had been a nightmare trying to push all of those fancy names into her aging brain for the floristry exam. And had she ever used them? Had she bollocks! The arranging, though—that had been vital.

"I thought I might experiment a bit," she told him. "There's all sorts of funky arrangements out there and I never really have the time to try them out, so now seems a good opportunity. But I need the plastic flowers." They both looked up at the loft hatch above them. Michael stretched out uncomfortably and Julie flinched. "Of course—your back. Sorry. Silly of me."

"Not at all. It's much better now. I'm sure it can cope with a ladder."

Julie felt awkward suddenly. There had to be all sorts of stuff up in the loft, stuff that, should they end up divorcing, they would need to divvy up. That wasn't a thought she wanted to face right now.

"The ceiling's very low up there," she hedged.

"I'll sit down."

"Don't worry, I can do it. You just—"

"Julie—I can sit down."

His voice was quiet but very, very sure. There was nothing to say but "Thanks."

She fetched the pole and reached up to hook the end into the trapdoor. It came down with a clatter, disgorging the ladder, and they both leapt back. Julie heard Michael suck in a pained breath, but when she looked at him he was very deliberately straight-backed.

"I'll go first."

She watched as he climbed slowly and carefully up the ladder into the roof space, disappearing bit by bit through the dark hole. She gripped the rungs and followed him upward.

Michael had sat himself down cross-legged in the middle of what could only be described as chaos. For far too many years they'd taken the "shove it up there and forget about it" approach, and stuff was all anyhow. Julie reached tentatively for the first box, pulling it toward her to see Adam's teddy poking forlornly out of the top as if plucking up the courage to escape.

"Adam loved this bear."

"He did. Remember when he nearly left it down in the Vendée?"

"God, yes! It had gone tree-climbing! Good job Briony spotted it was missing or we'd have got all the way home and then there'd have been hell to pay!"

Michael opened a bag and pulled out first one, then a second pretty dress. He held them up to the light from the bare bulb.

"These are tiny, Julie. They'll never fit the girls now."

Julie blushed. "I know that. I just kept a few of the prettiest ones in case, you know, there were ever any granddaughters."

Her gut squeezed at the word. If they split up, they would have to see any future members of the family separately, look after them separately. Michael had always been good with little ones. She could still hear the kids' giggles as he'd thrown them in the air. Not that he'd be able to throw them any more with his back. And not that they'd have any grandchildren round more than a few times a year. She couldn't build a life around that. It had to be about her now, about what she wanted.

"This breadmaker looks useful," she said, picking it up decisively and pushing it toward the hatch. "And I suppose I should be making use of these weights."

"For what?"

"I dunno. Keep fit and that. Better than Zumba."

"Zumba looked fun."

109

Julie plunged further into the piles of boxes to hide her discomfort; Zumba *had* been fun, especially the waltz.

"These yours?" Michael asked, and she looked up reluctantly to see him holding the Spanish language CDs she'd optimistically bought years ago.

"'Fraid so. Damn! Whose stupid idea was it to come up here? All we've done is find purposeful things I now feel I ought to fill my days with."

He laughed. "You don't have to, Julie. You could just take a rest."

"A rest?"

"It's allowed. You don't have to be like your mum."

Julie gasped. "What do you mean?"

He looked up at her, stricken. "Sorry. I wasn't being rude about Linda. I just...She wasn't exactly keen on sitting still, that's all."

That much was true. Linda had been forever on the move, almost as if some monster was chasing her that would pounce if she stayed still for too long. It wasn't a bad thing, though.

"She had to work hard, my mum, to bring us up on her own."

"I know that. She was amazing."

"And to keep our house together. God, it was a shithole and the landlord was a lazy bastard. Clare and I did shockingly little to help, too. I don't know why she didn't make us do more."

"I guess she wanted you to be able to just be kids."

She looked at him. "I guess so." She put a hand up to the low ceiling, feeling it pressing down on her suddenly. There was so little air up here, so little space. "That's probably enough for now, hey?"

He squinted at her. "We haven't even found the flowers yet."

"We have." She grabbed a long white box from behind an old highchair. "Here!"

110

"Ah. Good. But what about all this?" He waved a hand at the rest of the clutter.

Julie looked at it, feeling desperately weary. "I don't know, Michael. What's the point? The tip's closed and so are the charity shops, and we're not allowed to see the kids."

"True. Maybe you're right. Maybe we should just go back down, make a cup of tea."

"Maybe."

The air was getting low in here, it seemed. Julie heard her breath coming in short, sharp gasps and focused on the square of light that would let her out of here. Eagerly she stepped over a large cardboard box to reach it, but as she did so, her foot caught one of the flaps and it sprang open like some strange magician's trick to release a rush of silver streams. She froze amidst the sparkly explosion. Michael looked up.

"Is that…?"

"The decorations from our twenty-fifth anniversary party. Yes." The shock seemed to have kick-started her breathing again, at least, and she bent to pick up a handful of the streamers. She let them run through her fingers to catch the light drifting up from the landing and watched them glitter, transfixed. Twenty-five years: silver. She had filled the house with it to make it sparkle as much as their lovely marriage.

"It was a good party."

"It was."

"A good time."

"Ten years ago," she said into the foil cloud.

"Just ten years. It feels like a lifetime ago," Michael echoed, shaking his head. He was blinking hard and Julie peered at him through the streamers. "Dust," he said, scrubbing at his eyes. "Probably best if we get out of here."

"Probably," she agreed, and, shoving the streamers back into their box, she pushed it aside and scrambled for the exit.

Chapter Fourteen

April 2010

Michael stands in the middle of the kitchen feeling as if it's finally happened: Julie has finally actually whirlwinded him off the ground.

"Can you stand still for a minute, darling?"

"Very funny, Michael." She shoots past him balancing two big stacks of plastic pint pots. "Have you tapped out the barrel?"

"Of course. I did it last night. The beer needs time to settle."

And so do I, he wants to add. Whose crazy idea was it to have their twenty-fifth wedding anniversary party in their own house?

Ah yes—his!

"We should do it at home," he said when it first came up months ago. "We have a lovely house and it will be so much more personal this way."

What he actually meant of course was "How on earth are we going to afford any of those fancy places in the leaflets you keep bringing home?" Julie had been strewing the coffee table with glossy pictures of country house hotels, artisan pubs (whatever the hell they were) and bloody teepees, and he was starting to panic.

"Personal?" She stopped flicking through pictures of tree houses and looked at him, considering. "You know what, maybe you're right."

"Of course I am."

"And with all the money we'll save on a venue, we could have caterers, a DJ, maybe a cocktail waiter!"

"A barrel of beer?" Michael suggested.

"If you must."

"I must."

And somehow, that decided it. He worked hard to discourage the idea of the cocktail waiter—"Think how drunk everyone will get"—and the DJ—"Think of the noise for the neighbors"— but bit by bit Julie lost her nerve anyway and decided to do pretty much all of it herself. All that remains from that original list of treats is the barrel. Ah well—it's the best bit anyway. And he's going to need a few pints just to stay awake after helping Julie make sausage rolls and blinis until three a.m. yesterday after she had a panic that there wasn't enough food.

"They sell perfectly good sausage rolls in Tesco," he protested at midnight.

"Perfectly good for who? This is our silver anniversary, Michael. Don't you want it to be special?"

Michael was pretty sure that it would be more the people than the sausage rolls that would make it special but wasn't stupid enough to say so. He'd enjoyed the cooking actually, and three a.m. would have been OK if he wasn't also kicked out of bed at seven this morning to mow the lawn, despite the fact he only did it two days ago and it's only April so the grass doesn't even grow very quickly.

"I think we should get dressed," he says. "The guests will be here in less than an hour."

"But what about…?"

She looks around wildly, but even Julie can't actually find a streamer that isn't in the right place, or a table that isn't loaded with drinks or nibbles. Michael takes her gently by the shoulders and propels her toward the stairs.

"It all looks great. Take a little time for yourself."

She doesn't of course. Well, no more than half an hour, but she still looks amazing. He's kitted out in the sequined waistcoat she found in a charity shop, and although he was horrified when he first saw it, he has to admit he feels rather dashing in it now. But Julie! He suspects his jaw hits the floor when she steps out of the bathroom and shyly reveals her outfit.

She's been worrying for weeks about the girls showing her up, but she needn't have given it a moment's thought. Sophie, ever conservative, has gone for jeans and a discreetly sparkly top, and Briony, who's dating a goth, has opted for all black with hefty silver boots and metallic hairspray. They are young and more beautiful than Michael can ever quite believe, but tonight they're not a patch on their mother. She's in a full-on foil-effect dress that clings to her luscious curves in all the right places and feels unbelievably soft when he sneaks his arm around her shapely waist.

"Stunning," he whispers, going to kiss her, but she puts up silver-tipped fingers to stop him.

"Lipstick!"

He smiles. "Later, then."

"If you're lucky."

"I'm already the luckiest man in the world."

She kisses her fingertip, presses it to his cheek. "You brush up pretty nicely yourself. Shall we get down there? Prepare."

"Let's," he agrees, hoping that "prepare" means have an early drink, but they barely make it to the drinks table before the doorbell goes and there's Clare and her latest boyfriend.

"Thought we'd get here early so you're not kicking around wondering if anyone's going to turn up."

Julie laughs. "It's not a sixteenth, Clare."

"True, true. You look amazing, sis!"

She strikes a self-conscious pose. "Well, you're only silver once, right?"

He hears her say that a lot during the night, as they cross paths filling up drinks, chatting to friends and family, dishing out canapés. Clare needn't have worried—people come in their droves, bringing presents and drinks and lots and lots of happy chatter.

"Can't wait for the gold," so many people say, and Michael smiles and imagines his wife in something long and elegantly burnished. She'll be—he does the calculation quickly—sixty-nine. And he'll be seventy-three. But that's not that old, right? Easily reachable, especially once the kids all leave home and they stop having to dash around so much and can make a little time for one another. Sophie has been in her own house for two years now, Briony is off to university in September, and with Adam newly a teenager, he's so much more self-sufficient. It's not that their parenting job is done—will it ever be?—but perhaps the most labor-intensive bit is almost over.

They make a speech together, keeping it as a short, light toast to "the next twenty-five years," and then he leads Julie out into the middle of the room for a sort of first dance. Julie suggested "Hi Ho Silver Lining"—for the comedy value—but he put his foot down and insisted on them having their original first dance tune: "All You Need Is Love" by The Beatles. As he pulls her into his arms to whoops and cheers from their rowdy friends, she fits perfectly against him and he feels blessed.

The calm of their first dance does not last long, mind you. Julie gets "Hi Ho Silver Lining" on anyway and it opens the floodgates to the battle of the iPod as all their mates fight to choose tunes from their library. His own classier (or so he likes to believe) albums don't get much of a run-out, mainly because the men are far more interested in the rapidly emptying barrel

115

than the music selection, but Julie's mishmash of seventies and eighties cheese is widely tapped. The music finally grinds to a halt at four a.m., and after "one for the road" with the straggle of survivors, they limp up to bed together not long before dawn.

"It was a good party," Julie says as they hit the sheets with a happy groan.

"A great one. Everyone seemed to enjoy it."

"They did. Were there enough canapés?"

"Plenty. And the decorations were very..."

"Sparkly?"

"Yes. Very sparkly. They'll be hell to clear up tomorrow."

"We'll have plenty of help."

"Great way to spend our actual anniversary, hey—tidying up on a hangover."

"It's our actual anniversary already."

"So it is." He turns to her, takes her hand. "Happy anniversary, darling."

"Twenty-five years—who'd have thought it," she mumbles sleepily.

"I would," he says stoutly. "And the next twenty-five too. D'you know you'll only be sixty-nine for our fiftieth."

"Not so old, I guess."

"Definitely not."

She sits up suddenly. "Do you think I'm past my prime, Michael?"

He laughs. "No! Lord, no. You're just about to hit it, I'd say. In fact I was thinking about it earlier, looking at the kids all so grown up now."

"Scary, isn't it? It's happened so fast."

"It has. And it is. But it's exciting too. The next twenty-five years are for us, Jules. For you and me."

"How d'you mean?"

"Well, we've done most of the parenting stuff, so now we can focus on things we'd like to do, places we'd like to go, things we'd like to see."

"Sounds good."

"We're lucky—we found each other young so we've got plenty of oomph left."

"Oomph?" she giggles, but he's not be put off.

"Yes, oomph. It's a good thing. You've got bags of it. So come on, what would you like to do in the next twenty-five years? Actually, forget that—in the next ten."

She considers. "I'd like to get thinner."

"Julie! Proper stuff."

"That *is* proper. But OK, OK. I'd like to get to Greece at last."

"Yes! Good one."

"And I'd like to dance more."

"Me too."

She thinks, wrinkling up her nose in the way he loves. "I'd like you to get that promotion you want."

"Would you?"

"Of course. You really deserve it, Michael."

"It would mean putting in the hours."

"So go for it. Like you said, the kids don't need us so much."

"But what about you?"

She leans over and kisses him. "I'm going to work to make the shop really successful. It was an amazing gift, Mike, and I want to make the absolute most of it."

"You make the most of everything, Julie. It's one of the things I love about you."

"Oh yes?" She snuggles up to him, runs her hand down her chest. "Well, how about I make the most of *you* right now?"

"Sounds good to me," he agrees, pulling her closer, but it's very late and they've done an awful lot of dancing. Already they're drifting off, and they fall softly away from each other, worn out by the success of their sparkly party.

Chapter Fifteen

Day Twelve

Michael peered hopefully into the fridge just in case, as if by magic, some new ingredients had appeared since he'd last checked out its contents an hour ago. Needless to say, they had not. He was left with the unenviable choice of a last slice of ham, curled up and hard around the edges, a half-portion of rice left over from last night's dinner, and a brown banana. With a sigh he reached for the fruit and padded across to the bread bin. He used to love a banana sandwich when he was a young man, and if he was lucky, there'd be some of that amazing bread Julie had made in the recently unearthed breadmaker.

She'd clattered around in the kitchen for ages after the strange loft experience, making a lot of noise but ultimately producing a beautiful loaf. They'd had it for dinner with cheese and soup and at least its quality had given them something to talk about. Something other than the subject they should really have been addressing—the huge distance between that sparkly twenty-fifth anniversary party ten years ago and their awkward, tongue-tied existence as they approached their thirty-fifth.

With a sigh, Michael lifted the lid of the bread bin to reveal the crumbs of the home baking and one small crust of shop-bought. That figured. Unpeeling the banana, he shoved it onto the wizened slice, folding it over as best he could and trying to avoid the thought that it looked like a dog turd. It would tide him over until Julie returned from the shops, whenever that would be.

She'd sallied out mid morning with a list the length of her arm but she still wasn't back. He could only hope that was a good sign. They were out of milk and bread. The only meat they had was the strange cuts from the back of the freezer, and they were down to their last toilet roll. He'd been trying not to indulge in the strange mass hysteria over this most basic of goods, but he had to admit it was getting slightly worrying. He was all for eco measures, but wiping his bum with leaves was definitely a step too far. Everything, it seemed, was going to pot at the moment.

He took his sandwich out into the garden, hoping the sunshine would help soothe his agitation. He hadn't slept well. At one point he'd woken seeing the sparkly silver streamers raining down between them in the loft, and had lain awake, staring at the spare room ceiling, torturing himself over how useless he'd been. What he should have done was to leap up between the glittering strands, pull her into his arms and kiss her. But the sparkles had been so mesmerizing and the ceiling so low and he hadn't been sure that she'd want him to, so he'd hesitated and the moment had been lost. Idiot!

The dining room table and chairs were sitting incongruously on the lawn, as if the whole room had decided it fancied a change of scene, and he sank down onto a chair to eat. Yesterday Julie had talked him into carrying the table outside to distress it. It sounded a little cruel, but you couldn't be cruel to tables, right, and as it turned out, it was probably better she was out here attacking the furniture than rummaging around in the loft.

She'd thrown herself into it, and later, when they'd gone

out onto the street to clap for the carers, she'd been happily grimy and covered with flecks of old varnish. Mind you, their neighbors had been in an equally odd array of clothing. The woman two doors down had been teaming smart blouse and full makeup with scruffy joggers, the bloke from across the road had been in makeshift running gear that he looked to have last worn in the eighties, and old Mr. Jones on the corner had been unashamedly in pajamas. All of them, however, had been smiling and waving and Michael had found himself doing the same. He'd been unsure about the clap, worried that it was a bit American in approach, but had been surprisingly moved by the moment of simple appreciation. It had been nice, too, to realize that people were still out there for when this was all over. Today, though, they were all confined to their own gardens again.

Sandwich finished, he wandered restlessly over to Mr. Nibbles' cage and poked a crust through the bars for the old boy. Clearly the rabbit was unimpressed by the dried-out bread, because he didn't even bother coming out to sniff at it. Michael stepped back, suddenly seeing a young Briony sitting at the side of the cage chatting to her pet. God, she'd wanted that rabbit so much. She'd gone on and on about it for ages, years maybe, but it had taken Sophie leaving home to actually secure the deal.

Briony had visibly pined for her big sister. Michael had been very struck by it because he'd never really thought his daughters got on with each other. He'd lost count of the number of times he'd had to break up screaming matches over stolen mascara and broken shoes and unfathomable issues with pictures on social media. Whenever they'd gone anywhere in the car, they'd had to make sure Adam was in the middle to keep the girls apart.

"But you were always arguing with her," he'd said to Briony on the way back from a hockey match when she'd been bemoaning the fact that she had no one to check her outfit for some party later.

"I know!" she'd wailed. "But I loved arguing with her."

It had seemed a strange logic to Michael, but her pain had been clear and it had hurt him more than he could stand.

"How about," he'd said, "we swing round past the pet shop and see if they've got any rabbits?"

It had been reckless. He'd gone out on a limb without running it past Julie, but it had been worth it to see Briony's eyes light up at last.

"Really? Can we really, Dad? Now?"

Well, there'd been no backing out then, had there? They'd got home at least an hour later than expected with a great big hutch rammed into the boot and a tiny fluffy bunny cuddled in an ecstatic Briony's lap.

"What the...?" Julie had gasped but she must have seen Briony's recent misery too, because she'd put up surprisingly little resistance to Michael's off-piste decision. And standing there together watching their daughter chattering away to the rabbit, she'd turned to Michael and said, "You're an old softie, aren't you, my love?"

If he remembered correctly, he'd batted it away with something along the lines of "Less of the old, you," but now it seemed a bittersweet memory of a time when they'd slotted together so easily and naturally.

Restless, he went over to the border and began tugging up weeds in random Julie style. His phone buzzed in his back pocket and he pulled it out to see that a new message had come through on WhatsApp from Adam. Eagerly he opened it up.

You ever see Jimmy Greaves play, Dad? Been watching this documentary about him. He looks cool.

Michael smiled, typed swiftly:

Not just cool—the man was a genius! Saw him take
Spurs to a 5–1 win in the Charity Shield at Portman
Road in '62.

The answer came straight back.

You were there? Wow. That game was in the
documentary.

Should have looked more closely at the crowd for
your old man.

Old is right, Dad. Can't believe you were alive then. The
shorts were mental. Not to mention the haircuts.

Michael smiled. Adam seemed to be finding all sorts of retro
games on TV and was sending him endless questions about
them. It made him feel close, even way down in Kent. Sophie
messaged him regularly too, but he hadn't heard from Briony
in ages. Looking back at the rabbit's cage—he still hadn't
bothered coming for the bread—he pulled up her name and
pressed the video chat button.

"Dad?" She was there so fast he jumped.

"Briony!"

She laughed. "You called *me*, Dad."

"I know. Sorry. I just wasn't sure if you'd be able to answer."

"You caught me on a break. I was just watching stupid
videos on YouTube."

"OK. Great. I'm just feeding Mr. Nibbles."

"Oh, I miss him! Give him a cuddle from me."

He smiled. "Will do, Bri. How are you?"

"I'm good."

"Healthy?"

"Yep. And it's brilliant in the lab, Dad. I've been put on one of the teams researching a vaccine and it's going at rocket pace. I've never seen anything like it. Scientists don't usually work like this!"

Michael laughed. "So what are you doing exactly?"

"Well..." She paused. "Dad, is Mum there?"

"She's out shopping. Been gone for ages, actually. Why? What's wrong?"

"Nothing's wrong. I promise. It's just a bit hectic at the moment and I thought it might be easier to, you know, talk to you both at once."

"Ah. Right." Did they never do that? Of course they didn't. They were never usually in the house at the same time long enough for anything like a family FaceTime. "We could call back later. Oh, but, hang on..." Inside the house, the front door banged loudly. "That'll be her now. Wait a sec."

He headed back inside to see Julie standing in the doorway, arms held triumphantly aloft and clutching a nine-pack of toilet roll as if it were the World Cup.

"The heroine returns!"

"You got some!" He hurried down the hall, instinctively reaching out to hug her and then, at the last minute, hesitating. "Well done."

Was he imagining it, or was Julie leaning toward him?

"Er, hello?" a voice squeaked from somewhere between them, and immediately she jumped back.

"Bloody hell, what's that?"

Michael shook his head. "*That* is your daughter."

Julie peered at the screen as he held it up.

"Briony! Oh God, Bri, it's so good to see you. Are you well, darling?" She dropped the toilet roll as she snatched the phone. "Are you eating properly? Sleeping? Is it hideous in the lab at the moment?"

Briony laughed. "I'm fine, Mum. And no, it's not hideous.

It's . . . kind of exciting. I mean weird and horrible and all that, of course, but exciting too. If our team can find a working vaccine, we'd help so many people."

Julie sank down onto the floor, propping the phone on her knees to hold Briony up close to her face, and Michael had little choice but to edge himself down next to her. Together, backs against one wall and feet against the other, they watched their middle daughter.

"That would be great, Bri. But what about you? Are you safe?"

"As safe as I can be."

There was silence. Michael longed to shout "Please stop working and come home, where we can look after you," but he knew he was being ridiculous. Briony was an adult, and her knowledge and skills were crucial in the lab right now. Yet she was still his little girl.

"I'm fine, honestly," she said, "but I'm going to have to go, I'm afraid. My break's nearly up."

Julie gave a strangled cough and Michael pressed his shoulder more tightly against hers.

"Course, sweetheart. Stay in touch, yeah? And stay safe."

"I will. I promise."

"We love you," Julie managed.

"Love you guys too. Remember to give Mr. Nibbles a cuddle from me, Dad."

"Course I will."

"Fab. Take care. Speak soon."

And as quickly as she'd appeared on his phone, Briony was gone. Julie stared bleakly at the blank screen.

"She can't promise to stay safe, can she?" Her strong body was shaking slightly against his, and he felt an almost overwhelming urge to hug her. She looked at him, her eyes misted. "Can she?"

"She'll be OK," he reassured her, his arm creeping up the wall like a kid on a cinema date.

Julie gave a tight nod and closed her eyes. Michael stretched his arm slowly out behind her, but just at that moment she opened them again and glanced around with a dark laugh. "God, look at us sitting on the floor with our bloody bog roll! And with the shopping getting all hot in the car. We should get up."

She ducked out from under his poised arm and pushed herself to her feet. Michael let it drop limply to his side again and stared up at her.

"Was it OK at the shops?" he asked.

"It was. A bit odd with the queues all spaced out and everything, but people were very patient. And very polite. I had a lovely chat to the cashier about how her children made them a pub in their back garden with a sign saying 'Lockdown Arms.' How sweet is that?"

Her voice had risen, as it always did when she was trying to be jolly. Michael pushed himself up and touched her arm.

"You OK, Jules?"

She gave him a weak smile. "I'm fine. I just wish the kids were here to make a pub in *our* back garden. I worry about Bri. About them all."

"I do too."

"I know." She patted his hand. "I know that. Now come on, shopping—I got carrots so we can give Mr. Nibbles a treat from Bri."

"Here, bunny, bunny. Look what we've got for you!"

Michael approached the hutch, but Mr. Nibbles did not deign to come out and greet him.

"I reckon he's deaf," Julie said. "And no wonder. He must be, what, ten?"

Michael counted. "I make it twelve. We got him when Sophie left home, remember?"

"I remember. You gave in to Briony's pestering."

"I gave in because she was sad."

"True. And she did love him. For a while, at least. Then he became more yours."

"That's not true." Michael defended his daughter. "Well, not entirely."

Of course, as time had gone on, Briony had lost some of her avid interest in her new pet, but to be fair to her, she'd been great about feeding him and moving his hutch around the garden for fresh grass and even cleaning it out. And Michael had found himself rather taken with the little creature. There was something about the rabbit's stoical approach to life that appealed, and he'd often head out with a tasty bit of lettuce or carrot, enjoying the way Mr. Nibbles loped keenly across to it. Today, though, the crust was still lying untouched on the grass, so he moved round to open up the sleeping area.

"Hey there, old lad. Wake up. We've got a treat for you."

Mr. Nibbles didn't stir, didn't even give a twitch of his pink nose at the smell of the carrot. Michael felt a shudder of dread run through him. Behind him he thought he heard Julie say his name, but all he could focus on was the rabbit.

"Mr. Nibbles?"

Slowly he reached out and touched his back, gently, so as not to alarm him, but the moment his hand connected with the fur, unnaturally cold, he knew. He gasped and snatched his hand back.

"No!"

"Michael?"

"He can't be."

"Oh no," Julie said. "Oh, Mr. Nibbles!" He heard her give a little sob, and then her hand closed around his. "I guess he was old, love." Some part of him registered the term of endearment, as rare these days as her fingers in his. "And at least he was in his own bed, safe and content. It looks like he died in his sleep. He probably didn't even know anything about it."

All the words were making sense, but he didn't want sense right now. He wanted the rabbit. He wanted Mr. Nibbles alive again. He wanted Briony here to chase him round the garden, and Adam to shout at for using him as football target practice. He wanted Sophie to come back and say he was pretty cute for a poor captive creature trapped out of his natural environment, and Julie, his old Julie, to sit and drink an easy beer with as their kids ran each other around the garden.

He felt tears well and knew that this time there would be no holding them in. They'd been threatening for far, far too long and here, with the death of an ancient pet, they were going to have their day. Pulling away from Julie, he sank onto a dining chair, buried his head in his hands and let them flow.

"Michael! Oh God, Michael, don't cry."

He glared up at her, suddenly furious. "Why not? Why can't I cry?"

"You can. You're right. Of course you can. Sorry. I didn't mean it wasn't allowed. I just...I just don't want to see you sad."

She fluttered nervously around him and he wanted to stop, really he did, but it wasn't going to happen. All he could feel was the cold fur and the frozen rabbit beneath, as if that was his family—dispersed and in danger and no longer his to cuddle and keep safe and hold together. He looked up at Julie.

"It's all gone wrong, hasn't it?" He gestured around them, unable to say exactly what he meant: our life, our family, our marriage. "All of this. It's gone so very, very wrong."

She didn't say anything for a while. Eventually she managed a limp "The world's gone wrong at the moment, Michael." It

127

was no comfort. He felt for the world, really he did, but it wasn't that that was the cause of his tears.

"I'd better go back to work," he said gruffly, and leaving Mr. Nibbles dead in his bed and Julie standing helplessly beside him, he ran for Briony's room and the cold comfort of the still flowing tears.

Chapter Sixteen

Day Thirteen

"Gary? Hi. It's Julie Marshall, Michael's wife. Yeah, hi. Good, thanks. You? Good, good. Er, Gary, that bike part Michael's been waiting for, any sign?"

Julie waited a little desperately as Gary went off into the depths of his garage to check. She was worried about Michael. He'd taken Mr. Nibbles' death hard, and his words as he'd sat there on the lawn yesterday, tears flowing down his cheeks, were hitting her a pretty nasty blow too: *It's all gone wrong, hasn't it? It's gone so very, very wrong.*

She knew what he had meant, and he was right, of course. She knew that better than anyone. That was why there was a brown envelope lurking in her bedside drawer beneath *Great Expectations*. Should she just accept what he'd said, hand it over, start all the hard conversations now whilst they were shut away from everyone else and could hammer things out? Maybe it would be the sensible thing to do. And yet...

She remembered how she'd felt that very first afternoon when she'd tried to give him the envelope. She remembered the feel of the invisible force almost visibly shimmering around her, like something out of a *Star Wars* movie, stopping her from starting the process. Was that force just memories? Just the glitter of a family life that had once been so good, like those confusingly dazzling streamers in the attic? Or was it something more.

He's just upset about Mr. Nibbles, she told herself as she trod round the garden, trying not to look at the shoebox she'd stashed in the shade of the apple tree. If she was honest, his reaction had shocked her. She didn't know when she'd last seen him cry; possibly not since his dad had died, and this was hardly the same. It was just a rabbit, and a very old rabbit at that.

She'd done her best to cheer him up. She'd made his favorite curry last night and brought in a bunch of daffodils to put in a pint pot on his desk. She'd persuaded the chemist to give her some extra-strong painkillers for his back and made an extra effort to keep the house tidy. Small things, really, and ultimately useless, which was why she was now on the phone to Gary. Working on his bike had always been Michael's refuge, and if he could just get this stupid part, it might make him feel a bit better.

"Hello? You have! Brilliant. Can I collect it? Box outside the door? Perfect. He'll be so pleased. Thank you."

She hung up feeling a small sense of triumph. She'd go and pick the part up now and Michael would have it for the weekend, when his conference calls dried up and he was left with nothing to do but mope for Mr. Nibbles. Hopefully once he'd got Gertie going, he'd be able to face a pet funeral.

The garage was only five minutes down the road and it didn't take her long to drive onto the deserted forecourt, open the plastic chest Gary had described and pull out the grimy cardboard box that apparently held the precious oil pump. She looked at it for a moment. It was hardly what you'd call a romantic gift, but she knew it would mean a lot to Michael.

Turning round, her eye was caught by two motorbikes sitting in the garage yard, leaning into each other almost as if they were sharing a secret. She moved toward them, admiring the curves of the bodywork, the bulge of the big exhaust, the enticing promise of the little travel case on the back. *Come on,* it seemed to be saying, *chuck some spare clothes in here and let's just ride!*

Nasty, dangerous things, bikes, she reminded herself. She'd seen all the stats. And those she hadn't, Sophie had provided in her long-running and terminally unsuccessful attempt to get her father to give up his Guzzi.

"You might as well ask him to cut off his arm," Julie had told her gently after one particularly lively Sunday lunch years ago.

"Or his willy," Adam had provided with a teenage snigger.

"Don't be stupid, Adam," she had snapped.

He'd just smirked and she'd given up, but it was true. Michael's bike wasn't some macho thing, not really. He had a genuine affection for the big machine, partly because it had been his dad's and partly because of the "purity of the engineering." As far as Julie could see from her husband's long hours with a spanner, the engineering was pure shite, but he loved it all the same. It was a part of him, as she'd known right from the first time she'd seen him astride it in Budapest, blue eyes shining. Not that it made her want to go on it, not any more—Sophie's stats had proved far, far too accurate.

*

Julie looks down at the panniers on the bedroom floor, and across to the pile of clothing ready to be packed into them. There's a distinct mismatch. She's forgotten how small the traveling bags are. When they bought them for their honeymoon, she was blissfully certain she could get by for a fortnight with a bikini, a couple of summer dresses and a lightweight cardy in case it got chilly in the evenings. And she did. But that was over twenty years ago.

She goes downstairs to call up the weather pages on Ceefax. She's checked the Athens forecast loads in the last week and it still says the same—sunny and at least 20 degrees celcius. She'll need a bit more than a bikini but she can probably ditch the jeans. She smiles and gladly returns to their room to put them to one side. It's silly, really, to be packing when they don't fly for another five days, but she's so excited. At last she's going to get to the Greek islands.

It all started when Bett called up out of the blue last month and offered to have the kids for a week—not the sort of chance they should ever pass up. Michael's mum is a devoted granny, but in fits and starts, visiting five times in two months and then not at all for the rest of the year as she gets absorbed in some project or other at home. She's supposedly retired but she's got herself on every committee going, works part-time as a magistrate and is newly installed as ladies' captain at the golf club. All this leaves her with little time for any sort of reliable childcare, so it only took a matter of moments to say yes. Yes please!

Sophie may be eighteen soon, but Adam is only eleven and Briony, at fifteen, is going through a rebellious phase. Only last weekend they had to rescue her from a friend's house after the pair of them had decided to try out vodka. It wasn't pretty—though they found out, at least, that Briony is a happy drunk. It was hours before they could get her to stop hugging them all and go to sleep, and even if it was quite funny in the end, it's not something they want to leave poor Sophie to deal with. Bett, however, would be more than capable of handling any sort of teenage misdemeanors.

"Finally," Julie told Michael, "we can get to the Greek islands."

Michael frowned. "We won't make it to Greece and back in a week, Julie."

"No," she agreed. "We'll have to fly."

It didn't compute in his brain at first. "But what about Gertie?"

She took his hand, kissed him gently. "I think this time, Mike, we'll have to go without Gertie."

"Without…?"

His eyes widened in horror, but when she directed him to a motorbike hire website and he found an old Triumph Bonneville that was to his relative satisfaction, he relented. So here they are, flights booked, Bonneville hired, panniers all but packed.

"Julie, where are you?" Michael pounds up the stairs and into their room. He laughs. "You're packing."

"Certainly am! Bikini or swimsuit?"

"You're really asking me that?" He grabs the swimsuit off her and tosses it over his shoulder. "I love you in a bikini."

"What about the stretch marks?"

"What about them? They were made by our children, so I love them too."

"Very right-on."

"Very true. But listen, I've just dropped Adam at Maisie's party and Sam's mum says she'll bring him back, so I reckon we've got a couple of hours free."

"Really? Where's Sophie?"

"At that Save the Penguins rally in Nottingham."

"Oh yes. Briony?"

"Has already told me that she's got no interest in what we do with our afternoon. In fact, she doesn't see why Granny has to come next week, because Sophie can look after them, and if she's busy, Briony is more than capable."

"At fifteen?"

"So she says."

Julie laughs. "She'd soon change her tune if she started trying to feed Adam. I think he must be growing again, Mike."

"He's always growing. But right now he's busy ripping up someone else's house in the name of their birthday, so shall we grab the moment?"

"What do you suggest?"

"I'm going to take you out to the Green Oak."

"The pub up in the hills? With the garden that looks out over the whole valley?"

"The very same. Grab your leathers, honey, and let's ride!"

His enthusiasm is catching, so she shuffles into her leather trousers and follows him downstairs, snatching her orange and black jacket off the hook by the back door as she goes.

"Sure you'll be OK, Bri?" she asks her daughter, who is studying at the kitchen table. She gets an eye-roll in return. "See you in a bit, then."

And just like that, they're out.

"Good, this, isn't it?" Michael says over his shoulder as they mount the bike. "Just think, another few years and we'll be able to head out whenever we want."

It's a thrilling thought. Julie grips his waist and listens to the familiar roar of the engine.

"More to the point, in five days' time we'll be heading out around Corfu!"

"Can't wait."

He edges the bike out of the garage, fires the engine and they're off. Julie feels the familiar tug in her loins and shifts to get comfortable against her husband. She looks out at the suburban streets of home and imagines riding across Greek clifftops to watch the sun sink into the Mediterranean before heading to some rustic taverna to eat dolmades and drink rough red wine.

Last year, Michael surprised her with a trip to London to watch a musical called *Mamma Mia* that everyone was raving about. It was based around Abba songs and set on a Greek island, and she loved it. She's been singing Abba around the house ever since, all three kids protesting loudly, but soon she won't have to listen to any of them for five whole days. She bounces on the Guzzi's seat as Michael slows at traffic lights and pulls over to the left, but as they approach, the light changes to amber and then to green and he starts to speed up again.

As Julie settles against him again, she hears a growl behind her and flinches sideways as a big black Audi comes shooting up behind them, spotting a chance to accelerate through the lights. Apparently not even seeing them, it passes so close to Julie that the wing mirror brushes against her arm, and then, as the car tries to slew away, the back end hits them. The bike kicks sideways and Julie finds herself thrown into the road. She feels her body bump against the tarmac, hears her leathers scrape across it, and curls up small, dreading the impact of another car. She hears a squeal of brakes and shouts of fury, and slowly, very slowly, she uncurls. All of her seems to be working, but she's on the far side of the road from the bike. And from the other figure lying against it.

"Michael?" She's up and scrambling across. "Michael!" He's screaming, a harsh, desperate sound. At least he's not dead, she thinks, but he doesn't sound good. "Michael, speak to me."

"My knee," he gasps out. "He hit my knee."

She cradles him against her, looks desperately around at the cars stopped either side.

"Oh my God, are you OK? I saw it all. What a bastard!" A woman has leapt out of a silver car and is hurrying across. She's parked it firmly across the road to shield Michael as he lies groaning and clutching at his knee, and Julie looks up and sees two little girls' faces pressed to the window.

"He drove into us," she splutters to the woman. "He drove into Michael."

"I know. I saw. We'll get him for this, but in the meantime, let me look. I'm a nurse."

Rarely has Julie heard sweeter words. Someone else is already calling an ambulance, and now the woman produces a first-aid kit from her car and proceeds to cut Michael's leather trousers away to reveal a badly mangled knee, already deep purple and swollen. A crowd gathers. Someone puts a blanket around Julie, someone else produces a flask of tea. The ambulance screams up, blue lights flashing across Michael where he still lies in the road. The nurse gives the paramedics precise details in a clipped, efficient tone, and before Julie can truly process the fact that she's now on the way to the hospital rather than the pub, they are through the doors of A&E and Michael is on a morphine drip.

Julie is still shaken, but from somewhere she musters the mummy-energy to arrange for Sam's mum to keep Adam for the night. She tells the girls to look after each other at home, but within the hour they turn up at the hospital, and together the three of them sit with Michael as he hallucinates his way through the night on a cocktail of pain and drugs. And then suddenly, at around four a.m., just after the nurse has been to tell them that they're hoping to get him into surgery in the morning, he sits bolt upright and bursts into a rousing chorus of "Mamma Mia." It's so unexpected and so absurd in the sterile ward that they laugh and laugh, clutching at each other as he warbles "How can I resist you?" into the night.

She knows then that he's going to be OK, but she knows too that she'll never go on the bike again. It's just too risky. That Audi would only have needed to be another two or three centimeters over and the girls could have been sitting here with both parents in hospital, or worse. The next morning she goes home and, with a heavy heart, cancels the flights to Greece.

*

Julie stared at Gary's motorbikes, sadness welling up inside her. They'd sworn they'd rebook those flights, but with the bike issue it just hadn't happened. She'd never truly understood how Michael had been able to get back on Gertie after the accident, let alone go out on the roads again. She'd been angry about it. Furious even.

"How can you take that risk?" she'd demanded.

He'd been calm; so damned calm. "There's no more risk than there's ever been, Julie."

"True. There's always been *too much* risk. We just turned a blind eye to it. But we can't do that any more, Michael. What about the kids?"

"I won't take the kids on it."

She'd screamed at him then. "Don't be obtuse. I mean what about the kids if we had another accident? What would happen to them if we were properly knocked off the road, if we were rammed into a wall and left to bloody well die? What about the kids then?"

He'd drawn in a deep breath. "That won't happen, Julie."

"How do you know? Did you think some arsehole was going to side-swipe you at the traffic lights? No! So how do you know?"

"I'm a good rider."

"You can be as good as bloody Evel Knievel, Michael, but that doesn't stop other people being idiots."

He'd hung his head. "I know," he'd said, so quietly she'd had to lean in to hear him. "I know all that, Jules. But I love it."

"More than them?" she'd shot back.

"No! Of course not. Don't be stupid. But there's risk everywhere. I'm statistically just as likely to have an accident in a car."

"But statistically a lot less likely to die from it."

He'd had no comeback for that, but he hadn't given in.

"I love it," he'd repeated. And then, "It's my sanity."

And deep down she'd known that was true, so despite her anger, she'd given in. And then, feeling guilty, had signed him up to a Guzzi riders' club, where he'd found new mates to ride out with. Before she knew it, he'd been booking trips with hairy Rob and she'd just been relieved that she didn't have to go through the worry of another big bloody Audi coming up on them. Perhaps she'd focused too much on what could

137

have gone wrong and not enough on what had been so very, very right.

She turned away and made for her car. It was Friday afternoon. In a normal world she'd be looking forward to G&Ts with Clare in one of their favorite bars, and oh, how good that would be. It wasn't going to happen obviously, but she could FaceTime her at least. First, though, the oil pump.

"You got it!" Michael stared at the box with something like awe as Julie placed it on the desk before him, and for a moment she felt like whichever knight had chased down the Holy Grail. Perceval, wasn't it? Had he ever actually found it, though? She couldn't remember and it really didn't matter because she, Julie, had found the grail of the Guzzi oil pump and for the first time in days Michael's eyes were shining with something like pleasure. "Thank you so much."

"No problem. I just thought it might help you to, you know, get the bike going."

"Help me?"

"You've always been happiest with something constructive to do."

He gave his lopsided smile. "Penalties of being an engineer. You know me too well."

She shifted. "Yeah, well, I look forward to hearing that throaty roar from the garage again over the weekend."

"I'll do my best. It's not the easiest part to replace. The fuel injection line…" He caught himself. "I'll do my best," he said again. "Thank you. Really. I'd almost given up on this."

"No problem." She was grateful when his phone rang. "I'll, er, leave you to it."

She backed out of his office as he answered the call, but not before she saw him caress the box with his long, slim fingers and give a little smile. Retreating to the kitchen, feeling rather proud of herself, she took out her phone and FaceTimed Clare.

"Hey, sis, how's things?"

"Boring," Clare said grumpily. "Why haven't you done Zumba again?"

A memory of the waltz leapt into Julie's mind and, it seemed, all across her body. She pushed it away.

"You were right, Clare, it's silly."

"Fair enough. I've found a kick-boxing class now if you fancy it. Good for taking out any frustrations."

"That'd be bloody perfect! Just tell me when."

Clare leant in toward the camera. "You OK? How are you and Mike coping, just the two of you?"

"Fine," Julie said hastily. "Though his back's still not good. And Mr. Nibbles died."

"Briony's rabbit? He must have been ancient."

"Twelve," Julie told her authoritatively. "A good age for a rabbit, but he was well cared for. Especially by Michael."

"And now he's got nothing left to care for but you. And you're impossible to care for."

"I am not!"

"You are and you know it. Always whirling around the place refusing to be told what to do, or when to rest, or even what to eat."

"I'll have you know I eat whatever's put in front of me."

"Really? You've grown up at last then. Remember that year you'd only eat things that were white?"

Julie groaned. She missed Clare, really she did, but the problem with having a best mate who was also your sister was that they had all the dirt on you.

"I was eight, Clare."

"Maybe but you've always been a bit picky. Michael used to take that bike of his out for miles when you were first married

139

to find you avocados long before they became trendy. And when you were pregnant—Lord! The poor man had to go all the way to Norfolk to find those langoustines you were craving."

"He didn't mind," Julie said uncomfortably. "He's always liked an excuse to go out on the bike."

That much was true, but she had to confess she'd forgotten how far he'd gone out of his way to please her. She'd stopped being so fussy once they had the kids. There'd been no time for long trips out for exotic ingredients, and no money to afford them. Mince and carrots had been easily found in the local supermarket and were unlikely to elicit the sort of whining that made mealtimes hard to bear. She couldn't remember when she'd last had a langoustine and felt a sudden craving for them, almost as strong as when Sophie had been ripening within her. She'd have to crush that; the PM would not consider a trip to Norfolk for seafood essential.

She glanced at the clock: four p.m.

"Too early for a glass of wine?" she asked Clare.

"Never! Last one back from the fridge is a loser."

That was what she liked about her sister—always up for a good time. Julie leapt up and raced to the fridge. Bollocks—no wine. She spun round to the wine rack, relieved to see several bottles of white awaiting her pleasure. They'd be warm, but she had those silicon ice cubes in the freezer that would soon chill a glassful down. Pouring one out, she went back to the freezer to dig out the cubes.

"Loser!" Clare's voice crowed from the phone.

"Oh yeah?" Julie spun back triumphantly, brandishing her glass, now lit up like a Christmas tree. She'd forgotten the ice cubes were flashing ones. "Quality beats speed!"

"Fair enough. You win." Clare stared across the airwaves at Julie's psychedelic glass. "God, Jules, I want a night out so badly."

Julie smiled. Clare hadn't always been a party girl; quite

the reverse. Under their mum's stern fears for their idle hands, she'd always been bent over her books, only ever coming out of her shell on the sports field, where she'd played like a creature possessed. As a teen, she'd cultivated a small, tight-knit group of friends and, despite the urgings of her various teammates, had avoided the sort of wild parties that had drawn Julie like a magnet. It had been little surprise, therefore, that she'd come home from uni with an equally quiet boyfriend, a softly spoken land management graduate called Hamish. She'd married him and followed him to a sheep farm on a remote Scottish island without—perhaps crucially, as it turned out—so much as a hockey team to its name. The marriage had lasted fifteen years before Clare had suddenly broken free, not just a divorcee but a totally different woman.

She'd moved into a flat near Julie and thrown herself into work, trying a variety of careers and joining every sports club going. Julie had worried about her and been delighted when the shop had done well enough for her to take her sister on as her assistant. It was around then that Clare had discovered dancing (not as a sport) and Julie had found herself dragged into her new social life and suddenly back out in the bars she'd thought were a thing of the past.

"Are we turning into Mum?" she'd asked Clare once, horribly aware that she was about the same age Linda had been when she'd hit the tiles.

"No," Clare had replied without hesitation, "because we have each other."

It had been a good point, and God, it had been fun. It *was* fun. Julie loved those Friday nights out where she could have as many drinks as she liked, no longer having to worry about what time the kids would get her up in the morning, and dance as if she didn't have a care in the world. It was a shame really that Michael didn't like dancing. Although thinking about it, he'd definitely liked it when they'd first been together. And he'd definitely liked it when they'd waltzed the other day. Odd.

As if on cue, he came into the kitchen and gave a little wave at the screen.

"Hi, Clare."

"Hi, Mike. Julie driving you insane yet?"

"Not quite."

He grinned at her and Julie felt something tug at her insides. Michael and Clare had always got on well. In fact, she suddenly remembered, Clare had encouraged her to bring him out with them on those early dancing trips, but everyone else in the gang had been female and it hadn't felt quite right. If she was honest with herself, she hadn't wanted to be the steady wifey on those heady nights away from the family so she'd told him it was strictly girls only. Mean really.

"Have a drink with us," Clare was saying now.

"Tempting," Michael said, raising an eyebrow at Julie's still flashing glass of wine. "But I'm about to work on the bike, so probably best I wait an hour or two."

"*Plus ça change!*" Clare teased.

"*Plus c'est la même chose,*" Michael shot back. Julie looked at him in surprise. "What? I know my French sayings!"

"How?"

"I'm naturally cultured."

He was very bouncy. Clearly the oil pump was more restorative than even she had anticipated.

"And really?" she demanded.

He gave a sheepish grin. "Really there's a French girl on the team in this big new project I'm running and she says that sort of thing all the time. Best get on with this bike. Stay safe, Clare!"

"You too, Mikey-boy."

Julie watched as Michael bounded through the door to the garage, grimy box clutched happily before him. French girl?

What did that mean, "girl"? How old was she, with her sexy accent and her fancy sayings? She'd be an engineer, though, right? So surely thickset and serious and...Julie batted away her own stupid stereotyping and heard Clare laugh.

"What are you doing, Jules?"

"Nothing. Sorry."

"You OK?" She was leaning into the screen again, looking concerned.

"Course. Just need more wine. Hey, when d'you reckon they'll open the pubs and bars again?"

That distracted her sister. "Not soon enough, that's when. At least you've got Michael there with you. I'm going mad not seeing Dharmesh. We had phone sex last night. It was good, I guess, but it's not the same as actually having them there in your arms, is it? Julie? Is it?"

But Julie was diving into the fridge for more wine and didn't answer.

Chapter Seventeen

Michael's heart was in his throat as he straddled the Guzzi and turned the key. He hovered his foot above the kick-start, not daring to test out his repair in case it had failed, but that was just stupid. He could be here all night. Sucking in a deep breath, he tensed his leg and kicked down. Gertie jumped, stuttered and then seemed to almost audibly draw oil into her V7 engine. The throaty roar Julie had described when she'd so kindly brought him the part earlier filled the garage, thankfully covering his own shout of joy.

"Yeeessss!"

He'd done it. He'd brought her back to life. Again.

He glanced to the garage ceiling—one for you, Dad!—and then shook his head at himself. Was it weird that he still spoke to his father thirty-five years after his death? And why did he only ever talk to him about the bike? What would he make of the mess of his marriage? he wondered suddenly, and felt a little roar of something like anger deep inside. Ken and Bett had been married twenty-six years when the heart attack had taken him from her. They'd still been in the sparkles of their silver anniversary and had never had a chance to grind each other down. He remembered what Bett had said to him on the phone the other week: *I don't think your father and I ever argued as much as we did when you went to university. We weren't perfect, Michael. No couple is.*

Too right! He twisted the throttle and the engine gave a roar, as if Gertie was echoing his feelings. He looked to the garage door, resolutely shut. What wouldn't he give to take the old girl out for a spin. He could claim he was going to the shops, couldn't he? Strap on the touring bags that had once been filled with his and Julie's holiday clothes and head out to buy milk and bread and vegetables like every other bugger looking for an excuse to leave the house. He glanced at his watch. Nearly nine p.m. God, where had the time gone?

He looked again at the garage door.

"Sod it!" he said over the now quiet purr of the ticking-over bike.

He grabbed the remote from the side and pressed. The door slid slowly, enticingly upward. A moment to pull on his jacket and helmet, always kept ready on a hook at the side, and before he knew it, he was out. He eased Gertie down the drive, turned out onto the road and, with a rush of joy, hit the pedal. He'd rarely felt more rebellious.

He flashed past the first supermarket, and then the second. God, it was good to be out. He wouldn't describe himself as someone who needed physical challenges. He'd always loved rugby, first playing it and then watching, and he'd always kept fit, but he wasn't the sort of man who had to lift the heaviest weights, or climb the biggest mountain, or hit some spurious number of steps set by a dictatorial machine on his wrist. The bike, though—the bike had always got him.

He could still remember getting on the back of this very machine aged just ten, his mum fretting and his dad telling her not to worry, he was a natural. "You can't know that," she'd snapped, but Ken had been right. Michael had known instinctively to lean into the corners, to meld himself to the machine, to feel the road not just through his feet but through his gut. He knew motorbikes weren't safe—the accident had proved that—but when he spent the rest of his life being so damned sensible, it was good to have just one little risk to keep his heart pumping. Shame Julie had refused to join him in it any more. They used to have so much fun.

Glancing around like a criminal evading the police, he flicked the indicator on and turned left out of the town and any chance of a supermarket, and onto the open road into the Derbyshire hills. It was deserted. He'd say one thing for lockdown—it made for great riding conditions! He pushed himself hard, taking the corners faster than he usually would, letting himself go where the bike led and his anger feed into the road beneath him. It felt glorious.

A twinge in his back caused him to ease off a little, stretching it out. Now that he thought about it, he realized he was slightly out of breath too. Bloody old age. Spotting a vacant pub car park up ahead, he eased off the throttle and pulled in, looking up at the sign swinging over the door: *The Green Oak*. Julie used to love this pub. In fact, hadn't he been going to bring her here on their last ever ride out on the Guzzi? The ride that had ended in bloody A&E.

He dismounted hastily and removed his helmet, turning to look away from the pub and out across the hills beyond. It felt as if all of Derbyshire was laid out for him, and walking to the edge of the car park, he looked down into the valley, searching the myriad pinpricks of domestic lighting for his own home. Was Julie asleep, or was she still up, bottle of wine emptied and feeling lonely? He felt a sudden urge to turn round and rush back to her, but what for? He hadn't even kissed her for... how long?

He closed his eyes for a moment remembering the feel of her body against his when they'd waltzed in front of that strange exercise class, and then again yesterday when they'd sat together shoulder to shoulder, chatting to Briony—the child they'd made with a far greater intimacy that had been so natural to them both for so many years.

It's not too late, he told himself. He thought of his mum. *Talk to her, Michael.* She'd made it sound so simple. It *should* be simple. They were shut in the bloody house for day after day, so they couldn't exactly claim there was no time to chat. It wasn't chat, though, was it? It was talk, with all the weight that implied, and Julie was only just beginning to open up to him. If he'd learned one thing from Linda's death, it was that going in too hard just resulted in her closing him down. He had to tread carefully. But that was OK; he was a patient man.

And for now, at least, he had all of Derbyshire open and empty before him. He should stop worrying and just bloody ride. Yanking his helmet down, he leapt back onto Gertie and ripped the throttle once more.

Julie couldn't sleep. She'd heard the familiar roar of the Guzzi engine echoing around the garage hours ago and been pleased that Michael had got the old girl going. But then it had been followed by the whine of the big door opening, and before she'd had time to get up and go to the window to see, he'd been gone. All she'd caught of him was Gertie's rear light as he'd headed off down the road, and for a moment she'd felt cross that he'd gone out without her. Then she'd remembered that for nearly twelve years now she'd been refusing to get on the bike.

And yet she'd been unable to stop a twist in her gut at the thought of the throb of the engine beneath her, the rush of acceleration, the warmth of Michael's strong body against hers. Confused, she'd turned away from the window and gone back to the crappy drama she'd been watching on TV, but it had felt even crappier in comparison to the pervasive memories of road trips past, and she'd snapped it off and gone to bed. Sleep, however, had refused to come.

She clicked the button on top of her alarm clock and the figures glowed mystic blue: 1:58 and Michael still wasn't back. Julie wasn't sure whether to feel worried or jealous. Certainly she was surprised. Whizzing around Derbyshire in the middle of the night was most definitely not essential travel, and it was unlike Michael to break the rules. He loved a rule. He always obeyed no-entry signs, always followed a diversion, and got very tense if Julie so much as wandered off a marked footpath in case they were trespassing. So what was he doing riding forbidden roads in the middle of a worldwide pandemic?

Assuming, of course, that he *was* riding the roads. That he wasn't in a ditch somewhere, bleeding to death, or crushed up against a dry-stone wall with several broken bones. On a bike you were exposed, vulnerable, easy prey for any passing twat in a big Audi.

Stop it, Julie!

It would save you divorcing him, an evil little voice said in her head, and she hated herself for it and was almost relieved when her body rejected the thought with a physical shudder. She might have decided she didn't want to live with her husband any more, but that most definitely did not mean she wanted him dead. The very thought of seeing him laid out, cold and blue and—

Stop it, Julie!

She got up and went to the loo, not because she needed it but simply for something to do. She was being pathetic. Michael would just be enjoying being back out on the bike again and making the most of the empty roads. And why not? She needed to stop fretting about it and go to sleep, and in the morning he'd be back. Simple.

Apart from the going-to-sleep bit.

It was doing nothing all day that was the problem. Usually

she collapsed into bed exhausted at the end of a run of work and socializing and was fast asleep within minutes of putting her light out, but just kicking around the house all day, she wasn't expending enough energy. She'd go out for a good long walk tomorrow, sign up to that kick-boxing class of Clare's, dig the garden, clean the skirting boards. Whatever it took. And for now—well, she'd just have to put the light on and read her book.

She padded back to the bedroom but as she went, she thought she caught a sound outside—a low, throaty growl, getting louder all the time. She ran to the window and there, turning into their road, was Michael on Gertie. Thank God! She realized she was shaking and reached for her dressing gown as she watched him approach the house in the darkness, safe and whole and uninjured. Despite herself, she felt that tug of envy again. She'd loved that bike; part of her still did. She'd just got cautious in her old age, scared off an activity that had given her huge pleasure.

She stared out the window. Michael was still sitting on Gertie, checking something on the dials, presumably the oil levels, and he looked so natural on her, so much a part of the damned machine, that she couldn't tear her eyes away. As he kicked the bike onto its stand and dismounted, her breath caught. There was no denying that his fifty-eight-year-old body looked a little stiff, and no denying the peppering of gray in his hair as he took off his helmet and shook it out, but standing there in the night, shoulders broad and hips slim, he could almost have been the twenty-two-year-old Julie had fallen head over heels for in Budapest so many years ago. Her head told her that was nonsense, but her body wasn't listening and she felt a luscious tug deep in her loins that set her skin on fire.

"Bloody menopause," she muttered automatically, but it wasn't that and she knew it. This was a far more primal flush, and as she watched him wheel the big bike toward the house, she turned and looked at the door. Should she go down? Step into the garage and drop her dressing gown? Move up to him and kiss him as she'd done that first night at the campsite, to the smell of campfires and the soundtrack of "Hotel California" played on an out-of-tune guitar? He was pushing the bike up the drive, engine off so as not to disturb her, but she was already disturbed. And she liked it.

She took two steps toward the bedroom door, her heart beating, but as she opened it, she remembered the last time she'd tried to seduce Michael—here in this very room, high on Christmas love and ready to welcome him back into her arms. It had been going so well and then he'd just shut down on her, made it clear he didn't want her. Could she face that again?

She went slowly back to the bed and drew the divorce papers out of the drawer. She thought of his rejection that Christmas night, of his coldness over the sofa covers, of the humiliation at Sophie's wedding. So many times she'd thought they might reconcile and so many times she'd been wrong. Why put herself through it again?

Hearing Michael's slow tread on the stairs, she shoved the papers under the bed and burrowed determinedly beneath the duvet, but as he passed her door, her body still pulsed. She thought she caught the smell of leathers, warm and faintly sweaty, and yearned suddenly for a time when the thrill of that glorious bike had been greater than the fear. Maybe Gertie was just a symbol of her own sexual frustration—a sign that she should get out of the lockdown of her marriage and find someone new. Maybe, indeed, the bike was all it had ever been between her and Michael—the rub of leathers, the throb of an engine, the rush of acceleration.

It would be easy to think so, but the truth wasn't that simple. The truth was that they'd been much more than that. And that was why these papers, when she finally found the strength to deliver them, would cut so deep.

Chapter Eighteen

September 2006

Michael pulls up in front of the shop and cuts the engine. He looks over his shoulder at Julie, clutching tight to his waist.

"Ready?"

"I'm not sure." Her answer is muffled by her helmet, but he hears it all the same. He gets off the bike and gently removes it, kissing her long and slow.

"You're ready, Julie. It's going to be wonderful—both the day and the shop."

"Do you really think so?"

"I know so."

"We are lacking a good flower shop around here."

He smiles. "There's that, yes, but there's so much more to it. *You* are what will make this a success—your passion, your style, your sheer joy in life."

She blinks up at him. "Is that what floristry needs?"

"Yes! And it's what I need too." He kisses her again. "I love you, Julie Marshall. Now get off that bike and into that shop. We've got a party to prepare!"

She smiles and clambers off Gertie, drawing the shop key out of the pocket of her leather jacket.

"Is it really mine, Mike?"

He gestures to the sign above the door: *Julie's Flowers*. "It's really yours, my love. You open up and I'll pop the bike around the back."

"Don't. Leave her here. She looks cool."

He shakes his head. "No way. Not even my lovely Gertie is going to draw the eye away from your shop today. I'll put her round the back."

He goes to mount, but she puts out a hand to stop him.

"OK. But in a minute. I want us to open up together if that's all right?"

"All right? I'd be honored."

He puts the helmets down on Gertie's seat and comes with her to the door. He notices that her hands are shaking, and feels another rush of love, but she slots the key into the lock and turns it firmly. The door swings back with the tinkling jangle of the bell they went all over the place to find.

"Could we try just one more place?" she'd asked him.

"Course we can," he'd agreed, because another few miles out on the bike was never a hardship, but he'd understood, too, that she wanted to find the right sound to welcome customers into her shop. And at last they had.

"Sounds good?"

"Sounds perfect."

They step into the shop together and stand a moment looking round at the walls they painted evening after long evening, with the kids in bed and Linda babysitting. Michael was always tired after a day at work, but he tried not to say so; besides, the moment he got into the shop and saw Julie's delight in it coming together, all tiredness was swept away. He looks down at her, remembering the night he definitely wasn't tired.

"We've got to christen her," Julie said that particular time, tugging at his painting trousers, which had long gone baggy around the waist and were all too ready to respond to her advances. They weren't the only thing.

"People will see," he objected breathily.

"Not in here they won't," she said, dragging him into the kitchen at the back. The shop was well and truly christened.

He looks at her now and she winks at him, reading his thoughts.

"Shame we can't do that again right now," she says, "but all the food would get squashed."

They go through and look at the plates of little nibbles they brought down earlier. They took the car back for Linda to bring the kids in as near to the actual opening as possible to avoid spillages and/or tantrums, which is why they've come on the bike.

"I'll go and move Gertie now," Michael says. "You make a start."

He's only gone a few minutes, but in true Julie style she has laid out most of the food and is busily fretting at the flowers in the snazzy aluminum buckets. He smiles at the sight of the shelves. They took even longer to choose than the bell. Julie went round and round whether to go for metal, plastic or wood, and then, when she settled on wood, whether to go painted or natural. In the end she went natural and Michael thinks they look fantastic against the apple-white walls. They're elegant and unobtrusive and they let the flowers shine.

"It's beautiful, Julie," he says. "People are going to love it."

"If they come. What if they don't come, Mike?"

She's shaking again. He's not used to seeing her like this. She's always so confident, so loud, so unabashedly herself. It just goes to show how much the shop means to her.

"They'll come," he says. "I promise. And I'll be here."

She reaches up and threads her arms around his neck.

"That's all I really need."

"But it's not all you'll get. I'm not the only one who loves you, Julie."

Sure enough, there are people gathering outside before they officially fling the doors open at midday, and within twenty minutes the place is packed. Linda arrives with the kids, though the only tantrum is hers. It emerges that she has very kindly (her words) bought the girls flowery dresses for the occasion, and the girls—at 16 and 13—have objected. Strongly. Only nine-year-old Adam has toed his granny's line, in a flowery waistcoat, and he basks in her loud praise whilst the girls escape gratefully into the crowd. Clare turns up with Hamish, who looks totally bemused by the crowds. Michael supposes he's only really used to sheep these days and wonders how Clare copes with all that emptiness. In truth, he's not sure that she does. She seems snappy with the poor man and keen to abandon him to talk to anyone else she can find. She's spoiled for choice.

There are mums from the school gates and from the various scouting, sporting and music groups that Julie carts the kids around to on a regular basis. There are other local shopkeepers, customers from the café next door, curious passersby and various people clutching the leaflets offering 10 percent off, which Michael took around the area on Gertie. Sophie has invited some friends, and even Briony, who's been quite vociferous about flowers not being cool, seems to have asked a few along. No wonder they wouldn't wear their granny's dresses! People spill out onto the pavement and Michael is glad he put Gertie around the back to leave space. Julie's smile widens and widens. Her only worry is whether they're going to run out of bubbly, but Bett sorts that by popping down to the local Co-op for another case.

"She's a marvel, your wife," she says to Michael as he helps her carry it in and pop more corks.

"Isn't she just?" he agrees. "This is going to be a big success, I know it is."

Eventually, when it feels as if the poor little shop is going to burst at the seams, Julie climbs up onto a stool and taps a cocktail stick on her glass.

"Ladies and gentlemen, I'd like to say a few short words." There's a whoop of approval and she smiles shyly. "It's nothing more than a thank you so much for coming along today. As some of you know, this has been a dream of mine ever since I came home blubbing after dropping Adam off at primary school and signed up for a floristry course to keep myself from going mad in an empty house. Although it turns out flowers can be every bit as hard to handle as children." A laugh ripples around the crowd and Julie pauses before adding, "Though every bit as rewarding."

"That's me," Adam pipes up. "I'm her child."

The crowd laughs louder. Julie smiles down at him.

"I just have a few more thank yous and then I'll let you get on with the important business of drinking." A cheer.

"And ordering flowers," Linda calls. "Ten percent off today!"

Julie rolls her eyes. "Thank you, Mum! And whilst I'm at it, thank you for showing me what it is to work hard. And for looking after the kids whilst Michael and I painted this place. And whilst I made him take me all over to find the perfect shelves and bell and buckets. It's a good job my husband has the patience of a saint!"

"He's learned the hard way with you," Clare calls, and Julie sticks her tongue out at her.

"Thanks to Bett, too, for all her support—and for the extra bubbly! And to the kids for putting up with me talking nothing but flowers for weeks."

"Years," Briony mutters.

"Years," Julie agrees. "As I said, this has been a dream of mine for a long time, so the final thank you has to go to the man who's made it all possible: my patient, supportive, endlessly encouraging husband. Ladies and gentlemen—to Michael!"

"No," Michael protests, but no one hears him and in the end he has to step up and join Julie on the stool, placing an arm tight around her waist to stop either of them falling off.

"That's very kind of you," he says, "but the praise should not go to me today. This shop is called Julie's Flowers because it's the result of the dreams, ambitions and downright hard work of one woman. So thank you for your toast, my lovely wife, but today there is only one person to drink to: Julie!"

Her name echoes around the shop and she shakes her head at him but kisses him all the same. The stool wobbles and it's only thanks to the surprisingly fast moves of Hamish that they don't inadvertently crowd-surf. They step down self-consciously and Julie smiles at Michael then moves to her flowers, stroking them lovingly as the orders start to roll in.

Chapter Nineteen

Day Fifteen

"It's the first of the *MasterChef* finals tonight," Julie said as they sat opposite each other in the kitchen.

"My pad thai made you think of that?" Michael asked. He'd made an effort over the weekend to cook some nice food for them to share, and bit by bit spending time together was starting to feel more natural, but this was a step up indeed.

"No!" she laughed. "I saw it on Twitter earlier."

"Oh."

"Though this is very good."

He looked down at the hearty bowlful of Thai goodness. "Not deconstructed enough for *MasterChef* perhaps?"

"I dunno. Looks to me like they've gone off the whole deconstructed business this year."

"I take it you've been watching?"

"Hmm. On my iPad usually, when I can't sleep."

"Right."

"Not doing enough in the day to tire myself out."

"I know what you mean."

"Have you been watching?"

"Sometimes, yeah." He's watched every single episode

actually, sitting alone in the living room. "Did you see that poor girl do deconstructed beef Wellington the other day? All those smug critics were very scathing."

"Hypocrites! Two years ago they'd have been all over it."

"True, true. We were never keen, though, were we?"

He froze at the "we." It sounded odd, like an olde-worlde word. Julie looked at him across the kitchen table. Silence stretched between them and then she said, "No. No, we weren't. Why take a perfectly good dish and break it up for the hell of it?"

He relaxed. "Exactly! Good riddance to that trend. Still keen on the old chocolate fondant, though, aren't they?"

Julie chuckled. "Adam and I made those, remember? They were perfect. Total doddle. We didn't know what all the fuss was about. And then I tried to do them for a dinner party and they were a disaster. We must just have got lucky that first time."

"Try it again."

Another pause, shorter this time. Then, "I might. No. I will."

"I'll look forward—"

"I could drop them off for Sophie and Leo. Is that allowed? I could just leave them at the end of their drive."

"I'm sure that's fine." Michael fiddled with a bit of pak choi. "Don't fondants sink, though, if you don't eat them straight out of the oven?"

"Maybe." She looked crestfallen.

"I'm sure you could take Sophie something else, though," he said hastily. "What did she used to like?"

"She was always so picky."

"She had a sweet tooth, though, for sure."

"Yeah." Julie's eyes lit up. "D'you know, she was saying on the phone the other day that she misses my lemon meringue pie."

"You do make a great lemon meringue."

"D'you think we have the ingredients?" She got up and started rifling through the cupboards. "Eggs, yes, lemons—I might have to go without a slice in my gin, but I'll cope. Flour?" She dug around and pulled out an empty-looking bag. "There might be just about enough, and I could top it up with the bread flour."

"And make more bread?" Michael asked hopefully.

She laughed. "I noticed you liked it."

"It was delicious."

"Thanks. Bread it is, then."

"And lemon meringue. Not just for Sophie, though, right? We can have some too."

The "we" came out more easily this time, and Julie barely even seemed to notice it.

"We can."

It sounded as sweet as the promised dessert. As sweet as this— a proper conversation.

"Do you want to watch it?" he asked, as nonchalantly as he could manage.

Julie looked up from her assembled ingredients. "Watch what?"

"*MasterChef.*"

"Oh." She froze, an egg in each hand. "I want to get on with this really. I'll maybe catch you up."

She wouldn't, he knew, but he could hardly force her to sit on a sofa with him.

"OK," he mumbled, and shoving his bowl in the dishwasher, he padded out of the kitchen.

Julie looked over her shoulder after Michael's retreating figure and felt a pang of guilt. Ridiculous. It was just *MasterChef*, no big deal. He didn't even like watching telly with her—said she talked too much. To be fair, she *did* talk too much; there were always important things to discuss—the name of the actors, what else they'd been in, if they were hot or not.

"Just watch it!" Michael would explode.

Briony was the same as her father, Sophie and Adam more

159

inclined to chat. Julie smiled at the thought of family battles past and reached for the lemon squeezer. Sophie had left home so long ago it was sometimes hard to remember her here, and because she hadn't gone to uni there hadn't even been a transition period. Just *bang*—gone. Day visits only. Julie and Michael hadn't been very pleased with that particular decision.

"There's no point in me going to uni to be a journalist, Mum," Sophie had said with mock patience. "All I'll do is run up debt and waste three years in which I could be bagging bylines."

"But you got such good grades," Michael had protested.

"Grades are a flawed indicator of intelligence with no inherent worth in the real world."

She'd had all the talk, even at eighteen. She'd been offered a junior position on the local rag, had found two friends to live with and nothing was stopping her. Now she was a well-respected writer with regular commissions from all the big papers and magazines. She'd been offered several full-time jobs but they'd been in London and she was very scathing of the "smug, self-centered, inward-looking" capital so had turned them all down. Michael had nearly had a fit.

"It's a regular salary, Soph—holiday pay, sick leave, a pension!"

"It's a job I love, Dad—freedom, autonomy, quality of life."

"Security," he'd whimpered.

"I am my own security," had been the grand response.

Julie had been very proud of her eldest daughter then, albeit a little afraid for her. Doing something you loved was wonderful, but you needed money too. Perhaps, despite the early battles, she and Michael had brought her up with too much security? She had longed to give her children that, but maybe it wasn't as big a favor as she'd imagined.

As a child herself, she'd never been sure if there was going to be tea on the table and she'd hated it. Linda had worked so hard to keep her and Clare feeling safe and loved, but it had been far from a steady life. Employers hadn't been very understanding of childcare issues back then, and Julie had lost count of the number of times her mercurial mum had come home having lost her job. She'd always been straight out there finding something else, but for young Julie and Clare, money had been something that came in fits and starts rather than a nice steady stream.

"Save," Linda had always urged them. "Make sure you have something for yourself. Make sure you have security."

Julie hadn't wanted that sort of desperate pressure for her kids and she'd been glad to hear Sophie's confidence in her own abilities. She'd been right, too. Meticulous, organized and conscientious, she'd made a success of herself. And even when it had become clear that she was going to move in with a potter ("A potter, Julie!" Michael had wailed. "What's wrong with a nice lawyer or accountant?"), she'd given them no real cause for concern. With Briony also in a good job and Adam—results pending—on his way to becoming a surveyor, it seemed all three children were doing well. Which was good. Great, in fact. A job well done by their parents. But a job very much done.

You don't need children to define you, Julie reminded herself, beating the hell out of the egg whites. She'd known that all along. It was why she'd really gone for it with the shop, the best fortieth birthday present Michael could ever have thought of.

She beat the eggs harder.

He'd been so considerate then. He'd really seen her, known what made her tick. And he'd loved the shop, too. They'd spent hours together doing the place up—painting the walls, building shelving, designing the logo. Julie had gone round and round all sorts of fancy names and Michael had indulged her, but he'd always been quietly certain of the name. "It should be called Julie's Flowers," he'd said, "because it is." He'd won eventually, and still every single day when she opened up, the simple name above the door warmed her heart.

161

Of course he'd barely made it for the extension opening three years ago. Whizzed in at the last minute from some supposedly delayed flight. She'd done that all herself, with Clare's help. Using blood money. The second half of the shop had been secured by the poor bugger driving past a crumbling bingo hall at just the time her mother had staggered into the road. The memory came at her suddenly, as if a brick or two in the careful wall around it had somehow shaken loose. She saw Linda lying in the hospital, helpless and gray as Julie crushed her hand, trying desperately to transmit life back into her.

They said she was knocked out instantly. They said she didn't suffer. Certainly she'd never regained consciousness, not even for the minute it would have taken Julie to say—

"Julie! What the hell?"

She blinked out of the dark mists of a hospital bed and looked around. She was in her kitchen, a Pyrex bowl spinning wildly on the worktop and egg white all over the place.

"Sorry. God, what a mess! I got carried away. Sorry." She scrabbled for a cloth. Michael was going to shout. She couldn't take shouting. "I've got it. It's fine. You go and watch *MasterChef*."

"Julie." She felt two strong hands on her shoulders and froze. Michael was looking at her not with anger or even irritation but with something like care. "*You* go and watch *MasterChef*. I'll clean up."

"But—"

"It's OK. Really."

His eyes were so blue, like a tropical sea or a summer sky or a glassy lake. Soft. Calm. Kind. Mesmerized, she nodded. Her body felt ridiculous shaky now, as if she, like the damned egg whites, was splattered all over the place.

"Thank you."

The *MasterChef* contestants were somewhere deliciously hot and exotic, cooking at the edge of seas the color of Michael's eyes. She sank onto the sunflower sofa and let herself drift on prawn bisques and pineapple puddings. At some point Michael slid back into the room and they watched in silence. Half of Julie wanted him to challenge her, to ask what was wrong. The other half would hate him if he did. She closed her eyes as one of the contestants babbled on about their dream to run their own restaurant. God, she missed the shop!

She suddenly realized that she was shivering. Opening her eyes, she put a nervous hand to her forehead. What were the virus symptoms again?

"Michael, are you cold?"

He looked over. "Cold? Actually, I am a bit. Is the heating on?"

"I hope not," Julie said, "because if it is, I might be getting ill."

He stared at her, and the horror in his eyes instantly took her up a couple of degrees.

Michael peered at the boiler, wishing he knew more about it. People always asked him to look at this sort of thing. "You're an engineer, Mike," they'd say, as if that qualified him to under-stand every man-made item on earth. He'd try to explain that he was a structural engineer, who only really knew about bridges, and they'd nod and smile and then just nudge him toward whatever was broken.

He crouched down and shone his phone torch onto the white frontage. There were only three buttons available to him—one for water, one for radiators and one that presumably turned the whole thing off. Or on. Hopefully, he pressed it. The pilot light flickered, his hope with it, but there was no whoosh of gas and no lights on the tiny display. Great. This was all they needed in lockdown. Were plumbers even still working? Certainly not this late at night, they weren't.

"Is it buggered?"

He turned to see Julie behind him.

"Looks that way to me."

"Shit!"

"I'm sure it's fixable."

"Are you? It's pretty old. God—remember when the last one went?" He frowned, trying to recall. "The New Year's party, Mike. The frigging millennium!"

"Of course! We had all the neighbors coming over."

"You wanted to cancel."

"And you said we'd make it into a jumper party."

"Yep. It was Bridget Jones time; Christmas jumpers were just becoming a thing."

"You offered a prize for the most outrageous one."

"And it went to Tommy Markinson, who..."

"Came in his kid's school jumper," they finished together. "Oh God, what a night!"

*

"Jumpers?" Linda says. "What on earth did you say jumpers for? I'm roasting."

Julie and Michael stare at her, slinky in spray-on trousers and a tight cashmere sweater in festive red. She looks amazing but very flushed.

"We thought, with the boiler broken, that it would be cold," Michael explains.

Linda grins. "Parties are never cold. D'you remember when we used to have everyone at ours for New Year, Jules? It was so hot one year we had to have a Hawaiian theme the next."

"Complete with sand on the floor and a real palm tree," Julie says, nodding.

"Sand?" Michael asks, horrified.

"Murder to clean up," Linda confirms. "Julie refused to help."

"Because I said it was a stupid idea in the first place."

"It *was* a stupid idea, but a bloody fun one. I seem to remember you were quite happy building sandcastles with that Marcus Tyler all night long."

"Is that a euphemism?" Michael asks.

"No!" Julie says, poking him in the ribs. "I was about ten."

"Plenty old enough to help tidy up," Linda says tartly. "But you wouldn't have it. There was poor Clare on her hands and knees with the brush, whilst you had your feet up and—"

"Perhaps we should do Hawaii next year," Michael breaks in as Julie bristles. He's seen this too many times and he wants them to get through the party without any disputes.

"At least then I'd be in a bikini," Linda agrees easily. "And not cooking in a blinking jumper."

"So take it off," Julie says.

"I can't." She leans in, hisses, "I've only got a bra on underneath."

Despite herself, Julie giggles, relaxes.

"I'm sure it's a nice one, Mum."

"Of course it is. La Senza's finest. But it's still a bra."

"Shall I lend you something of mine?" Julie offers, but Linda looks horrified.

"Lord no! I'll survive, thank you very much. It's just that you said it was going to be cold."

"We thought it was!"

Julie and Michael look around at their millennium party. It's in full swing now and the house is crammed with happy guests bopping away to Destiny's Child. Linda's right—they needn't have worried about the lack of heating. At least half their lovely friends turned up with portable heaters of some sort or other, and those, combined with the sheer body heat of fifty partygoers, has made the house virtually tropical. Most of the Christmas home-knits have been cast to one side and everyone is living it up in vest tops, T-shirts and slinky blouses.

"Bet the boiler's sulking now," Michael says to Julie. "Shall we dance?"

She nods and they push into the middle of the living room to join the pulsing group as the music shifts to Bon Jovi and people start whirling their hair around like the rockers they undoubtedly aren't. Julie laughs and ducks behind Michael as Tommy Markinson bounds onto the dance floor, still in his son's primary school jumper, his hairy belly wobbling exuberantly where the fabric fails to cover it. It's stretched so tight the school logo looks like some sort of spaceship, and hair is protruding from holes under his armpits where the seams are giving up the fight. He'll have to buy a new one when term starts again but for now no one cares, least of all Tommy.

"Nearly midnight!" someone calls, and Jon Bon Jovi is mercilessly clicked off to give way to Jools Holland and Coldplay on the telly. Tommy Markinson keeps on dancing anyway. Everyone gathers. Glasses are hastily filled. The kids emerge from upstairs, where they've been doing who knows what while their parents throw themselves around the dance floor.

"Ten, nine..."

Michael and Julie look around their friends as they scream out the numbers.

"Eight, seven..."

Seven-year-old Briony slides in next to them, wide-eyed with the excitement of staying up this late. Sophie arrives too, with little Adam on her hip.

"What's he doing up?" Julie demands.

"Six, five..."

"He woke up. He wants to see the new millennium in with us."

"Four, three..."

"Well done him," Michael says. "It's good to be together for this."

"Two, one...Happy New Year!"

The room erupts in laughs and cheers, and party poppers

cast their tiny, impossible-to-tidy-up strands all over the discarded jumpers, but no one cares, for the new millennium has arrived.

*

"Oh, it was good," Julie said.

"But messy. The state of the house the next day!"

"We hung all the jumpers up outside for people to reclaim when they surfaced, remember?"

"God, yes. And had a bloody drink with every one of them to celebrate still being alive."

"We'd avoided the millennium bug, but talk about hair of the dog!"

"It was a good party."

"Yeah. But the boiler was kaput. Cost us a fortune."

Michael grimaced and pressed the button again. Julie gasped as the pilot flared, but it didn't fire up. "We'll have to try the plumber in the morning and hope he's still working. Will you be warm enough until then, do you think?" She gave him a sideways look and he swallowed. "I just meant..."

"I'll be fine. Thanks."

"Right. Good." He stood up, very aware of her proximity on the narrow landing. "It's just, they said there might be a frost tonight, so, er..."

"Thick pajamas?"

Was she teasing him? It felt as if she was. He was definitely teased, especially in certain areas, though perhaps that was just the memories playing havoc with his old body. He carefully closed the boiler cupboard door and they stood there, adrift in the freezing corridor.

"How about a cup of tea?" Julie offered. "I'll stick the kettle on, shall I?"

Michael snatched at this modicum of normality. "Great. I'll get us some warm clothes."

"Cool. I'll, er, see you in the kitchen then."

It sounded weirdly like a date. He went into the bedroom and rootled through Julie's wardrobe until he found a fleecy white cardigan he knew she loved. Most of his own jumpers were over in the spare room, but at the back of the drawer he found a navy cable-knit she used to admire him in, and feeling a little self-conscious, he tugged it on and headed downstairs.

Julie was adding milk to two mugs of tea as he walked into the kitchen, leaning into the meager warmth of their steam, and her eyes lit up at the sight of the cardigan.

"Perfect! Thanks, Mike." She paused. "You look nice."

"This old thing?" He tugged at it, then told himself to stop being pathetic. "Thanks."

She gave him a quick smile and busied herself pulling the cardigan on whilst he took his tea and sipped gratefully at it.

"Do you remember my mum, Mike?" she asked suddenly.

He looked at her, confused.

"Linda? Of course I remember her. How could I not?"

"Why do you say it like that?"

"Like what?" He could feel the mood slipping away from him again and tried desperately to hold onto it. "I loved your mum. She was great fun."

"She was a hard worker too. Really hard. Often had two jobs on the go."

"I know."

"You only ever saw the fun side of her."

"She was a woman who threw herself into whatever she was doing. I've no doubt she was like that with work before... before..."

"Before she discovered partying."

"There was nothing wrong with that, Julie."

"And booze."

He swallowed. "We all like a drink, don't we?"

168

"Yes, but not so much that we don't even notice a car hurtling toward us."

"No. That was terrible. Julie, are you OK?"

"Fine. I'm fine, thanks. Just... Too many memories, hey?"

"We can talk about it if you want."

She looked at him, opened her mouth as if about to take him up on the offer, and then gulped at her tea instead.

"No. Thank you. I'm tired. Bed for me."

His heart sank into his stupid slippers.

"Julie..."

"Night, Michael."

She headed out of the kitchen, her shoulders tight beneath the white cardy and her mug of tea held in front of her like a lantern.

"Night, Julie," he said sadly, blowing the words out across the surface of his own tea and wondering how he'd got that so very wrong. Again.

Chapter Twenty

August 2016

Michael stirs awake to see Julie already up and standing at the wardrobe, pulling out clothes at random. In the gloom he can see a pile of dark items building up on the floor until suddenly she snatches at something and yanks it on. Even in the darkness of the early morning, the neon of the pink blouse shines out. He suppresses a moan. Ever since Linda's death, Julie has been wearing relentlessly bright colors. She and Clare requested them for the funeral, and people arrived in such varied shades that the church looked like a rainbow parade. Michael saw how it fitted Linda's vibrant personality, but he'd have preferred the safety of black.

"It doesn't feel right," he muttered to his mum, who had come in a pretty lilac.

"Michael," she said, squeezing his arm, "today what *you* feel isn't the point."

She was right, of course, and Michael did his best to support Julie, but her persistent choice of lurid colors is starting to worry him. She's wearing them like armor against her grief, and even a week after they buried Linda it's proving remarkably impenetrable. He forces his weary body out of bed.

"Julie, darling, it's very early."

He's no idea of the exact time, but the sun is still pale around the edges of the curtains, and that means it's definitely too soon to be getting up.

"I need to get into work. There's a lot to do with Clare away."

Away. It's a curious choice of word. Clare came to the funeral in a long dress of deepest purple and wept copiously through-out, leaning helplessly in against her rigid-backed sister. At the wake she was taken in hand by two old university friends who swept her up in their kindly arms and carried her off to their Cornish retreat. Michael has found himself curiously jealous of how Clare submitted to their caring, for Julie, it seems, is not as ready as her sister to be looked after.

"I could come with you to the shop."

"Why?" She frowns at him as if he's some sort of stranger rather than her husband of thirty-one years.

"Why not? I used to help out there after all."

"But you don't any more."

"Well, I haven't done recently, but I could. I'd like to."

"What about your own work?"

He has to resist shaking her. "I've told you, Julie, I've taken time off."

"Oh yes. Why?"

"To look after you, of course."

He thinks she's going to ask why again, but she stops herself. Just. The sun tops the horizon outside and a ray creeps round the edge of the curtain, lighting her up. Her eyes are glassy. It's scary. She's not dealing with this, he knows. What he doesn't know is what to do about it.

"Come back to bed, hey?"

"Why?"

"For a cuddle. It'll be nice."

She looks unconvinced but allows herself to be led to the bed.

171

He takes her in his arms but she lies there stiffly instead of curling into him as she's always done before. The neon blouse is made of some synthetic material, and static sucks it against his bare skin. He longs to yank it off her but forces himself just to lie there, stroking her hair, praying she'll relax against him. She doesn't.

"Can I get up now?" she asks eventually.

"In a minute, darling. Let's just...talk."

"About what?"

"Maybe about...your mum?"

"Why? She's dead. What's the point in talking about her?"

"OK. About you then, about how you're...feeling. How you're coping."

"Coping?" She looks at him angrily. "I think I'm coping fine, thank you very much. The funeral was good, wasn't it? Everyone said it was good. Lots of people came. The vicar did that lovely speech and people liked my poem, or they said they did. There was enough food at the wake, and the beer, so I'm told, was excellent."

"Julie..."

"Was it? The beer?"

"It *was* excellent," he confirms obediently, "but that's not the point here. You need—"

"And now I'm getting on with things. That's what Mum would have wanted. That's what she always did. If things knock you back, you pick yourself up and get on."

"Well, yes, and that's very commendable, but it's fine to take a little time for yourself first. Like Clare has."

"You want me to go and bow to the morning sun and eat mung beans? That will make it better, will it?"

"No. But you can stay at home, rest, let me look after you."

She lets out a long sigh and for a moment turns into his arms, but then she says, "I'm not good at resting, Michael," and is up again and reaching for a red skirt to clash with the blouse.

172

Michael watches her, feeling useless. His own grief when his father died did not operate this way. With the heart attack two weeks before their wedding, he did have to get on with things, as Julie is doing now, but every happy moment was followed by an equally sad one that had him seesawing constantly from smiles to tears. Julie seems to have neither—it's like she's flat, numb to everything.

As he lies there, he remembers waking on his wedding day in his old single bed back home, his body filling with the glorious awareness of the day ahead before being hit by the painful real-ization of his mother next door, all alone and no doubt weeping into his dad's empty pillow. He remembers going to see her and lying on the bed, just as he used to do when he was small, except that this time there were no longer two bodies to squirm between and it was his arms that went around her. But at least she found comfort there, unlike Julie now.

He leaps up and follows his wife to the kitchen like a shadow.

"Let me make you some breakfast," he says.

She sits obediently and he hurries to scramble eggs, keen to at least offer her physical sustenance. As he looks at her, hands folded in her lap, pink blouse bright against her pale skin, he remembers his first sight of her as she appeared at the back of the church. He hadn't been nervous, but with Bett sitting alone just behind him, he *had* been sad—right up until he heard the rustle that told of Julie's arrival and was instantly washed through with happiness. He'd had no idea what she'd be wearing. It could have been classic white, rebellious black, or polka dot. He'd have put nothing past her and he'd loved that. In fact, she'd gone traditional in swathes of rich cream, the skirt so big it brushed against the pews on both sides and tangled in Linda's legs as she proudly offered her daughter her arm. They looked at each other, smiled, and strode out together, and that was when he saw them—the bright red shoes that marked her little rebellion.

Julie has always loved color, but now it seems as if she is more color than Julie, and it's blinding him.

"I'll come to the shop," he says decisively.

She looks at him as if she might resist, but it seems she doesn't have the strength for it.

"OK then."

It's only as they pull up in the little parking space that he realizes how long it's been since he was last here. After they agreed he should go for promotion, he's been so wrapped up in his work that he's not paid much attention to hers. It's been going well, he knows that. She even, now he thinks of it, muttered something about expanding. He follows her round to the front and notices that the café next door, once a vibrant little place full of kooky colored chairs and pots of daisies, is empty.

"What's happened to the café?"

She stops dead, stares into the grimy window. "It shut down. A while ago now."

He stands back, considers it. "You could take it on, Julie, extend into it."

Her stare swings from the café to him. Her eyes are glassier than ever and she seems to look straight through him.

"Mmm, yes, what a great idea." There's an edge to her words that he doesn't like.

"Julie, please." He reaches for her hands. "Have I done something wrong?"

"No, you haven't."

But she's pulling away and clattering her key into the lock and he can't get her to face him again.

He follows her into the shop, still a shadow—formless, useless. The rich smell of the place hits him instantly—the sweetness of the flowers with the musky undertones of the greenery and the sharper tang of the cellophane and ribbons used to dress them up for the romantics of this world. He should buy her flowers,

174

he thinks. It always seems a pointless exercise, but he sees now that that's wrong. If she likes flowers, she should have flowers.

Their wedding leaps into his head once more. Julie had a glorious bouquet that day, red, of course, to match her shoes, but orange too and yellow and every shade of green. It sat across the front of their table as they ate and he remembers brushing against it as he led her out onto the floor for their first dance, releasing a scent so rich it made him giddy. But as soon as he took her in his arms, to the soft chimes of The Beatles singing "All You Need Is Love," the rest of the overdecorated room faded into soft focus.

"I love you," he whispered to her.

"I love you too," she said back, louder. "And I always, always will."

She linked her arms around his neck and pulled him close and he couldn't believe how happy he was. But then the music shifted into the chorus and she pulled back to wave the others onto the dance floor. His mum hovered alone on the edge and his heart cracked, but it was Julie who stepped away from him and went to Bett, who took both her hands and danced with her. It was a simple, natural act from his new wife, but it swelled his heart almost to the bursting point—and if it didn't quite mend the crack, it at least held it together long enough to start to heal. Why can he not, then, help to heal hers now?

"What can I do?" he asks, looking around.

"I'm not sure," she says, staring into the distance. "I'm not sure there's anything you can do."

Chapter Twenty-One

Day Sixteen

"Tea."

Michael sidled into the room, proffering the mug like a bone to a hungry animal, and Julie sat up hastily and took it with a smile. She'd not slept at all well, haunted by the look on his face when she'd pushed him away last night, and was relieved he'd kept to their new morning routine.

"Thanks, Mike. And sorry I, er, ran out on you."

"It's OK."

She sips her tea. "That's perfect."

"Nice and strong."

"Exactly."

She smiled shyly at him. She'd never understood people who drank weak tea—if you were going to do something, do it properly. She could still remember how pleased she'd been when Michael had asked for his "well stewed" when she'd invited him to her house a couple of weeks after the end of her Interrail trip.

She'd been so nervous. She'd had three nights with him in Budapest, three glorious nights and two blissful days before Susie had had a mardy about being left on her own the whole time. Two years later, at their wedding, her best mate had made a hilarious speech about how she'd so nearly broken up true love, but the truth was they'd exchanged numbers—landlines back then—on that first dawn when they'd woken up tangled together. Nervous as she'd been about whether it would be so perfect away from the glamour of Budapest, nothing would have stopped her inviting him over. Or, as he'd told her within moments of her opening the door to him, stopped him coming to find her. And then there'd been the tea.

"We're made for each other!" she'd cried, clinking her dark brew against his. And he'd smiled a slow smile and taken her in his arms. Not much of that tea had been drunk.

She shifted beneath the duvet, suddenly hot.

"We could maybe make that lemon meringue today?" she suggested.

"That would be great," he said, but then his brow creased. "I've got to work, though. Conference call at eight."

"Do you have to start that early?"

He gave an awkward shrug. "It's with China. They're nearly at the end of their day already. I'll hurry them along as best I can."

"No rush."

"OK. Thanks."

He edged out of the room and Julie sat listening to him head down the corridor and into Briony's room. A little later she heard the low rumble of his voice start up as another international business dialed into his expertise. With all that had been going on in the last five years, she hadn't noticed quite how impressive he'd got. She wondered if the French girl was part of this call, and hot again, she kicked the duvet off and leapt up to open the curtains.

Another beautiful day greeted her. Perhaps she'd walk a little further today, get to the woods where the bluebells were blooming with glorious abandon. She liked it there and almost always saw other people. They steered careful paths around each other but it was nice to smile at someone, to chat briefly across a stream, to remind yourself that other human beings still existed. Mind you, there was a distinct early-morning chill she hadn't noticed before the boiler had given up on them, and she hastily dressed in her warmest jumper and made for the kitchen.

The pie ingredients were all still out and she self-consciously wiped a tenacious bit of egg white off the wall, remembering Michael rescuing her last night. He was being so nice to her at the moment. It was confusing, like thinking you were drinking tea and finding out it was actually coffee, but nice too. She decided to make the lemon meringue pie, then maybe he'd have finished with China in time to come with her to Sophie's. She set to with pastry and sugar and vibrant lemon, and soon she was coaxing gentle waves into the meringue and placing it in the oven to cook. Sophie would surely be up, cutting her kohlrabi or milking her oats or whatever it was she and Leo did for breakfast, so she called her.

"Morning, Mum." Her daughter sounded surprisingly sleepy.

"Did I wake you?"

"No, no, no." Julie was pretty sure that meant yes and grinned. "I was just, er, doing yoga."

"Right. Well, I won't be a minute. I've got a present for you."

"A present?"

"Yep. Something you'll like."

"I'd hope so if it's a present. What is it?"

Julie wanted to be mysterious, but she was far too impatient for that, always had been. Keeping birthday or Christmas presents secret almost killed her, and many was the year she'd let vital information slip with just days to go.

"It's a lemon meringue pie."

"Wow!" Sophie made a strange noise, almost a sob.

"Soph? Are you OK?"

"I love lemon meringue pie."

"I know. That's why I made it for you."

"That's very kind, Mum." She sounded almost tearful. Julie frowned down the phone. "So I thought if I brought it to the end of your drive, you could get it from there. And we could maybe, you know, have a chat. Two meters away, obviously. Ten meters even. It would just be nice to, well, to see your face."

"And yours, Mum. Really."

"Good. Well then, once it's out the oven and cooled, I'll—"

"But we shouldn't."

"What?"

"It's not essential food, is it?"

Julie stared at the oven. "Well, not essential, no, but it's very nice."

Sophie gave a low moan. "I know it's very nice, Mum. But what about the plate?"

"The plate?"

"It might be contaminated."

Julie sank down onto a chair, picking one in the sunshine coming through the window for warmth.

"Sophie, sweetie, your dad and I have been at home for over two weeks now and neither of us is ill. I'm sure we can safely drop off one little pie."

"Yes, but... It's Leo, you see. And his asthma."

Julie frowned. "Sophie, is everything OK?"

"Yes, fine, just trying to be extra cautious. I bet the lemon meringue looks beautiful. Send me a picture, hey, Mum?" There was a strain to the words that Julie didn't like.

"Sophie, something's wrong. I can hear it in your voice."

"Nothing's wrong, I promise. I'd love some of your magnificent pie, but we've only got to be patient a little longer."

"They're talking about weeks more—maybe even months," Julie said, hearing her own voice wobble.

She'd wanted to take the pie as a treat for Sophie, but now

179

that Sophie was refusing it, she was realizing how much of a treat it would have been for her too. Behind her, the oven timer pinged.

"Is that it?" Sophie asked. "Is that the pie?"

"Yep. Here, I'll switch to video call and you can see it."

"Mum, that'll just be torture. That…"

But Julie was already switching the call over. She propped the phone on the side and drew her creation out of the oven to set it before her virtual daughter.

"Oh!" Sophie said, as much a groan as a sigh now. "Oh Mum, it looks amazing."

"Doesn't it?" Julie agreed, pleased with herself. "Look, Soph, it'll be easy. I'll put it on a paper plate and you can just lever it off with a spatula or something and—"

"No! You can't come here, Mum."

"Why on earth not? Sophie, what's wrong? Have you been feeling ill?" She peered at the screen. Sophie did look rather flushed.

"No, Mum." She glanced sideways, as if checking for her husband, then visibly shook herself. "Just don't come. Please."

"Sophie, is everything OK? Are you…frightened?"

"No! God no, Mum. It's nothing like that. I promise. Oh Lord, you're going to make me cry now."

"Cry?" Julie was horrified. Her eldest child never cried.

"I have to go. The pie looks wonderful. Enjoy it for me, OK?"

"Sophie…"

"Please, Mum."

"OK!" Julie put her hands up in surrender. "Can I call you again? Soon?"

"Course." Sophie wiped a tear from her eye, gave a watery smile. "Course you can. Sorry. It's just all this virus stuff, you know. Weird times. Let's talk again soon. Very soon, yeah? Bye, Mum. Love you."

And then she was gone. Julie stood there, the pie cooling in front of the now blank screen, wondering what the hell was going on. Not only did Sophie never cry, but she wasn't much of a one for I-love-yous either. Seeing her like that was enough to shake anyone up, and especially someone who'd already been feeling pretty wobbly.

She glanced at the ceiling. She could hear the faint murmur of Michael on his conference call and suddenly desperately wanted to talk to him again. Maybe he'd been in contact with Sophie. Maybe he knew what was going on with her. She was his daughter too, after all. She'd take him up some pie. He'd like that.

She put the kettle on to make coffee as the pie cooled, and even dug out the old cafetière they used to love and rarely bothered with these days. Ten minutes later, perfect coffee brewed and a large slice of pie wobbling beautifully on a plate, she headed for the stairs and knocked politely on Briony's door.

"Come in."

She poked her head into the room. He was sitting at the desk in that lovely cable-knit jumper that set his eyes off a treat.

"Thought you might like some of this," she said, stepping inside and presenting the pie with a flourish.

"Wow! That looks great." Michael sat back as she set it on the desk. "Coffee too. Thank you." He picked up the spoon and took a big bite. She stood there waiting. "Delicious."

"Thanks."

He looked at her. "Are you OK?"

She perched on the end of the bed. "I am. yes...Mike, have you heard from Sophie recently?"

"Sophie? Only the odd message here and there—much like usual."

"Like usual? Really?"

"Well, yes. She sends me links to worthy articles explaining how I ought to be running my life more effectively."

Julie gave a tight smile. "She does that to me too. Did you get the one on why vegetarianism is the only way to save the planet?"

He shook his head. "She's given up on the anti-meat thing with me. Mine are more on renewable energy and, lately, cholesterol levels—old-man stuff."

"Right." He looked so pissed off that Julie almost laughed, but then she remembered Sophie's strange mood earlier. "And nothing's changed?"

"No. This morning she sent me one on sea levels, I think. Why? What's going on, Julie?"

"I don't know. I called offering to take her the pie and she was adamant I wasn't to go anywhere near them. And then she cried, Michael."

"Cried? Sophie? Are you sure?"

She was grateful for the response. Only Michael knew Sophie well enough to understand.

"Dead sure. I saw her wipe away a tear."

"Is she ill?"

"I don't know! Whatever it is, she won't tell me. I've no idea what to do."

Tears welled and she fought them, but one escaped, dropped onto her jeans and spread across the fabric. She rubbed at it. Why couldn't this stop? Why couldn't it all just go away? Another tear fell, and this time she let it.

"Oh Jules." Michael slid onto the bed beside her and took her hand. "She'll be OK, I'm sure of it. She's strong as an ox, our Sophie."

Our Sophie. The gossamer web reached around her as tightly as Michael's hand in hers and she leant against him gratefully.

"You promise?"

"I promise." She knew he couldn't do that, but she had to believe him or she'd be screaming a track up and down the garden within minutes. "Pie?" he suggested, and she gave a tiny laugh and nodded.

He fed it to her with his spare hand and she opened her mouth like a baby, like a little Sophie playing choo-choo trains in her highchair. The dessert burst across her tongue, sweet and then sharp with the buttery pastry as a rich follow-on. God, listen to her—she was like a frigging *MasterChef* voice-over. And yet for this moment it was a relief just to focus on the intricacies of the food. She swallowed.

"Not bad, if I say so myself."

"It's delicious! Sophie would love it, the silly moo."

Julie looked at the remains of the pie. "Maybe I'll just go over there anyway."

"Why?"

"To see her. Properly."

"You know she won't allow that."

"She won't bloody stop me. I'm her mother."

Michael gave her a look so long that she squirmed beneath it. "What?" she demanded.

"You're a great mother, Julie. You love so...fiercely." He paused, then added, "Just like Linda did."

Julie froze. "What do you mean by that?"

"Just what I said. The way you love Sophie—and Briony and Adam too—that's the way Linda felt about you."

"I'm not sure that's true, Mike. We argued. All the time."

He nodded carefully. "I'm not saying that she always liked you, or you her—but she always loved you. Always."

Julie lay back on Briony's bed and looked at the ceiling. Was he right? Every memory she had of her mother was tangled— half sweet, half sour. But maybe, just maybe, all this time she'd been focusing too much on the sour.

Chapter Twenty-Two

July 1999

"Are you sure we can do this, Julie?"

Julie looks at Michael's concerned face and laughs.

"Sure I'm sure. All the locals are at it."

"But that's because they know what to do."

Julie laughs again and looks around at her young family, poised by the rocks with their plastic buckets in their little hands.

"And so do we. Come on, we've cooked mussels loads before."

"From a shop."

"And where d'you think the shop gets them from?" She waves a hand to the glorious crop of dark mollusks crowding the Breton rocks, and finally Michael smiles.

"You're right."

"Of course I'm right." She reaches up and kisses him. "Now let's go, kids! An ice cream for whoever picks the most whole mussels. And another for the biggest, fattest, juiciest one."

"And a third," Michael adds hastily as the girls shoot off, "for the prettiest shell."

Julie looks up at him. "Three ice creams—good plan."

"Self-preservation. Also, it gives me more chance of winning."

He winks, swings little Adam onto his hip and heads after the girls.

Julie follows more slowly, loving the scene. They've been camping in Brittany for a week now, but she feels like she could stay here forever. The weather has been largely kind and the kids largely sweet. The days drift and stretch deliciously. She watches nine-year-old Sophie's long legs leaping across the rocks in search of the best place to harvest—the best place for her always being away from the rest. Briony, at six, has already given up trying to follow her sister and settled to methodically plucking mussels from the nearest spot. She will win the "most mussels" prize, no doubt about it. Adam, at only eighteen months, is a little young for the job, but he insisted on having his own bucket and is now tugging keenly at shells with his podgy hands whilst Michael steadies him. The midday sun is shining down and she's delighted with her pick-your-own-lunch challenge.

She glances back to their area to be sure their stuff is safe. It's chaotic. Every time they arrive at the beach, Michael lays their towels out in a neatly squared-off line, sets up the umbrella and tucks the cool box and bag of toys beneath it. It always looks perfect—for about a minute. Then the kids fall out with each other and move their towels, disgorge the toys everywhere and open up the cool box for food, despite having had breakfast barely minutes before setting out. Michael is always very patient about it, collecting up their scattered goods on a regular basis and keeping his own towel on the edge of the madness, but she suspects that he sometimes craves the quiet order of their pre-kids beach trips.

"You'll miss them when they're gone," she said to him this morning as they pulled up the carefully laid-out towels.

"Not this bit," he replied through sand-gritted teeth, but he's happy now, helping Adam put mussels into his Thomas the Tank Engine bucket. And he'll love setting the fire needed for cooking. Julie has a pan in the cool box, pre-chopped onions, white wine, cream. It's going to be a feast.

"Come on, slowcoach!" Michael calls, and she stops watching her family on the rocks and rushes to join them.

"I've got the most. I've definitely got the most. My bucket's full to the very top."

Briony dances up and down, waving her sparkly purple bucket under Julie and Michael's noses and sending mussels flying. Julie puts out a hand to steady it.

"You do have a lot, Bri."

"Only 'cos her bucket's so much smaller than mine," Sophie objects indignantly.

Julie looks at Sophie's bucket. At most it's a centimeter taller than Briony's and is barely half full.

"It looks like you've got very big ones, Sophie. You must have chosen with care."

"Of course. You can't pick the baby ones, can you? That wouldn't be fair. They've got to live their life before we swoop in and eat them."

Julie looks at the rocks, considering this.

"What sort of life do you think it is for them, Soph?"

"I don't know, do I? I'm not a mussel."

"Fair point."

"But I'm sure they like it. More than they like being boiled alive, that's for sure." She looks at the pot on Michael's fire and frowns. "Actually, isn't this cruel?"

"Oh no," Michael says quickly. "I read a study about it before we came away—mussels have no nerve endings so can't feel pain."

Sophie looks at him uncertainly.

"It must be true," Briony puts in, "because you don't hear them screaming, do you?"

186

"That's because they haven't got mouths, stupid!"

"Or nerfs."

"Nerves."

"Yeah. Those. And anyway, they're all we've got for lunch, so eat them or die!"

Sophie's lip wobbles. "You're so cruel, Briony. Don't you care about these poor creatures?"

"The mussels? No. Why should I?"

"'Cos they can't care for themselves."

"Doh! If they can't—"

Julie steps in.

"They don't suffer, Soph, but if you don't want any, that's fine. There's lovely fresh bread."

"And ice cream after," Michael puts in. "Because look, Sophie, you definitely have the biggest one here."

He pulls a truly huge mussel out of her bucket and Sophie beams, cruelty forgotten in the glory of victory.

"And I get one for having the most," Briony says.

"You do. And look, Adam found this really shiny one with such pretty patterns." Michael holds out a half-shell Adam has bagged and tips it to the light so the pearlescent lining shimmers.

"That is pretty," Briony says.

Sophie rolls her eyes. "They're all like that inside," she says loftily, but then relents and crouches down to her little brother. "But it is lovely. Good job, Ads. Ice cream for you too."

"Yay!"

Adam celebrates with a mad toddle around the perimeter of their chaotic camp. Sophie chases after him, Briony follows and Julie sinks down next to Michael at the fire as their children swirl around them giggling.

"We won't need all that white wine for the mussels, right?"

"Dead right," he agrees, leaning back to pull two garishly colored plastic cups from the cool box. "Elegant glass, my lady?"

"You spoil me!"

She pours and they chink—well, clunk—their cups as the first batch of mussels starts to open enticingly in the pan.

"We do know what to do," he says, putting an arm around her. "You were right."

"Of course I was right."

He laughs and kisses her quiet.

"Lunch is up, kids! Grab a plate."

They're on the second batch when a voice calls, "Cooee!," and Julie turns to see her mother coming down the beach toward them, elegant in a fifties-style swimsuit, carrying a large bag and swaying slightly.

"Uh oh," she says to Michael in a low voice. "Here's trouble." He gives a pointed look to her own cup of wine and she relents and waves. "Hi, Mum! You're just in time for some fresh mussels."

"Mussels?" Linda looks down at the pan in horror. "Good God, what are you thinking of, Julie? You'll poison the children."

Sophie instantly drops her mussel onto her plate. "Poison?" she squeaks.

"Nonsense, Mum," Julie says. "All the locals are doing it."

"That's because they're French."

Julie feels her irritation rising. She loves her mum, really she does, and on the whole she's been great on holiday so far, entertaining the kids, doing her share of the chores and regularly taking herself off to give them all space. They were sort of hoping she'd babysit a couple of times to let them go out together, but on the first night they sent her for takeaway chips and she found a bingo club behind the campsite bar. She's been off out to that every night since.

It hasn't mattered, though. Julie and Michael have been happy sitting in front of their tent with Briony and Adam asleep inside and Sophie deep in a book, sharing a bottle of wine and watching the world go by. And Linda has her own one-man tent so she can come in without waking them and sleep on in the mornings. In many ways, they've agreed, it's a glimpse into what it will be like having a teenager. So yes, on the whole it's been good having her along, but sometimes she can just be so damned obtuse.

"The French are people just like us, Mum," Julie says, fighting to keep her voice low and even.

"Not *that* much like us, love," Linda says, flopping onto the sand and moving the bowl of empty shells disdainfully away. "They don't have proper loos."

"Actually, I think you'll find that the crouching toilet is much more hygienic."

"And they eat frogs! And horses."

"Horses?" Sophie stares at her aghast.

"Mum," Julie hisses.

"But they do, Julie. There's no point in lying to the kids, is there?"

"We haven't had horse, have we?" Sophie demands, rounding on Julie and Michael. "You haven't fed it to us?"

"No!"

"Are you sure, love?" Linda asks. "That beef casserole we had last night tasted lovely and rich to me."

"Because we bought good stock!" Julie shouts. "It was definitely beef."

Michael puts a calming hand on her knee and she fights for control. People are looking over.

"Why don't you try some mussels, Linda?" Michael suggests in his politest, calmest voice. "They go beautifully with a glass of white."

He lifts the bottle out of the cool box and Linda's eyes light up.

"Don't mind if I do." She accepts a cup of wine, but when Michael goes to dish her up some mussels, she raises a hand.

189

"No. Thank you. I have my own lunch. A good old English ham sandwich."

Adam looks up at the magic words. He loves a ham sandwich.

"It's hardly English on a baguette, Mum," Julie says tightly.

"Ah, but look what I found in the campsite shop." Linda pulls a perfectly square, anemically white sliced-bread sandwich out of her bag. Adam drops his mussel immediately and reaches for it. "Oh no you don't," Linda says. "You've got your lovely shellfish."

"Ham," Adam says, reaching again. "Ham. Ham!"

"I'm going vegetarian," Sophie announces. "And so should you all."

She attempts to take Briony's mussels off her and Briony, furious, kicks out. Sand flies up, landing in the last of the mussels, in the wine and in Sophie's eyes. She wails. Adam wails. Julie leaps up.

"For God's sake, Mum. Thanks a lot!"

Linda looks around at the chaos, wrinkles her nose in the way Michael always teases Julie about, and rises gracefully.

"Fine. I'll go then."

And taking her plastic sandwich and her sandy cup of wine, she floats off down the beach, leaving Julie and Michael to deal with the fallout.

"Ice creams!" Michael suggests, and Julies leans against him gratefully and nods.

Later, they come back to the tent after showering everyone down after a thankfully enjoyable afternoon on the beach to find beautiful canapés laid out on the table in the evening sun, a bottle of bubbly chilling in one of the kids' buckets, and a contrite Linda.

"Sorry about earlier, Jules. The sun went to my head, I think. I love France really. And the French. Horse's doofers, anyone?"

"Horse's what?" Sophie gasps, but Linda is quick to it this time.

"Just Granny being silly, sweetheart," she says. "Hors d'oeuvres. It's French for 'fiddly little mouthfuls of yumminess.' Look, these ones here are all veggie." Mollified, Sophie sinks into one of the chairs and takes a tomato and cheese stick. Briony loads a plate with one of everything and Linda draws Adam onto her knee. "These are ham, Ads, for you." His eyes light up at the tiny triangles of ham and white bread, and Julie has to smile. How has Linda made these look elegant? "Glass of bubbly?" her mum suggests, her eyes pleading.

"Lovely," Julie agrees, taking her own seat. "Thank you."

Linda's eyes soften with relief. "I'm a bit of an idiot sometimes," she says quietly.

"Aren't we all?" Julie replies. "Cheers, Mum."

"Cheers, love."

Chapter Twenty-Three

Michael sat awkwardly on the bed at Julie's side, watching her. She'd been lying in the same position for a while, her eyes closed and her lips moving slightly, and he was dying to ask her what she was thinking. He didn't quite dare disturb her, though, and was relieved when a flurry of beeps revealed action on the family WhatsApp group. He opened up the messages.

> Hey folks!

This from Sophie, unusually jolly, especially given that she had apparently been in tears just a short time ago.

> How's about a family Zoom tonight? Would be great to see all your ugly mugs.

A family Zoom?! What was going on with his eldest child? The others had been very quick to reply.

Adam:

Speak for yourself, I'm as handsome as they come. Can do 8 if you all can?

Sophie:

8's good for us. Bri?

Briony:

Can we say 8:30? Work's manic.

Adam:

Show-off.

Briony:

Layabout.

Sophie:

Mum? Dad?

Michael looked at Julie. Her eyes were still shut.
"Julie?"
She blinked up at him. "Sorry. Miles away."
"Good miles?"
She shrugged. "I'm not sure."
"I have something that might help a little."
"You do?"
He held out his phone and she quickly scanned the messages, then looked back at him.
"What d'you think's going on?"

"No idea, but it looks like we might find out tonight—if you're up for it?"

"I guess so. I mean yes, of course. That would be good."

Michael typed:

We'll be there.

Sophie came back straight away:

Cool! Can't wait.

"Cool?" Julie said. "Sophie never says things like 'cool.' Oh God, I hope she's OK. Ask her if Leo will be there."

Michael dutifully typed the question and Sophie replied immediately:

Of course.

Adam was straight there:

Good. At least he's not ugly.

Sophie sent back a tongue-out emoji.

Michael smiled, set down the phone and looked at Julie.

"They're good kids."

"They are. We're lucky."

"We worked hard, Julie. Did lots with them, you know. And we were...we were happy. Weren't we?"

"We were." She sounded pleasingly certain. But then she added, "It's hard, isn't it?"

Michael wasn't quite sure what "it" was, but he felt like they were getting somewhere and he had to keep going.

"It is, yes. We've been very busy."

She nodded. "Too busy, do you think?"

"Not too busy, no. We've done so many lovely things—as a family, with our jobs, as a couple."

"Hmm."

He felt the conversation sliding away from him, as it seemed to have done so often before. How would he deal with this if it was someone from work? he wondered. It felt callous to approach this vital conversation as he might a professional assignment, but he needed some sort of way in. Facts, that was what he'd look for. Actual solid core facts. He drew in a deep breath.

"I think perhaps we've struggled since…since…" Come on, Michael, he urged himself. Just bloody say it. "Since your mum died." There was an icy pause, but he battled on. "I know I failed you then, Julie. I know I did. But I still don't know how. I'm sure it was my fault, that I was insensitive or stupid or something, but I couldn't reach you then and it feels like I never have since."

It was the most he'd said to her in ages. He looked at her desperately and willed her to say something.

"I was grieving," she stuttered eventually.

It was something. He shifted closer to her.

"I know. Really, I know. I understand what it feels like to lose a parent, remember?"

"You don't, though."

"What?"

Her whole body tightened visibly before him.

"You don't know what it felt like for me."

"Well, no, I don't, but I lost Dad. And it hurt. It hurt like hell. I wouldn't have got through it if it hadn't been for you."

"Oh, you would. You would, Michael, because your grief was so perfect."

"Perfect? How could it be perfect, Julie? Dad died two weeks before our wedding."

"I know! Two weeks before our wedding and a day after you and he had been on your father–son bonding pub crawl and come staggering in arm in arm."

"What? What's that got to do with it?"

She shook her head wildly, flailed her arms in the air. "Everything. It's got everything to do with it, Michael. Your grief for your father was so...so pure."

"Pure?" he echoed, stunned. He'd wanted answers, but now that she was flinging them at him, they were harder to fathom than the great blank that had gone before.

"Yes! Perfect. Unsullied. Pure. Blissfully, exquisitely, painfully pure."

"Julie." He reached for her but her arms were still flailing around and he couldn't grasp her hands. "Julie, please. I don't understand."

"I know!" she wailed at him. "And you have no idea how lucky that makes you."

"So tell me!" he begged. "Please, Julie, tell me what you mean."

She leapt up and reached for the door. "I can't, Michael. Somehow I just can't."

And then she was gone, crashing down the corridor. Moments later, he heard the bedroom door bang shut behind her and knew he'd blown it. Again.

Chapter Twenty-Four

July 2017

Julie rubs her eyes and looks up, pulling herself slowly out of her reverie. This has been her grandest creation ever and has taken all her energy, but it's worth it. She stands back to survey the arrangement. It's all white and green. There's not a speck of color, not even a whimsical touch of sky blue to break up the purity, but she's used every white flower she's been able to get her hands on, so that despite the monotones, it bursts with variety. Tonight, as the sun starts to drop, she will take it to Linda's grave. Clare is coming too, once she's back from scouting Leo's pottery for business, but the flowers are from her alone. They're a gift, an apology, a peace offering. They're also the marker of a hard year done and, she hopes, a new one ready to unfold.

She has not grieved well, she knows that. Clare did far better than her, weeping out her grief and letting her friends take her to Cornwall to make peace with it. She came back a new woman, still sad but able to laugh over the cold dawn swims, the meditations and even the expressive dance classes, which, despite her gentle mockery, quite clearly helped her heal.

Julie sighs.

"Penny for 'em."

She jumps and looks up to see George, their friendly plant supplier, standing in the doorway, a big tray of begonias in his strong arms.

"George! Sorry. I was miles away."

"Clearly." He comes in and sets the plants down. "If you don't mind me saying, it didn't look the happiest of places."

She sighs again. This is the sort of half-question that she usually bats away, but working on the flowers has loosened her guard and George is looking at her so kindly that for once she allows herself an answer.

"I was thinking of my mum. It's a year today since her death."

"I'm so sorry." He comes a little closer. "Are those flowers for her?" She nods. "They're beautiful, Julie. Very elegant."

Julie gives a little laugh. "Probably not quite right then. My mum was never really elegant. Fun, yes, joyous even— but not elegant."

"Well, it looks to me like you've made her elegant now."

She looks down at the flowers, suddenly shy.

"Thank you. I...I wanted to strip it back." She waits for him to probe, but he just stands there quietly and she finds herself offering more. "At her funeral we went for color. Lots and lots of color. It felt very her—she was a very colorful person—but I think maybe it was also...oh, I dunno..."

"A protection?"

"Something like that, yes. I didn't want to be sad."

She runs a finger along the soft petal of a rock rose and thinks about Linda. George stands quietly at her side, and for once she feels no need to fill the silence.

"Tell me about her," he asks gently.

She looks up, surprised by the sudden swelling of emotion inside her. George doesn't fuss, doesn't suggest making cups of tea or sitting down. He just stands there.

"OK." She smiles at him and sighs. "She was quite complex, my mum."

She looks down at the flowers, plucking at a snapdragon as memories come flooding back in.

"She had us young," she tells George. "Her parents were very straitlaced and it sounds like she was your classic rebel. Wild clothes, crazy hair colors, piercings, parties, unsuitable boyfriends. One in particular—my dad, Shawn. They married the day after her twentieth birthday. She had me just over a year later and Clare the year after that. I think they were happy. She used to say they were, at the start, but my dad was a gambler. He talked her into putting all their money—which wasn't much—into some business venture that went horribly wrong. The whole dodgy-lenders-at-the-door-with-baseball-bats horror. In the end he left. Told her he was doing it to protect us, but if you ask me, he was just running away from his responsibilities."

"Your poor mum."

Julie nodded. "Yeah. It must have been awful. We didn't see him again after that; didn't try to see him either. As far as Clare and I were concerned, Mum was all the parent we needed, but it was hard for her. She battled to bring us up on her own, said there was no way she was letting another man into our 'girls' house." It was understandable but it left her with everything to do, which took its toll. She was…unpredictable. And she had to juggle so much it was hard for her to hold down a steady job. I think she hated herself for that.

"She was always telling us to work hard and to save, to make sure we had something to fall back on, but it wasn't advice she followed herself. God, I can remember her coming home one day with a bonus and taking us out for a Chinese. All dressed up and wide-eyed over our sweet-and-sour chicken we were. She spent so much that we were on baked beans for weeks, but we had a great night. That was Mum!"

She stops and lets her fingers run down the trailing snapdragons. She's not spoken about Linda in this much detail all year but it's easier, somehow—less cluttered, perhaps—to capture the essence of her with someone new.

"She sounds fun," George says, and she pulls herself away from the flowers and looks at him. "But a bit difficult, perhaps?"

"A bit?" Julie permits herself a bitter little laugh. "We argued," she admits. "A lot."

"Mothers and daughters often do."

"Yeah? Well, we were always at it." She bends down and sniffs at the peonies at the heart of the arrangement. "We argued the night before she died, actually."

The words are out of her mouth before she quite realizes she's said them. They hover in the air, dangerously, but then George puts a hand over hers where it rests on the counter. It's warm and soft and so, so gentle.

"They say that when people die, their lives flash before them, you know. And they say, too, that the human mind is kind—it's always the good stuff that surfaces."

She looks up at him. "Really?"

He nods. "They've done surveys of people who were pulled back from drowning or on operating tables. Near-death, it seems, is largely a happy place."

"I hope so, George. Oh God, I hope so." She feels a tear break loose from her eye and puts a finger to it in wonder.

"Oh no," he says. "I'm sorry. I've made you cry."

"Don't be sorry. Really." It's one of the first tears she's shed since that call from the hospital last year, and it feels like an oasis in the desert.

"May I...?" He holds his arms open and she nods and steps forward. They close around her, strong and safe, and she leans gratefully against him.

"Sorry," she mumbles. "I'm not usually like this."

200

"Then maybe you should be," he says softly.

"Mum would be horrified. She didn't like crying. Said it was a waste of time. Why cry when you can laugh, that's what she'd say."

"And she was right. But maybe sometimes you need to cry before you *can* laugh."

"You're very wise, George."

"For a gardener?"

"For a man."

He gives a little chuckle. "Is that what your mum said too?"

"She wasn't the biggest fan of the male of the species, certainly. She used to swear about them like a trooper." She puts a guilty hand to her mouth. "I shouldn't speak ill of the dead."

He strokes her back. "I'm not sure why. Are people different just because they're dead? I mean, it doesn't suddenly render them perfect, does it? I hope when I'm six feet under people will still be able to say, 'God, he was a grumpy sod in the mornings.'"

This time Julie's laugh is genuine. She pulls back to look up at him.

"Are you?"

"Absolutely. Don't go near me until I've had at least one coffee."

"I'll remember that."

There's a pause. George bites at his lip and Julie feels something shift between them.

"Right," she says, stepping hastily back. "I'd better get on. Are those begonias for Clare?"

George nods, looking suddenly awkward. "That's right. Is she here?"

It's patently obvious that she's not, that it's just the two of them in the tight little shop.

"She's off looking at pots, but she'll be back any minute."

"OK. I'll just leave them here, shall I?"

"Thanks. Oh, and George..." He's halfway to the door but he stops straight away. "Thanks, too, for, you know, listening."

"Any time, Julie." He smiles. "Take care of yourself, OK?"

The bell chimes out as he pulls the door open and Julie stands there watching his blond head pass along the front of the window until he's gone. She's not quite sure what just happened, but she feels better than she has done all year.

Chapter Twenty-Five

"Hey all!"

Sophie waved enthusiastically as one by one the squares on the screen came to life and the Marshalls gathered. Julie drank them in—her babies. *Their* babies. Adam was there in front of Chelsea's parents' geometric curtains again, but his hair was so cutely all over the place and his eyes so bright that she barely even noticed them. Briony was in her kitchen, apparently making tea. Her screen sat at an awkward angle, showing mainly the cooker and some sort of stir-fry in progress, but she raised a glass of wine and gave a cheery thumbs-up.

Sophie, Julie was pleased to see, was cuddled up with Leo, though to be fair she and Michael were sitting camera-close too, so that wasn't saying much. They'd been treading around each other ever since her outburst this morning, and now, it seemed, they were back to putting on a show. She sucked in a deep breath and plastered on a smile.

"How's everyone then?" Sophie asked.

Neither Julie nor Michael answered. Luckily the kids were more forthcoming.

"Great," Briony bubbled, dumping stir-fry onto her plate

and carrying it and her phone across to the table before taking them all back to fetch her wine. "Work's so cool at the moment and the city's amazing. It's deserted, especially in the evenings. Yesterday I walked down the middle of Oxford Street at ten o'clock. Extraordinary."

"What were you doing out at ten?" Julie asked her.

"Finishing work, of course."

"So late?"

"We're working to find a vaccine, Mum—it takes a lot of time."

"I understand that, but you do need to look after yourself, Bri. Stay well."

"I am. Believe me, walking through locked-down London is exceptionally cathartic. And very safe."

Julie smiled at her. "Fair enough. And you're eating well?"

"What do you think?" Adam put in as Briony lifted a laden fork to the camera.

Julie looked at him. "How are you, Ads?"

"Oh, I'm fine. A bit bored, you know. But very fit. I'm running a lot along the beach and Chelsea's got me doing all sorts of stupid Hollywood workouts. You'd wet yourselves laughing if you could see me."

"Have you got a leotard?" Briony asked.

"A thong one," Sophie suggested.

Adam stuck his tongue out at them. "No. And definitely no. I have football kit. And I tell you what, I cannot wait to play football in it again. I've done enough lunges and planks and bloody grapevines to last a lifetime."

"What's it like with Chelsea's folks?" Briony asked.

Julie tensed, but Adam gave a diffident shrug and said, "It's OK. They're very nice. Very kind." He glanced sideways, presumably to check he was alone, and then leant in confidentially. "They're all very polite to each other, though. I miss you lot taking the piss out of me."

204

"Always happy to oblige there," Briony said, mouth full. "Where shall we start, Soph? How about his hair? You know you look like Kevin Keegan on a bad day, right?"

Adam ruffled his hair and struck a silly pose.

"Can't believe you know who Kevin Keegan is, sis."

"Only because Mum used to tell Dad he looked like him when he was too lazy to go to the barber's, right, Mum?"

The memory flashed at Julie: Michael with his dark hair flopping across his face, hiding his blue eyes. She glanced at him.

"It was the only way to get him to go."

"I hated Kevin Keegan even more than I hated the barber's," Michael confirmed.

Everyone laughed and for a moment it was as if the wonders of Zoom had taken them not just across space but through time. Julie looked at her precious brood before her and thought of the divorce papers hiding upstairs. If she cut the link between her and Michael, she also broke the ring of them all. They'd work it out, of course they would, but it wouldn't be the same. She'd cut out the ease, sever the natural togetherness, run a knife through the memories, setting them adrift on a sea of "then" instead of keeping them anchored to the shore of "now."

"Mum?" She blinked to see Sophie staring at her. "You in there?"

"Sorry. Yes. Just, you know, remembering. I wish you were all here. I wish I could hug you."

"I wish I could hug you too, Mum," Adam said instantly. "No one hugs like you and Dad."

Julie felt dangerous tears prickle as Briony raised her glass and said, "I'll drink to that."

"Me too," Sophie agreed, lifting a tumbler.

Adam groaned. "Is that water, Soph?"

"Sure is."

"You know we're in lockdown, right? Drinking's virtually obligatory."

"For some, maybe."

"Tell me you've not decided alcohol is bad for the environment? You can make it yourself, you know, from parsnips and that. Granny's got her own still going with her lockdown mates. She's promised me loads of free gin!"

Sophie laughed.

"We do a bit of home brewing ourselves," Leo said, raising a glass of something dark and suspiciously cloudy.

"What's that?" Michael asked.

"Pear cider. Delicious. And lethal."

"So why aren't you having any, Soph?" Briony demanded.

"Well…" Sophie said, her lips curling into a shy smile, and suddenly Julie knew what was going on with her eldest daughter. Suddenly it all slotted into place.

"You're—"

She felt Michael's hand on her knee and stopped.

"Let her say it," he whispered.

So he knew too. She put her hand tentatively over his and together they leant forward.

"It's just possible," Sophie said, "that there's a new member of the family on the way." She looked at Leo, and he beamed and put his arms around her as, in their respective homes too, too far away, both Adam and Briony leapt up.

"Yay! A baby!"

"Nice one, Soph."

Julie looked at Michael and to her surprise saw a tear quivering on the edge of his eye. He wiped it hastily away.

"That's wonderful news, Sophie."

"Wonderful," Julie echoed.

"That's why you're on water!" Adam said.

"And why you were so careful about isolating," Julie added.

Sophie wrinkled her nose in the way Michael always used to tell Julie she did. "That's right. I was reading all this scary stuff about the possible impact of the virus on fetuses, and we didn't want to take any chances. But as we also didn't want to tell anyone until twelve weeks, we kind of used the asthma as an excuse."

"Twelve weeks," Julie breathed. "That means you're due when? November?"

Sophie smiled at her. "October the twenty-third. I'm only actually ten weeks, Mum, but after this morning I knew I couldn't keep it a secret any more. Sorry for being so weird on you."

"You're always weird, Soph," Julie heard Adam say, but only as background chatter, because her eyes were locked with her elder daughter's in new understanding, not just of this morning but of all that was to come.

October the twenty-third! This was a new date for them then—a new marker on the family calendar. And something else Julie would wreck if—

"Bubbly!" Michael cried. "We must have bubbly."

He leapt up, pulling his hand from under Julie's, and dashed off. Julie sat there, staring at her children as Briony and Adam insisted on seeing Sophie's tummy.

"See, I reckon I'm showing already," she told them, turning sideways to reveal a ridiculously flat stomach.

"Rubbish! I look more pregnant than that after a full English," Adam told her.

Sophie visibly blushed and they both looked curiously at her.

"What?" Briony demanded.

"I've a confession to make," Sophie said.

"Excellent!" Adam rubbed his hands.

"I've been desperate for meat. Bacon especially."

Her siblings stared at her.

"Wow!" Adam said. "You've come back over to the dark side at last."

"I have not, I—"

"Shut up, Adam," Briony said. "Don't worry, Soph; it's just that you need protein to grow the baby."

"That's what Leo said," she admitted, looking to her husband. "So the other day…I had a bacon sandwich."

"Good!" Julie cried, re-entering the discussion.

Sophie looked at her, her eyes full of anguish.

"Do you really think so, Mum?"

"I really, really do. That's your body telling you what nourishment your baby needs, Soph, and it's vital you listen to it."

"But I've been veggie for over twenty years."

"And you still are—it's just baby who's the little carnivore."

Sophie let out a laugh then, a little watery perhaps, but a laugh all the same.

"You're right, Mum."

"Of course I'm right."

That made them all laugh. Those words had been her chorus throughout bringing them up, and they'd all groaned at it every time.

Chelsea landed beside Adam and he turned to her.

"Hey, Chels, I'm going to be an uncle. A blinking uncle! How good is that?"

"Brilliant," Chelsea agreed. "Congrats," she added to the screen.

Sophie smiled. "Thanks, Chelsea."

"Poor kid, though," Briony said, "with an uncle like Adam."

"Oi!" Adam objected. "I've got vital skills to pass on—how to do backward keepy-uppies, how to burp the national anthem, where to hide things you don't want your parents to find. Then, of course, there's my superior stock of swear words."

Sophie groaned and Julie sat back, watching her kids tease

each other, seeing Leo and Chelsea joining in. Already the family was expanding, and now there would be a baby.

Michael returned with a tray and set it down, and Julie saw that he'd brought six glasses.

"Michael…"

"One for everyone," he said firmly. "Oh, hi, Chelsea. You'll have to share with Adam, I'm afraid."

"No problem!"

Adam reached out comically to the camera. Briony clapped. Michael popped the cork and solemnly poured out six flutes, adding a tiny bit to the sixth. "Just a mouthful for you, Soph." Then he set them out in front of the screen, handed one to Julie and lifted his own. "To Sophie and Leo," he said, "and to their new addition—the luckiest baby in the world."

"The luckiest baby in the world," everyone chorused, mock-drinking.

Julie felt the bubbles fizz in her mouth and the sweet taste of champagne burst across her tongue. It chased up her nose and, inexplicably, into her eyes.

"Aah," Briony called, "Mum's crying."

"Happy tears," Julie said, batting at them. But as Michael put a tentative arm around her and she dared to lean into him, she wasn't sure they really were. Didn't this just make things even harder?

When the call finally ended and the kids' chatter shut down to a dark, silent screen, Julie and Michael faced each other. They were two glasses of bubbly down each and Julie felt giddy and disorientated.

"We're going to be grandparents," Michael said.

"Yes."

He squared his shoulders. "That's a big responsibility, Jules. And it's one…it's one I want us to face together."

Julie swallowed. "I do too."

"But things aren't right between us. I know they're not. And I really want to sort that out." He paused. "You have to talk to me, Jules, tell me what's on your mind."

He looked into her eyes with his own blue ones and she longed to feel that same rush of love they'd always set going in her so easily before, but it just didn't seem to come any more. There was a wall inside her stopping it. A Linda-shaped wall. She remembered what Michael had said earlier about Linda loving her in the same way she loved Sophie. And now Sophie would have her own child to love and the chain would grow. She swallowed again.

"When Mum died…"

"Yes?"

There was such kindness in him. Linda had seen that straight away, she remembered.

"The day before Mum died…" she started again.

He blinked but didn't flinch.

Her throat was clogging up. She had to say it.

"The day before Mum died, we argued." Her throat loosened instantly. "I went to see her to…to ask her for something. She said no. Just like that. No. Didn't even really listen to me. Just shut me down. I got angry straight away—she always pushed my buttons so easily. I shouted. Said some horrible things. And she shouted back. Told me to bugger off. So I did. I swore at her and I buggered off and the next day…the next day…"

She burst into floods of tears and Michael just put his arms around her and rubbed her back as they soaked into his jumper.

"I'm here, Julie. You can tell me about it."

It was so tempting. He was wearing the cable-knit sweater again, and it was so soft and warm and it smelt of him—of kindness, of safety, of a time long past when things weren't all so confusing. She hunted around in her head for the words to tell him what had happened, but every place she tried to start seemed to burn a hole in her throat, and in the end she broke away from the warmth of his embrace and with a garbled "sorry" fled for the safety of her own empty bed.

Chapter Twenty-Six

July 2016

"Money?" Linda looks at Julie across the pub table. "You want money? From me?"

Julie fiddles with a bar mat. She knows that tone. Knows it all too well.

"A small loan, Mum. An investment. You see, the café next door to the shop's gone bust and there's a twenty-year lease available. If I buy that, I could knock the two shops together and expand the business. I've talked to Clare about it and we think we could branch out into plants and pots and floral accessories. People love all that stuff and it's a slightly different market to bouquets so it ought to expand our customer base. I've done a business plan if you—"

"Business plan? I'm not a bloody bank manager, Julie."

"I know that. I just thought you might be interested."

"You just thought I might be gullible is what you just thought." Julie glugs back her Bacardi and Coke in one big swallow. "Is this because you think I'm old?"

"What?"

"You don't think I need my money now that I'm approaching

seventy, is that it? I'm not interesting enough to actually spend any of my hard-earned cash on anything but you?"

"No, Mum, that's not it. I just thought that with Clare and me both working there you might like to invest. You know how you always said we should create something for ourselves—well, here it is, and you could be part of it. It would just be a loan and I would pay interest."

Linda, however, doesn't seem to be listening.

"Is this an inheritance grab?" she demands. "Do you think it's your money already?"

Julie looks desperately around the pub. Why didn't she bring Clare along? Because Clare doesn't even know she's asking, that's why. Clare thinks she's speaking to Michael about the money, but he hasn't picked up on her very obvious hints about wanting to expand. So now she's going to do it her own way.

"Mum, please. Calm down."

But Linda is up on her feet. "Another drink? I imagine you will, if I'm buying."

"No thank you."

She tosses her hair and goes to the bar, deliberately standing for ages chatting to the barman. Julie's glad. It gives her a chance to collect herself, and when Linda finally returns she thinks maybe it's given her a chance to think too.

"How much money?" she asks.

"Eight thousand, to cover the first year."

"Eight thousand?" She sniffs. "That's a *lot* of money."

Julie sucks in a deep breath and forces herself not to rise. She knows that Linda has over ten times that in savings from her parents' legacy, but it was stupid of her to call on it.

"It doesn't matter, Mum. Forget it. It was wrong of me to ask."

"How can I forget it now? Eight thousand! Do you know what a gorgeous cruise that would get me?"

"You don't like cruises."

"What on earth makes you say that?"

"Oh, I don't know—perhaps you always telling me that you can't see why on earth anyone would want to spend their holidays floating around the sea in a giant tin can?"

Linda glowers at her. "Yeah, well, maybe I've changed. And it's not just about cruises, is it? I want to drink nice wine now I'm older, not crappy five-quid-a-bottle stuff. I want to buy designer shoes and a new sofa—a cream leather one with one of those fold-back ends. Do you want me to die on that horrible beige thing I've had since you were a kid?"

Julie bites her lip. Linda bought the horrible beige thing about three years ago. She had designer shoes for Briony's graduation last year and she much prefers spirits to wine. But Julie gets the point, really she does.

"Of course I don't want that, Mum. If you need the money, don't worry. Forget it. I'll talk to the bank."

"Or Michael? Why can't you talk to Michael? He's rich, isn't he?"

It's the "he" that gets to her. The implication that all their money is his. But then again, perhaps that's why she's here in the first place. She puts her hands flat on the table, leans forward.

"First off, Mum, 'his' money is *our* money. He may have earned it but he could only do that because I stayed at home with the kids when they were little. It was a joint decision and a joint effort. Secondly, I was hoping to do this part for myself. I thought you of all people would appreciate that. I thought you brought Clare and me up to be independent, to fight our own corner, to keep our idle hands busy and make our own money."

"But this is *my* money you're talking about."

"It would be a loan, Mum. An investment—in the business Clare and I have created. A way of being involved that I thought you might like, but apparently not."

Linda stares at her for a long time, then shakes her head.

"This is the problem with being a mother," she says. "It never bloody stops."

"Oh, for Christ's sake!" Julie leaps up, suddenly furious. "Why does this have to be all about you, Mum? I didn't realize that by 'independent' you meant 'selfish,' though God knows why— I've lived with the proof of it all my life. Well, I apologize for clogging up your precious life with my own. I apologize for daring to think you might be interested in helping me instead of just yourself. In fact, I apologize for ever being born. I often think you'd be happier if I hadn't been, so I won't take up any more of your time. Enjoy your pissing cruise and I hope you trip up on your bloody designer shoes and fall overboard. Good night."

There's an elation to letting loose those words—a dark, thrilling release. It carries her home and through the night. It carries her through the next day in the shop, where she clatters around making high-speed bouquets and staring into the empty café next door. She even thinks of more things to add when she talks to Linda next. She's so angry with her mum for latching straight onto the money when it was meant to be about so much more than that, but by the evening the energy of the argument is dissipating into a low cloud across her mind. The only thing that can penetrate it is the shrill ring of her phone.

"Julie Marshall? Are you next of kin to Ms. Linda Jenkins? I'm afraid there's been an accident."

Chapter Twenty-Seven

Day Seventeen

Michael looked round the garage and nodded, satisfied. Not bad at all, if he said so himself. He'd been awake half the night trying to think of something he could do for Julie, and this was it. Not his finest structure ever, but the best he could manage in lockdown. He crossed his fingers, a kid again, and went to fetch the final pieces of his plan.

In truth, he was still trying to process what she'd told him last night. Not so much that she'd argued with her mum—that had been commonplace in all the years he'd known her—but that she hadn't felt able to tell him. Linda had died nearly four years ago and Julie had kept this buried from him that whole time. He understood why she thought his own grief for his father was so pure, if she'd been carrying the guilt of angry last words for so long.

He reached into the fridge with a flutter of nerves. What if she hated this? What if she thought it was a stupid idea? He drew out the box he'd stashed in there earlier and looked down at it. He'd snuck out to the supermarket at first light, and though he'd been annoyed to find that he'd hit "old folks' hour," he'd been even more annoyed when no one had paid him a glancing bit of notice.

"I'm not even sixty yet!" he'd wanted to shout, but where would that have got him? So he'd shuffled in with his sore back and joined the other elderly shoppers. It had been peaceful at least and the shelves had been bulging with stock, which had been ridiculously exciting. He'd wandered the aisles picking up the bits and pieces on the list he'd remembered to grab from the kitchen and looking for the special elements to complete his plan. The deli had been closed, but the freezer had proved surprisingly helpful. He smiled and took the box through to the garage, placing it next to the other things. Nearly time.

He'd hurried home from the shop to make Julie her morning cup of tea, but she'd been fast asleep and, suspecting she hadn't slept much either, he'd left her to lie in. Oh, it had been so tempting just to slip in beside her and put his arms around her. But he'd have scared her. Crazy, after nearly thirty-five years of marriage, but he was now seeing the chasm they'd allowed to open up between them, and he wasn't stupid enough to think he could leap that with a quick cuddle. His current plan seemed a pretty poor effort too, but it was all he had to try and show her how much he still loved her and wanted to repair their marriage.

Come on, Michael, he told himself. It was now or never. Even if she didn't want to talk to him, or if what she had to say was too horrible, it still had to be done. They couldn't creep around each other in a cold war any longer; it was damaging them both. He went back to the kitchen and looked out. Julie was in the garden, putting the finishing touches to the table. He had no idea why it was called "distressing," as the table looked amazing, not so much distressed as invigorated. Whatever she'd done had drawn out the natural grain of the wood so that it looked more tree than table. He loved it.

He put his hand on the back door, pulled it slowly open.

"Julie!" She looked over straight away. A good sign? "I've got something I'd really like you to, er, to see."

She looked annoyed. Damn.

"Now?"

"Shortly. Whenever you're ready, really."

She put down a pot of varnish. "I'm ready. This is done."

"It looks amazing."

"You think so?"

"Absolutely. Like it's alive again."

She smiled with genuine pleasure. "That's what I wanted."

"Well, you succeeded."

"Thank you." She came toward him. "What is it?"

He drew in a deep breath. "I've been thinking about what you told me about, you know, your mum. And what you said about the purity of my grief."

She fiddled with her hair. "I shouldn't have said that, Mike. It wasn't fair. It's not your fault that you got on well with your father, bless him."

"No, I know that. But I've been thinking about what a support you were to me when we lost him, and at the wedding and on our honeymoon. I can remember so vividly you dancing with my poor mum so she wasn't on her own. It was lovely of you."

"It was the least I could do, Michael."

"But I didn't give you the same support when you needed it."

"No, I didn't let you. Mum died at a far more...complex time for us both."

He jumped at that. "She did, Julie. She did. And today I want to take you back to a simpler one."

"What do you mean?"

"Wait and see."

She looked intrigued. Good. His heart was beating ridiculously fast, but he'd started this now and there was no choice but to finish it. "Come to the garage in ten minutes, will you?"

Her eyebrows furrowed. "The garage?"

"In ten minutes. Please. Oh, and bring your jacket."

"My biker jacket?"

"The very same."

"Michael..." she started, but he had to go before he lost his nerve. Last night had been a wonderful step into the future for them as a family, but now it was time to see if they could be a couple once more as well.

"Ten minutes, Julie," he repeated, and fled.

Julie watched Michael hastening up the garden, marveling at the changes in him in these last weeks. Or perhaps the changes between the two of them. She'd so feared being locked down with him when the PM had made his initial announcement, but stuck in here together they'd started chatting more naturally than they had in years, sharing memories, laughing even. She remembered the strange rush of intimacy when she'd had to help him up off the floor, and then the joy of standing shoulder to shoulder at the window watching the lambs leap. She remembered him taking her in his arms to dance the crazy Zumba waltz and placing his hand over hers as they'd anticipated Sophie's announcement. The happiness they'd been able to share shot through her anew and she swallowed. She didn't want to break up her family. That was perhaps what had been stopping her doing anything for so long before, but there was more to it. It wasn't about the kids now; it was about Michael.

He'd looked at her so intently up in the loft between the sparkles of their silver wedding decorations. She'd thought for a moment he was going to kiss her. Would she have kissed him back? Her body was certainly responding to him in long-forgotten ways. If someone had asked her when she'd stood in that shiny divorce lawyer's office what color her soon-to-be-ex-husband's eyes were, she'd have said black. But the light was back in him somehow and they were shining as blue as they had that very first time she'd seen him. It was enticing.

219

Hastily she put away the varnish and brushes and went back into the house. She paused outside the door into the garage but could hear nothing within. Her heart beat a little faster. What was he up to? She went through to the corridor and pulled her biker jacket off the peg, remembering the feel of it against her skin the other day, the way it had taken her so effortlessly back in time. Slowly she pulled it on. It didn't make her feel younger today but perhaps, even so, a little stronger. Nervously she retraced her steps and knocked on the garage door.

"Come in."

She put her hand to the handle, pushed the door open and stepped inside. The sight that met her was astonishing. The main lights were off, but two desk lamps shone down onto Gertie, making her glow gloriously red in the middle of the darkened room. Michael was astride her, helmet on, and in front of him, covering the big garage door was a white sheet onto which he had projected the image of a sun-drenched road. It stretched out in front of the bike, wide and open between craggy scrubland and leading to a tantalizing glimmer of sea on the horizon.

She put her hands to her mouth, unable to believe it.

"I can't take you back through the years, I'm afraid," Michael said, "but maybe I can take you somewhere nice right now. Will you come? It's quite safe. We're not actually going anywhere. And I've got all the windows open for ventilation." He looked so sweetly nervous.

She swallowed. "I'd love to."

"Oh good!"

He lifted her helmet up off the side and held it out to her. It glinted with a new shine—and with older memories.

"Where did you get that?"

"Oh, I've kept it in the cupboard. Just in case, one day... Not to pressurize you. Just that, well, I never liked riding with anyone as much as with you, Julie."

220

"What about Rob?"

"Rob's a smelly old biker who goes too fast and picks terrible places for lunch."

Julie laughed. She stepped forward and took the helmet, instinctively tucking her hair behind her ears before she slid it on. She looked at Michael through the visor, seeing him framed in front of her as he'd been framed so many times since that first amazing meeting in Budapest.

"OK?" he asked, his eyes shining with care.

"OK."

"Then, please…"

He patted the seat behind him and, heart pounding louder than ever, Julie stepped up and hooked her leg over the back. She sank onto the seat and the leather gave a tiny, happy sigh, as if Gertie had been waiting for just this. The curve of it pushed her toward Michael and she felt the achingly familiar press of his back against her body and dared to sneak her arms around his waist. His hands closed over hers for a moment, squeezed, and then, in a single fluid movement, he grabbed the throttle and kicked the bike into life. The engine roared and the sound echoed around the garage and filled Julie with the perfect reverberations of easy happiness.

She looked at the screen in front of her, and to her astonishment, it started to play. Michael must have a remote control in his hand, she thought, but then she didn't care how he was doing it, because the road was rolling under them as if they were traveling along it, and as they headed toward the horizon, the sea grew closer. Michael gently revved the engine and tipped the bike just a little as the road rose up and over the ridge of the hill, and suddenly before them was the curve of a beach, and along it, dotting the hillside, a cluster of beautiful white buildings.

"Greece!" she gasped. "Oh Michael, it's Greece at last."

The video paused with the glorious vista laid out before them, and Michael quietly killed the engine. For a short time they just sat there, Julie drinking in the sight and, far more wonderful than that, the effort that Michael, her husband, had made to bring it to her. Locked down in a garage in suburbia at what had felt like the back end of their once golden marriage, he had somehow transported her to the place of her dreams.

Eventually he drew off his helmet and looked over his shoulder at her.

"Ready for a bite to eat?"

"Here?"

"Of course."

He held out his hand and she took it and let him guide her off the bike and over to two of their old camping chairs she'd not noticed before. Between them was a table laid with a bottle of red wine, two glasses and a plastic picnic box. As she sat down, he lifted the lid.

"Dolmade, Chiquitita?"

She giggled. "Please."

"And a glass of red? It's not Greek, I'm afraid, but it's as rough as I could find."

"Perfect!"

He poured and took his seat opposite her. Julie bit into the vine leaf. It was still a little frozen in the middle, but she didn't care. It tasted of escape and hope.

"How on earth did you get these?" she asked.

"I gatecrashed the old folks' early-morning shopping," he admitted.

"Michael Marshall, you rebel!"

"I didn't do it on purpose. And d'you know what, no one told me I was too young. No one, Julie! Do I look that bad?"

"Of course not," she said, straight away, because that was what you did, but actually he didn't look old at all. A bit tight-backed,

222

perhaps, but that was just his injury pressing on him—and possibly his emotionally stunted wife.

"I think maybe I do," he said. "I can feel it coming, you know, the sixty thing. And I don't like it. I think it's made me grouchy. Unnecessarily grouchy. I'm sorry."

She sucked in a breath at the unexpected admission.

"You're not the only one," she said softly. "I thought this grumpy old woman thing was a myth made up by comedians, but it's not. Stupid things make me mad these days. I hear myself tutting under my breath at nonsense like falling-down jeans. Why do they matter? I should count myself glad to get a glimpse of a young man's boxers, right?"

He gave her a small smile. "Right. You know what *I* hate?"

"What?"

"The boomer thing. Someone muttered that when I was in a café at the airport a while ago. I'd only said something about not getting a free muffin with my coffee—because they'd been handing them out the day before—and this lad behind me muttered, 'Bloody boomer.' I wanted to turn round and sock him one! I didn't, because I hate violence, obviously. And also because he could have floored me with one punch. I still hated it, though, especially as I've had none of the advantages of a proper boomer. Neither of us has—not a final-salary pension in sight."

Julie grimaced. "No."

Michael bit into a dolmade. "That's why I've worked so hard, you know, these last years. It's not because I wanted to be away."

"I know."

"Do you, though, Julie? Because I never said it. I should have said it." He looked at her. "I'm saying it now. It's been really good being at home these last weeks. I mean, not good, because of the virus, and it would have been nice to be able to see the kids and Mum, obviously, but good for me. To be home, with you. I hate hotels."

223

She stared at him, a lump forming in her throat. She wanted to tell him that she'd enjoyed it too. She wanted to tell him that she liked hearing him talking in Briony's office, that she liked watching him pottering in the garden, or cooking in the kitchen. She wanted to tell him how she'd felt when she'd seen him step off his bike beneath the stars. But before she could form the words, his phone rang. He pulled it out of his pocket, annoyed, but when he saw the caller ID, he snatched it up.

"Hello," he said eagerly, then, "Yes. Yes please!" He turned to Julie as he ended the call. "That was John, the plumber—he's on his way."

"Now?"

"Any minute. He's in the area and got off another job quicker than he'd expected. I need to go and look out for him. I'll be right back."

He rushed off, and Julie sat sipping her wine, staring at the Greek sun and letting the calm of the beautiful place settle around her. All morning she'd been rehearsing words to explain what had happened between her and her mum—not to mention all that had come after—and in this beautiful bit of fake Mediterranean, she thought it might finally be possible. From far off she heard Michael letting the plumber in, and then he was back.

"OK?" he asked, settling opposite her again.

She nodded. "I'm good. Thank you, Mike." She poured herself more wine, then, forcing her voice to stay steady, said: "I want to tell you what my mum and I argued about before she died."

"If you're ready?"

She nodded, raised her glass to him. "Here goes then. It was over money." She saw him blink in surprise, but he kept his mouth clamped shut. "I wanted money to buy out the café and extend the shop." Michael's eyes widened, but still he managed not to interrupt. "I know what you're going to say," she rushed on. "Why didn't I ask you? I sort of did. That is, I dropped all these hints around my fiftieth about the café closing down. I even pinned the estate agent's details on the kitchen board. I thought I'd been so blinking obvious, but then you—"

"Bought you the fancy restaurant meal instead." He smacked a hand against his forehead. "How stupid was I?"

"Not stupid, Michael. It was a lovely gift. Completely lovely and very thoughtful."

He shook his head. "But not what you really wanted."

"I just thought you would understand me. That you would know, better than anyone else, what I was trying to ask for."

"And I should have done. I'm sorry. Is that why you asked the kids along to the meal?"

She sighed. "Sorry about that. Silly. I was using them as... oh, I don't know what. Armor or something. I was struggling a bit with them leaving home, to be honest, though I didn't want to admit it at the time. Nothing more boring than an empty-nester."

"Well..."

"Take it from me, it's true. Such a cliché. And I really didn't want to be a cliché. I wanted to be strong and autonomous and all that stuff. I didn't want the kids worrying about me and I didn't want other people muttering that I was purposeless without them. The shop seemed the obvious answer, especially when the café went bust. But after you didn't... After my fiftieth came and went, I went to Mum. I went to Mum and it was a terrible mistake."

"In what way?"

She groaned. "In every way. I asked her to loan me eight thousand pounds. It was stupid. I can see that now. She's always been so careful about her money, so keen to keep hold of it, and given her history, I know why. I knew why then too, but I was so caught up in my own plans for the shop that I didn't think about her. Stupid, hey?"

Michael shook his head vehemently. "It's not stupid, Jules. I understand why you asked. If one of our kids asked us for support with something and we could afford to help, I know we'd both jump at the chance."

She smiled at him. "I know, but money was different for Mum. She was terrified of losing everything again. Not that it stopped her spending when the mood took her, but that was always a spur-of-the-moment thing. And she always regretted it." She drew in a long breath. "She blew up the moment I suggested it. I should have known she would. I should have prepared for it, but I didn't, and I...I blew up too. I said all these hurtful things to her, about how selfish she was and how Clare and I didn't matter to her and how I hoped she fell overboard on her precious cruise. And then...and then she died thinking that was what I felt."

"Oh Julie, she knew you didn't mean it."

"How?"

"Because those were just words, not a life lived together. Sure, you rubbed each other up the wrong way, but you were amazing together too and she knew that."

"You think?"

"I know!" He reached out a hand, but she had hers clasped so tight around her wineglass that she didn't seem to be able to let go. "Why did you never say, Julie? I knew something was wrong. I knew I couldn't reach you, but I just didn't know why."

She looked at him, her eyes filling with tears.

"I felt too guilty. I told her I hoped she'd die, Michael."

"You told her you hoped she'd fall overboard. In a day or two she'd have found that funny."

"Except that she didn't get a day or two, did she? She died thinking I hated her. I couldn't bear that, and I especially couldn't bear anyone else knowing. If I said it out loud, it would be real. I'd be judged."

"Not by me! I wouldn't have judged you, Julie." He looked at her. "All you did was ask her. If she didn't want to help you out, she just had to say no. But your mum liked an argument, you know that. That was just the way she was."

Julie allowed herself the faintest of smiles.

"That might be true. But I shouldn't have risen, Michael. I shouldn't have shouted at her, shouldn't have said all those horrible things, not when she was about to die."

"You didn't know that!"

"No. But what do they say—never go to bed on an argument?"

They looked at each other, and Julie was sure he must be as aware as her of the irony of that particular statement. Was that not what they'd been doing for the last few years? Longer even.

"I hate that you didn't feel you could tell me. I'm your husband, Julie, your life partner."

The words sat between them, as fat and loaded as the Greek sun burning on the bedsheet. There'd been precious little partnership these last years. She stared at him. Again he reached for her hand, and this time she took it off her glass and edged it onto the little table. Their fingertips touched.

"This isn't about what happened with your mum, Julie. I mean, it is. I'm not belittling that; it must have been terrible for you. But years ago you would have told me straight away."

She nodded. "I know."

"So what went wrong? Why couldn't you tell me about the argument, and that you wanted to buy the café?"

She shrugged miserably. "I think we just did that whole drifting-apart-when-the-kids-were-older thing and...and..."

"Never drifted together again?"

She nodded.

"Can we still?"

227

She thought about it. She pictured the divorce papers upstairs, remembered how hard it had felt to hand them to him on that first afternoon when she'd brought them home. Was the force that had been stopping her love? Was it enough? She looked at the Greek sea sparkling enticingly across their garage door.

"I don't think we can drift together," she said. "Too much water under the blinking bridge. But I think, if we really want to, if we're really prepared to try, we can maybe turn the tide."

His fingers crept further over hers, and then, from somewhere around them, they heard a strange clicking noise, as if, Julie thought, momentarily creeped out, something between them was locking back into place. Michael, less fanciful, gave a slow smile and looked up at the pipes running round the top of the garage.

"That's the heating," he said. "Hallelujah, Jules—the boiler's working!"

His hand closed over hers and they leapt up together and ran into the kitchen to feel the radiator. Sure enough, warmth was creeping up from the base, and now John appeared down the stairs.

"Hello there." He came to the kitchen doorway and looked at them. "You can feel it, then?"

"We can feel it," Michael agreed. "Fantastic."

"It was just a broken airlock. I've replaced it, so you should be fine now."

"Fantastic," Michael said again. "Thank you so much."

"I'll bill you electronically, if that's OK?"

"Fine. Great."

"And I'll see myself out. Have a good rest of the night, folks, and I'm glad I could get you back in action."

John spun round and headed off. Julie and Michael stood there, tight up against the radiator. Julie felt her fingers wrapped in his, her bum warm against the metal, then her body even warmer against his chest as he turned to her. He was so close, his eyes so blue. Her heart beat as hard as the restored boiler pump, and she turned her face slowly, deliberately up to his.

"Back in action, hey?" she murmured, and then his lips were on hers and he was pulling her against him, his hands running over her body as if he could never get enough.

"Jules," he said against her lips, "my Jules."

Her own name reverberated through her and she tugged at his sweater, wanting more of him. Wanting all of him. He pulled back to let her yank it up over his head, and then his hands were on the buttons of her shirt, undoing them one at a time. She moaned, and impatiently he ripped at the last couple and threw the garment aside.

"I want you, Julie."

She ran her hands downwards and felt him hard beneath her touch.

"I want you too," she gasped.

She undid his belt and pushed his trousers down as he released hers in turn. Stumbling a little, they kicked them off and she pressed herself against him again, loving the feel of his skin on hers, his hands running down her back and over her bum, pulling her even closer—but not yet close enough.

"Bed," she begged.

"Too far," he groaned, pulling her instead into the living room.

And as he pushed her down onto the sunflower-covered sofa and lowered his mouth to hers, the tangles of the past few years faded away and nothing seemed to matter any more but the glorious here and now.

Chapter Twenty-Eight

April 1985

A crowd gathers to see Julie and Michael off on honeymoon the morning after their wedding. Someone has tied tin cans to the back of the bike on a string and Ken is not there to carefully remove them "for safety," but Michael doesn't mind. He likes the crazy rattle as they pull away, likes even more the feel of Julie at his back, her legs pressed tight against his as they have been most of the night before, and her veil attached to her helmet and flapping gloriously in the airstream behind them. They stop in a lay-by just down the road to untie the cans (he is his father's son still) and she goes to detach the veil as well but he stops her.

"Let everyone see what a lucky, lucky man I am to have such a beautiful bride on my beautiful bike."

She still takes the helmet off, but not to remove the veil, simply to kiss him. It takes a while to get going again and they nearly miss the ferry. Luckily the operators see the veil, smile indulgently and wave them on. They park the bike and rush up on deck to wave goodbye to Blighty, but Blighty is barely out of sight before they make for their cabin, eager to finish what they started by the roadside.

"Every night," Julie says to him as he frantically tries to peel the leathers off her. "We can do this every single night for the rest of our lives."

"Tonight will do for now," he gasps as the trousers finally yield to his desperate hands and she's there before him in all her glory—his wife. God, he's a lucky man.

France unrolls before them over the next few days, the spring sun getting hotter and hotter as they head south, away from the sadness of his father's death, away from the organization of their beautiful wedding, away from the loving attention of family and friends—away from everything but each other and the open road into their future. They ride all day and make love every night, stopping in little motels with old-fashioned decor and wonderful food and rickety beds that squeak out their joy to the other residents so that they eat their breakfast croissants with pink cheeks every morning.

"*Lune de miel?*" one patron asks with a wide wink. Michael nods, and he slips them extra croissants. "*Pour la fortitude, mes braves!*"

They laugh all the way to lunch.

It is even hotter once they cross into Italy, heading up over the Jura mountains and through scenery they find nearly as breath-taking as each other. They have only a few days before they need to turn back to be home in time for Ken's funeral, and they ride hard. Eventually Michael pulls into the open gateway of a deserted field and lifts off his helmet with a sigh of relief.

"Hot, isn't it?"

"Very," Julie agrees, her face turned to the sun. She's always loved heat.

"Aren't you sweaty?"

"A bit, but I'll cope. How far to Monferrato, do you think?"

"Half an hour or so, I'd say."

231

"Doable."

"Hmm," he agrees, but he's looking down the gentle slope of the field to a river running along the bottom of it, sparkling prettily as it ripples between low trees.

"Michael?" she questions.

He grins at her. "I just thought...I know how much you like a swim."

"In there?"

"Why not? There's no one around."

"I haven't brought a cozzie." He raises an eyebrow and she giggles. "You want to go skinny-dipping?"

"Don't you?"

She looks around. The odd car goes past, but the slope of the field should drop them below the eyeline of any drivers, and the Italians drive too fast to look out the window anyway.

"Go on then."

She's straight up on her feet and racing off down the field, but Michael isn't slow to react and shoots after her, chasing her gorgeous bum in the wonderfully tight leather trousers. He makes a grab for her but she picks up her pace and dodges him, giggling wildly.

It's not a big field and within moments she pulls up at the riverbank. In all honesty, it's more of a stream. This won't be swimming so as much as wading, but the water is sparkling in the sunlight and making that soft plinking sound as it curves around the stones, and Michael can't wait to feel it against his skin.

"Last one in's a rotten tomato," he challenges.

It's all he can do to focus on removing his own clothes as she tugs off her boots and then her trousers, hanging them in the branch of a tree to keep dry. Her jacket is next, then her T-shirt. She looks nervously around, but there's no one in sight, and when she spots him already pulling off his boxers, she chucks her knickers and bra into the tree. Michael is ahead of her, but she grabs at his hand.

"You holding me back, rotten tomato?"

"Yep!"

"Fair enough. I'll be rotten with you any time." He kisses her hard on the lips. "Ready?"

"As I'll ever be."

It's not exactly a romantic run into the water. The bank is soft enough to half slide down and the stones beneath the surface make it tricky for them to find their footing, but it doesn't matter. Giggling madly, they step carefully in, and oh God, it's cold! From sun to ice in one foolish move. Julie gasps and Michael bends down, scoops up a handful of water and splashes her.

"You bastard!"

She curves away as the myriad droplets hit her warm skin, then she's bending too and scooping up her own handful and they're splashing each other over and over and it feels so good. She trips and falls into the water with a gasp and he pounces, falling down at her side and clasping his arms around her as they lie in the freezing shallows together, laughing and kissing.

"I'd make love to you, my gorgeous wife," he says, "but I'm not sure the water temperature allows!" He looks down with a rueful grimace and she laughs again.

"We've still got a week, Michael. Still another whole week!"

Already it doesn't feel enough.

They check into their hotel an hour later, hair wet and molded into the most unflattering shape possible by their helmets, trousers uncomfortably ruched where the leather resisted their damp skin.

"*Va bene?*" the receptionist asks doubtfully.

"*Mucho bene,*" they assure her, in pidgin Italian, looking cheekily at each other.

She gives an earthy chuckle and lifts a key off the hook.

"*Camera migliore,*" she assures them. "*Grande letto.* Beeg bed!"

She winks broadly and leads them up to the finest room either of them has ever been in. It's so beautiful that it seems churlish to leave it, so they pull wine and crisps out of their panniers and devour them along with each other. The moon that night, and every one that follows, is honeyed indeed.

Chapter Twenty-Nine

Day Eighteen

Michael blinked out of a half-doze of blissful satiation, feeling momentarily disorientated. He looked at the colorful duvet on which he was stretched out and then, with wonderfully dawning realization, across to the woman at his side. Julie was fast asleep, one hand curled under her face, the other arm flung wide in delicious abandon. She looked utterly, perfectly luscious and he could have lain there all day just drinking her in.

He stretched luxuriously across the bed. Last night, after the desperate fury of their first lovemaking on the sofa, they'd stumbled upstairs and come together again, far more slowly and tenderly, taking their time to rediscover each other in a way they hadn't done for far too many years, even before they'd stupidly wandered into separate beds. Having teenagers in the house had made it hard to make love in anything more than a hurried, whispered way, as if they were doing something illicit, but last night they had more than made up for it. And pray God, tonight would be the same again. And every night thereafter.

Grinning like a Cheshire cat, Michael slid his legs round over the side of the bed. He was desperate for a wee—old age again!—but if he was careful, he could sneak out and return without waking Julie. Then he could watch her sleep, and perhaps, when she woke up...

He put his hands behind him and pushed himself carefully up to standing, but at the last minute, his foot slipped from under him and he bumped down again. The mattress gave and Julie shifted but didn't wake. Phew!

He looked down to see what he had stepped on. It was a piece of paper, A4 and glossily thick, with tight black words typed across it. Curious, he bent to pick it up and saw there were several more shoved loosely under the bed. He gathered them all up and ordered them with the helpful page numbers at the bottom. And there, on page one, he found a string of long names and a fancy crest, and beneath that, in bold and underlined: *Application for Divorce.*

He stared. Divorce? He cautioned himself to take his time, not to overreact, to read this properly before jumping to conclusions. Perhaps Julie was looking it over for someone else, or...or...But no. With mounting incredulity, Michael read his own name, filled in with some clerk's fussy writing, and then Julie's.

"My God!" he cried, and at his side, Julie started awake. She looked amazing, all soft and sleepy-eyed, but it was hard to see past the cold, hard words on the pages before him. "A divorce, Julie?"

She was instantly awake.

"Michael..." She stared at the pages. "Michael, listen—I got that ages ago. Before lockdown."

"Oh! Before lockdown. That's OK then."

"Is it?"

"No! No, it isn't. You want a divorce?"

She flushed and tugged the duvet around her naked body.

"*Wanted*, Michael. Or at least I thought I did."

He looked at the fancy crest.

236

"You did more than think about it, Julie. You've been to a lawyer. You've filled out the forms."

"Actually, they—"

"Whoever wrote the bloody names in the boxes isn't my concern right now, thank you very much. My concern is that you've had this by your bed all these weeks and said nothing."

"It didn't seem the right time. And it wasn't, was it, 'cos look, we're—"

"Shagging again?" She flinched, but he didn't care. He felt stupid, vulnerable, used. "Why are you keeping them here, Julie? So you can stroke them at night and remind yourself you can be out of here soon? Give yourself strength to be nice to me for just a little longer?" Something dug into his brain like a glass shard. "Was this a . . . a *pity* shag?"

"No!" She scrambled up onto her knees, reaching for him. "Truly, Michael, it wasn't. I *was* considering a divorce, I admit it. I've been thinking about it since Sophie's wedding."

He paused. "I see." He'd been pretty mean. He was ashamed of that. But at least he'd been open. Too open, arguably, but surely that was better than these lies of hers? A memory popped unwelcome into his head like a text message onto a phone: *Happy Christmas, Julie. I've been thinking a lot and you won't see me again.* He faced her. "What else aren't you telling me?"

"Sorry?"

"All these secrets. First the argument with your mum, then this divorce. What else don't I know?" He *was* stupid. And vulnerable. And definitely used. "There's someone else, isn't there?"

"No!" She was so vehement it startled him.

"Well there was, then," he hedged.

She stared at him. "What are you talking about?" It wasn't a denial. His happy heart shrank instantly.

"I saw a text. That Christmas. When we were last here," he gestured around them, "about to do *this*. I saw a text from

237

someone saying they wouldn't see you again. Saying you were 'beautiful inside and out.'"

She looked instantly guilty. "You saw that?"

"Yes! Who was it from?"

She sighed. "George."

"George?" He scanned his memory. "The plant supplier? The one you said Clare fancied?"

She nodded.

"And all along it was you who—"

"No! Nothing happened, Michael."

"How do I know that?"

She stared at him, eyes brimming with tears. "I guess you just have to believe me. To trust me."

Michael felt sadness swelling up inside him like a tsunami, sucking away his breath and pushing all the churned-up emotion forward on a fierce wave that threatened to carry the flotsam and jetsam of the last years of hurt with it. His eyes stung and he covered them with his hands.

"Michael, please." She put a hand on his shoulder, but he shrugged her off. He couldn't bear her touch, not now. All he wanted from her was the truth.

"What happened, Julie?" he demanded. "Please. Tell me what happened."

Chapter Thirty

Christmas 2017

Julie is drunk, drunk on Prosecco and cocktails and shots of spiced rum. She's so drunk that the city of Derby—wonderful for a cozy pint of real ale but not usually known for its glamour—looks like New York itself. The lights are bright, the music is gloriously cheesy and she could dance all night.

Clare and her mates are bopping away around her and some total genius of a DJ just put Chesney Hawkes on, and, yes, she *is* the one and only! Yes, there *is* no one she'd rather be! Things have been complicated. OK, worse than complicated, but she's had too many cocktails to locate more in-depth words. Dark maybe. That's what things have been—dark and confused and sad. But not right now. It's Christmas—a time to be happy and merry and jolly and all that. And she is. Merry especially. She's going to put all that sadness behind her. The extended shop is doing so well now. Surely Linda would approve of the use of her inheritance if she could see the place; or at least the balance sheet?

"I am the one and only!" she shouts with every other middle-aged idiot in the club, bouncing up and down on the shaking floor. And that's when she sees him. "George!"

He's right in the center, striking a silly pose with a couple of other blokes. He freezes, mid Superman-point.

"Julie!" He fights through the bouncing bodies between them. "Fancy seeing you here! Happy Christmas."

He gathers her up in his arms and she feels his strength, smells his aftershave, hears his low laugh rumble in her ear. It's a sound she's got very used to over the last few months. He comes to the shop at least once a week and always stays for a cuppa. It's nothing untoward. Clare is always there. In fact, Clare likes George. And Clare is single. But it seems to be Julie that he wants to talk to. Right now, though, giddy with Christmas cheer, it feels great to have someone who wants to talk to her, especially someone who wants to talk to her about something other than his bad back. She gives him a quick kiss on his cheek.

"Drink?" he suggests, and she nods and follows him off the dance floor to the marginally quieter bar area. "What d'you fancy?"

She feels giddy already.

"Just water, please."

He raises an eyebrow but makes no comment. She perches on a stool and watches him fight his way to the bar. He's a big man, tall and very broad. It must be from carrying plants around all day, she thinks idly. And he's blond. She never fancies blonds. Not that she fancies George. She's married. She's not like that. He does look cute, though, in his Rudolph T-shirt that shows off his muscular arms.

He turns round, seemingly to check she's still there, and his eyes light up when she gives him a little wave. Her stomach lurches rather pleasantly. She's forgotten what it feels like to have someone look at her the way George is looking at her. Like she's something to be desired. Plus, he really is very good-looking...

"Your water."

"Thank you."

She gulps it down. He watches, smiling.

"You needed that!"

"I've done a lot of dancing. And a lot of those rum shots they keep bringing round."

"Why not? It's Christmas. You deserve a treat. What you've done with your shop this year is amazing."

It's loud and he has to lean close for her to hear. The word "amazing" brushes across her earlobe like a caress.

"Thanks. It's important to me."

"I can tell. That sort of love permeates a shop. People are drawn to it."

"Love?"

He shrugs. "Don't you love it?"

She considers. The water seems to be chasing the rum around her bloodstream at pace.

"I guess I do. I bought it when my little boy went to school. It was something to do but it became more than that. It became, well, part of my identity, I suppose."

"Julie's Flowers."

"Yes."

She brushes away the memory of Michael insisting she call it that, but George must sense her hesitation, because he leans in close again.

"I especially like the plant section—though I would say that, I guess, because it means I get to come and deliver to you. It's the highlight of my week."

"My plant section?"

"Yes," he agrees, though his eyes suggest something more.

She looks up at him, at big, burly George with his smiley eyes and his floppy blond hair and his gardener's muscles. This is the sort of man she'd have imagined herself with as a teen—before she came out of a café in Budapest and was caught by a pair of blue eyes—and unconsciously she leans toward him.

"You're so beautiful, Julie," he whispers.

"Nonsense!" She gives him a little shove.

"You *are*. Beautiful inside and out."

She smiles. "That's a bit soppy, George."

"A *lot* soppy. I know. I can't help it—it's just how you make me feel. You're a very special lady."

She swallows. She doesn't feel special these days; just old and tired and a little bit sad.

"Thank you," she murmurs, and then suddenly he's leaning toward her, dipping his head to kiss her.

For a moment she's caught, and then she remembers herself and pulls back, instantly sober. The bright lights look tacky suddenly, the people half mad as they dance around them, and George—George just looks young. He blinks, shakes himself.

"Sorry. Oh God, I'm so sorry. It's just…"

"It's OK, George."

"It's not OK. I got carried away. You're just so sweet and fun and pretty. And you have this sadness about you that makes me want to help you feel better."

Julie's heart swells. "That's lovely, George. And in another time, you know, another place, it might just have done so. But right now, kissing you—lovely as I'm sure it would be—would only make things worse."

"Course it would. Course. Stupid of me. Sorry."

"George, don't apologize. If it's any consolation, you *have* made me feel better, just perhaps not in the way you'd think."

He gives her a sad smile. "I don't think *I* feel better," he says.

"And for that *I'm* sorry. Clare's around if…"

But he's shaking his head and backing away.

"Happy Christmas, George," she calls after him. "See you in the new year."

"Maybe," he says. "Or maybe it would be better not. For both of us."

And then he's gone, leaving Julie with nothing but the sickly swirl of memories and too much spiced rum.

Chapter Thirty-One

"That's all it was," Julie told Michael, begging him to believe her. "He tried to kiss me and I said no. I said nothing could happen between us. That's why he sent me that text. That's why he said he wasn't going to see me again. That's all there was to it." She closed her eyes. "We were friendly; he got confused. I'd told him some stuff about Mum dying and I think he thought it meant more than it did."

"What stuff?" Julie flinched and he leant in. "What stuff, Julie? Did you tell him about the argument?"

She opened her mouth to deny it, but what was the point now? He'd asked for an end to the secrets and she owed him that much.

"I'm sorry, Michael."

He stared at her, stunned.

"You told him, but you couldn't tell me."

"I'm sorry," she said again. "He caught me at a low time and it just felt . . . good. I think perhaps it was easier to admit it to a stranger."

"A stranger you nearly kissed."

"But didn't, Michael. Because of you."

He closed his eyes. "I just don't get it, Julie. If it felt so good to tell this George about your mum, why didn't you try it again with me?"

"Because you kept avoiding me. Even on Christmas night you turned cold on me."

"Because of the bloody text!"

She sucked in a sharp breath. "Right. You saw it at that exact moment."

"Yes. When you showed me Briony's photo."

She sighed. "What a mess. We just couldn't connect, could we?"

"*You* couldn't," he said coldly, and he was right. He was so, so right.

She thought of him over these last few weeks, cooking for her, coaxing her to open up to him, taking her to bloody Greece in his own garage. He'd been nothing but kind and she'd repaid him with secrets and lies.

"I'm sorry, Michael," she said. "Truly. I don't know why I told George about Mum. It just slipped out one time in the shop. It didn't mean anything."

"It means something to me. And so do these divorce papers. You were planning to leave me, Julie. Without even talking to me about it."

"I know. And I'm sorry. Everything between us was all wrong. But now it feels...right. Doesn't it?"

He looked at her, infinite sadness in his eyes.

"It certainly did until I saw these."

He dropped his head to look at the divorce papers in his hands. She hated seeing him like this, broken and confused. She wanted to pull him back into her arms and cover him in kisses, but he'd shifted away from her and was sitting there so stiffly that it felt impossible.

"What can I do to make it up to you?" she begged.

"I don't know, Julie." His voice was low and calm, horribly

245

calm. "These last few weeks I've been trying, in my own limited way, to build a bridge back into the past so we could find each other again. Last night I thought we'd done that. I was so happy, Julie. So bloody ecstatically happy. But it turns out that there's more in the past than I thought—that there's more in *you* than I thought—and I don't know if I can take any more lies, any more secrets. I know you've been hurting, Julie, and I hate that, but I've been hurting too. And right now, I still am."

He stood up, naked, and crossed to the door.

"Michael," she cried, "where are you going?"

"Away," he threw at her. "Away from you."

And then he was gone, the door slamming behind him, and she was left curled miserably in the sheets in which they'd tangled together so joyously just a few short hours ago. She stared at the divorce papers he'd scattered across the bed. How had she let this happen? Why hadn't she hidden the damn things properly?

But she knew already that hiding them wasn't the answer. *I don't know if I can take any more lies*, Michael had said, and he was right. You couldn't build a marriage that way. It was time to let it all out.

*

"Julie Marshall? Are you next of kin to Ms. Linda Jenkins? I'm afraid there's been an accident."

Julie looks up from the phone to see Michael staring at her. "An accident," she stutters out to him. "She says there's been an accident."

He's at her side instantly. "Who does?"

"The lady at the hospital."

She waves the phone frantically and Michael takes it, talks into it with quiet, calm urgency. He's always so bloody calm. She appreciates it, needs it, but sometimes she wishes he'd just fall apart for once—because then she could too.

"Come on," he says, putting an arm around her. "Let's go."

246

She lets him lead her to the car, drive her to the hospital, but by the time they get there, she's adjusted, she's taken it in. There are things she needs to do; things she needs to say. Private things.

"Drop me at the door, please."

"Julie, I don't think—"

"I can manage, Michael. I'm a grown woman, remember?"

"I know that."

"So drop me at the door. Please. It will save time."

He doesn't argue further, just pulls up as close to the doors as he can get without obstructing the clutch of ambulances parked outside.

"I'll be with you as soon as I can."

"Thank you," she manages, and then she's out and dodging round the ambulances and through the big glass doors. There's a queue, but she ignores it and rushes up to the desk. "Linda Marshall," she gasps out. "My mother. She's had an accident."

There are some very British rumblings amongst those waiting, but a passing nurse hears the name and gathers Julie up.

"This way."

The queue gives a murmur of something like respect. In the world of A&E there is a hierarchy of emergency, and Julie is clearly near the top. It is not a comfort. The nurse leads her at a brisk pace between a run of curtained cubicles and stops right at the end. She puts her hand on the edge of the curtain and turns to Julie.

"It was a nasty accident, I'm afraid," she says. "Your mother seems to have walked into the path of an oncoming car. The driver had no time to stop."

"Was she drunk?"

The nurse gives her a sad look. "It seems that way. The only good thing is that that would have made her loose—an unresisting body often copes with injuries better."

An unresisting body—it's a term that Julie already knows will stay with her for a long time.

"Is she in pain?"

The nurse visibly gathers herself. "She's not conscious, so no."

"Was she conscious when...when they got to her?"

She shakes her head. "No. She probably knew very little about it. Suffered very little."

"But she will, I bet, when she wakes up. She's not good with pain, my mum." The nurse is looking at her with stifling compassion. Julie knows what it means but doesn't want to face it yet. "She's a right wuss with pain. Even minor cuts and that. When we were little, I used to have to fetch her a brandy if she so much as stubbed her toe." Still the nurse looks at her. "Not that she was an alcoholic. Not then. Well, not now either. She likes a drink and all, but not, you know, at breakfast. Not..."

The nurse draws back the curtain, and the sight of Linda lying on the bed dries Julie's foolish babblings up instantly. Her mum looks tiny in there, wired up to a heart-rate monitor with tubes coming out of both arms. There's a bandage around her head, starkly white against the heavy makeup that seems to be slipping off her poor slack face even as Julie takes her in. Her left cheek is heavily bruised and her body beneath the thin sheet looks horribly twisted.

"She's not going to wake up, is she?"

The nurse puts a hand on her arm. "It's unlikely, I'm afraid."

"Not even for a little while?"

"Maybe for a short time. It's hard to tell. But she may be able to hear you even now."

"Really?"

"There are many studies that suggest so."

Already Julie suspects these "studies," but they are all she has and she springs forward.

"Mum?" Nothing. She looks back at the nurse. "Can I touch her?"

"Of course. If you're gentle."

Julie takes Linda's hand in hers. It's limp and unresponsing but still warm.

"Oh Mum." She hears the nurse slide away on her cushioned soles and is grateful. She remembers, too late, that she should have called Clare, and hopes Michael has thought to do it. But for now it's her and Linda and she has things to say, important things. "Can you hear me, Mum? I hope you can. I hope you can hear me in your heart if not in your ears. I'm sorry. I'm sorry I asked you for that stupid money for the stupid shop. And I'm sorry I got cross when you said no. Why shouldn't you have a cruise? Why shouldn't you have fun? That's far more important than selling stupid plants to people. Far more important than proving to your husband that you can run a successful business, too."

She clutches Linda's hand tighter.

"I wanted you to be proud of me, Mum. Idle hands are the devil's tools and all that. I've worked so hard, honestly. I've worked all my life, like you told me to. And I know it's only a little flower shop, but it's doing well, really it is—and that's because of all that you taught me. Clare too."

She looks desperately at Linda's face, but there's not so much as a flicker in the mascaraed eyelids.

"I love you, Mum. I didn't want you to fall overboard and I don't want you to die. I want you to wake up and to shout at me and laugh with me and make hot chocolate overstuffed with marshmallows with me. I want to show you my homework and have you tell me it's not good enough and I'm to do it again. I want to scream at you that it's not fair that I'm not allowed out after midnight. I want you to criticize the length of my skirt and the color of my hair and the state of my bedroom. I want to tell you my spotty boyfriend is perfect and roll my eyes at you when you ask me if I know about condoms, and I want to crawl into your arms when he ditches me three days later. I just want to crawl into your arms full stop. Don't die, Mum, not now, not like this, not thinking that I hate you, because I don't. I don't hate you, Mum. I love you."

The machine drowns her out with a sudden insistent wail, and instantly there are people piling into the cubicle. Julie is pushed aside as they grab the electric paddles, just like you see on the TV. Linda's tiny body pulses once, twice, three times, but the machine does not stop wailing.

"It's no good," someone says. "She's gone."

The words batter at Julie's head, trying to get in. She's gone. How can that be possible? Only last night, Julie was sitting across a pub table watching her down Bacardi and Coke and rage about designer shoes.

The nurse puts an arm around her to shield her as the team quietly and efficiently detach Linda's unresistant body from the tubes and wires that were trying—and failing—to keep her alive. And when Michael comes rushing in to find her, Julie is sitting at the side of a silent, still body, quietly holding a dead hand. She looks up at him.

"She's gone."

"Oh Julie." He embraces her. "I'm so sorry. Did you get to speak to her?"

It's a far bigger question than he knows. She looks up at the man she married thirty-one years ago. She used to tell him everything, but she can't seem to find the words to explain. It would only make it more real, and it already hurts too much.

"I did," she says.

It's true, after all. What she doesn't want to tell him is her dark, dread fear that her mother never heard her. That she died with her daughter's furious words in her ears.

Chapter Thirty-Two

Julie couldn't think properly. Everything seemed to be swirled together—her mum's death, her near kiss with George, her marriage. She had a sudden burning need to get out of the house and go to her shop, to open the door below the pretty Julie's Flowers sign and step inside and just be there. She'd been locked down in this house for far too long and she couldn't breathe properly here any more.

Throwing on some clothes, she ran downstairs and grabbed her car keys. They felt alien in her hand, and when she got into the driver's seat, she felt almost wicked. She slotted the key in, praying the car would start, and breathed a sigh of relief when the engine spluttered happily into life. Maybe it was as pleased as her to be back on the road.

It was a five-minute trip and Julie passed not one other car. She pulled into the tiny parking area feeling as if she'd stepped back in time. It had been three weeks since she'd last been here, since the world had stopped, and she was almost giddy with the joy of being back. She jumped out of the car and rushed round to the front door, pausing, as always, to look up at the sign: *Julie's Flowers*.

The door gave a familiar rattle as she pushed it open and she was instantly hit by a wave of earthy green smell. A single gerbera lay faded but still colorful in the middle of the floor, and in one of the buckets a sprig of gypsophila had withered and dropped its tiny white petals in a confetti puddle. Julie walked into the middle and spun slowly round, taking it all in. It wasn't big, hardly a kingdom, but it was all hers.

"Make sure you have something of your own," Linda had always told her and Clare. "Make sure you have security."

Julie could see why her mother would have felt like that. It was advice from the generation who'd had to bust so many holes in the walls of the patriarchy, but was it the right advice for her? What did Michael have all of his own? The house was shared fifty-fifty. Every bit of his salary went into their joint account. Even his bike, his precious bike, he was happy to share with her. And maybe that was because he was lucky enough to be a man, born out of centuries of privilege, but maybe, too, the need to have something of your own was as damaging as it was secure. At least for Julie. Maybe bit by bit, over the last five years, she'd withdrawn into things of her own and not left enough room for them both.

"Shit!" she said to the empty room.

How had she got into this mess? It was almost laughable. Linda would certainly have laughed at her.

She had to put a hand to the wall to steady herself against the sudden wave of grief—not for the unresponsive body in the hospital bed, but for the living, breathing, shouting, laughing Linda.

"Oh Mum," she sighed. "How do I fix this?"

She pushed herself off the wall and forced herself to move through to the other side of the shop. Pausing in the alcove, she remembered the builders cutting it into the brick, carving the elegant curve, plastering it into perfect smoothness. She remembered her and Clare painting the walls and glanced back to the

252

original side. She and Michael had done that, working away at night whilst Linda had watched the kids. Both experiences had been enjoyable, but maybe the shift from her husband to her sister told her something.

She snatched up her phone, dialed.

"Julie?"

"Hi," she said and heard her voice wobble.

"What's up?" her sister demanded instantly.

Julie closed her eyes, ran her hand up and over the alcove.

"Do you miss Mum, Clare?"

"Do I...? Course I do, you silly moo. All the time."

"Right. Good."

"Julie, where are you? You sound strange."

Julie looked around the empty space. "I'm in the shop."

"The shop? OK. I'll be there in ten."

"Clare, you don't have to—"

"I'll be there in ten, Julie."

Julie was sitting cross-legged on the floor when her little sister let herself in. Clare rushed toward her but then stopped herself and stamped her foot.

"Stupid social distancing!"

Julie smiled up at her. "It seems a terrible sort of world to live in where we can't even hug each other, doesn't it?"

"Tell me about it." Clare moved around her and went to sit in her own half of the shop. "There, safe!" She gave Julie a wave. Julie waved back. "So, what's going on with you? Why are you here, Jules? And why the questions about Mum?"

Julie decided to start somewhere easy.

"Sophie's pregnant."

"Sophie is? Wow! That's wonderful news."

"Isn't it?"

"You don't sound very happy."

253

"Oh, I am. I'm *very* happy. I just can't see her. Tell me we'll be out of all this by the time the poor little mite is born?"

"Course we will. God, we'd better be. If I can't see Dharmesh soon, I am going to physically burst. There's only so much a rabbit can handle!"

Julie laughed, then remembered herself and Michael in bed last night and flushed scarlet. God, it had been good. So familiar and yet so very, very new.

"Julie?" Clare probed. "This isn't about Sophie, is it? What's made you think about Mum?"

Julie tapped anxiously on the painted floor. The gerbera was still lying there, and she picked it up and plucked at the orange petals.

"Remember when you got to the hospital after the accident, Clare?"

"Do I? Poor Mum, all still and gray. It was horrible."

"Not like her at all."

"No." Clare gave a quiet laugh. "She was always so noisy—chatting, laughing, shouting."

Julie nodded, her throat tight.

Clare leant in toward her. "There's something you're not telling me, isn't there?"

Julie nodded again.

"So…?"

She rolled her eyes.

"Don't roll your eyes at me, Julie Jenkins."

"Marshall!"

"Jenkins too, madam. Jenkins first. What are you bottling up this time?"

"What d'you mean, this time?"

"Oh, come on—you've always loved a secret. Remember that diary you used to keep? It had *two* padlocks on it. And you were always changing the hiding place so I couldn't find it."

"How do you know?"

"Because I was always looking, of course! I was dying to know what you were writing about me."

Julie shook her head. "It was rarely about you, Clare."

"I bet it was. When we were younger, at least. *Clare bagged the best biscuit, Clare told on me to Mum, Clare wore my dress and made it dirty.*"

"Exciting stuff!"

Clare leant in again. "Did it say things like that?"

"Probably," Julie admitted. "But later it was mainly about the boys I fancied."

"Which was why I wanted to find it even more!"

They looked at each other fondly, but Clare was on a mission and not to be distracted.

"So if you were writing a diary now, what would it be about?"

Julie groaned. "Good question. Far too much and far, far too boring. I don't go around fancying people these days."

Her mind, as if in deliberate defiance, presented her with a picture of Michael taking his bike helmet off under the stars, and her body stirred.

"What about George?" Clare asked, and it was as if someone had poured icy water over her nice warm memory.

"George? I don't fancy George. Never did really."

"So nothing ever happened with you two?"

Julie grimaced. "He tried to kiss me once. In that nightclub at Christmas. But I stopped him. It wasn't what I wanted."

"Good!"

"Yes, good. This isn't about George."

"No?"

Impatience surged up inside Julie, taking her by surprise.

"No. This is about Mum. I argued with her, Clare."

"At the hospital?"

"No! The night before. I took her to the pub and asked her

to loan me money for extending the shop, and she said no, 'cos she needed it for shoes and cruises. I shouted at her. I shouted at her a lot."

"Oh."

Julie stared at her sister.

"You don't seem very surprised."

"That's 'cos I'm not!" Clare held out a hand toward her. "Oh, come on, Jules, you and Mum were *always* arguing. Too similar, that was your problem. You always went charging in asking for things and she always refused. At first."

"She did?"

"Remember that pink bike you wanted?"

"Well…"

"And the roller blades?"

"Yes, but—"

"And the karaoke machine, and the double bed, and the metallic-effect bloody curtains? Lord, the rows over those went on for ages."

Julie stared at her sister. "And your point is?"

"My point is, that's how the two of you were set up. Take it from someone who watched it far too many times. And it worked the other way round too. She'd ask you to tidy your room, you'd scream about the liberation of your personal space. She'd ask you to come home at eleven thirty, it would be midnight. She'd ask you to cook dinner for six, we'd eat at eight."

Julie shifted on the hard floor. That did sort of ring a bell.

"But Clare, Mum died."

"I know, Jules. And that's really sad. But if she hadn't, she'd have been round to you within a day or two, check in hand. And before you knew it, she'd have been in here criticizing your color choices and your stock and even the curve of the frigging alcove."

Julie felt tears well in her eyes and sighed. Not again! She

256

was a walking fountain at the moment. Her mind blindsided her with a picture of Michael sitting on their bed, tears running through his fingers as he tried to cover his face.

"You think?" she managed.

"I know! And she'd have known too. Did anyone check her handbag? It probably had the check in it already written out. Oh Julie, sod this." Clare crossed the space between them and clasped her sister in her arms. "Mum loved this shop."

"She did?"

"Are you being particularly obtuse today or what? She was always banging on about it. Julie this, the flower shop that. Aren't you lucky, Clare, that you have such a fantastic big sister? Hasn't she built up a wonderful business? Isn't it great that she took you on?"

"She said that?"

"All the frigging time!"

"Not to me."

"No, well, that was you two all over, wasn't it!"

"Oh Clare." Julie leant into her, loving the forbidden luxury of the contact. "I'm so lucky to have you."

"Yes you bloody well are." Clare ruffled her hair. "And I you, Jules. Please, please don't be so hard on yourself. Why didn't you tell me about the argument?"

"I didn't tell anyone."

"Anyone? Not even Michael?"

Julie sucked in a harsh breath. "Not even Michael." She waited for the sharp comment, but it didn't come. Clare just stroked her hair and waited. Damn. Now she'd have to tell her about that mess too. "We've, er, not been getting on all that well recently."

"You and Michael? Really?"

"Oh, come on, Clare, you were at Sophie's wedding. You heard his speech."

257

"His speech was lovely. Oh—you mean that strange bit later on. I didn't think that much of it." She frowned. "Max was being a bit of a prat that night, as I recall, and I guess I wasn't paying much attention to anyone else's relationships. I guess maybe I never do. Oh God, Julie, that's awful of me."

"Rubbish."

"It is. You're my sister and you've been unhappy and I haven't even noticed."

"And I'm glad."

Clare stared at her. "Oh, come on, Jules, you don't need to protect me any more."

"Are you sure?"

Clare gave a sheepish grin. "Well, maybe a little bit, but it's no excuse. You should have been able to talk to me. I feel awful now."

"Don't, Clare. Really. I couldn't talk to anyone."

"But now you can?"

Julie drew in a deep breath. "Now I'm trying," she corrected. "Things have been...bad, the last few years. Since Mum died. They weren't great before that—it was difficult when the kids grew up and it was suddenly just the two of us—but after Mum died I guess I found it too hard to let him in, to reconnect. Michael and I were social-distancing way before everyone else."

"Trendsetters, hey?"

"'Fraid so. We've been sleeping in separate rooms for over two years."

"Christ, Julie—I could shake you, I really could. Why didn't you say? No—don't tell me. I know. You didn't want to look like a failure."

"What? How—"

"How do I know? Because I'm the expert failure, aren't I? Cocked up my marriage, went from useless man to useless man, couldn't stick at a job until you handed me this one. I'm your A1 failure, sis."

"You are not!"

Clare gave her a pat on the head. "Cheers—but think about it. If I'm not, then you definitely aren't."

Julie pulled back. "You tricked me!"

"I'm your little sister—it's what I do!"

She shook her head, tears falling now, and hugged her sister close. If anyone walked past, they'd look mad, crouched here in the middle of an empty shop, clutched together as if they were in danger of drowning.

"Do you still love him?" Clare asked.

Julie sighed. "I do. But it seems there's a difference between loving someone and being able to live with them. I've never stopped loving Michael, but these last few years I'd started to accept that perhaps our relationship had run its course—we didn't seem to work any more, we didn't seem to make each other happy. I'd imagined this bright future for us after the kids left, but everything was all...wrong." She paused, remembering this morning and how right it had felt to wake up next to him. "But recently, I don't know, things between us have felt... different. Better."

"You and Michael—you're great together, Julie."

"We used to be." She looked at Clare. "D'you know, when Michael's dad died, just before our wedding, he told me that I was his happiness."

"I'm sure you were. Still are."

"But that's hard work sometimes."

Clare slapped her hand against her head. "Oh Julie, you aren't his happiness because of what you do, just because of who you are. You don't have to actively make that happen. You just have to be."

"Be?"

"Yes. Be. Be still, be you."

"Be still? I'm not so good at that. Except perhaps when I'm sitting on the back of the bike."

"With Michael?"

"Yes."

"Because Michael is good at being still. He's got this calm about him, this certainty. And that's what's always been so good for you. If you're his happiness, then he is definitely your stillness."

"He is?"

"D'you know what, Julie—I honestly never thought you were this thick."

"Cheers."

Silence fell over the shop. Julie heard her heart beating, her breath filling the room. She remembered the feeling of sitting behind Michael on Gertie yesterday. The stillness of it. She'd always loved the way she could just *be* when they were riding, but in truth it wasn't actually the bike that had given her that; it was Michael.

"Oh Clare, I've made such a bloody mess of it all."

Clare sat back, wiped the tears from her face and looked at her intently.

"Messes can be cleared up with a bit of work, sweetie. And maybe a bit of imagination."

"Imagination?"

She smiled. "You love Michael, right?"

"Right," Julie agreed, suddenly more certain of that than anything else in this whole topsy-turvy world.

"Then you've got to find a way to show him."

Julie paused, thinking. "You're right." She jumped up.

"Where are you going?" Clare asked.

"The fields!"

"The fields? Julie, have you gone mad?"

She shook her head. "Quite the reverse. I've just thought of a way for the madness to stop."

Chapter Thirty-Three

Michael paced the spare room—up and down, up and down. He'd wear a line in the beige carpet at this rate. It was five hours now since he'd stormed out on Julie, and he'd heard nothing but the front door banging some time back. Was that it? Had she just gone? Surely not.

Up and down, up and down. He glanced at the window. The sun was dipping but it was still a lovely day. He should go outside and do some gardening, but he didn't seem to be able to tear himself from his pacing. Was this the end of his marriage? He wasn't sure he could bear it and was furious with himself for how he'd handled it. Was it any wonder, given all the crap of the last few years, that she'd gone to a lawyer?

He thought back to him bumbling into her shop reopening so carelessly late, to her trying to seduce him at Christmas, having just turned down a far more interested man for his sake. He recalled her re-covering the sofas and setting up a romantic night and him tossing it back at her with childish remarks about triffids. And then, of course, that horrible, horrible speech at Sophie's wedding. It was a miracle, in all truth, that she hadn't filed for divorce sooner.

Up and down, up and down. He paused. Had he heard something?

"Michael!" He had. "Michael, I'm out here!"

What on earth…? He went to the window, and there, standing at the bottom of the garden, just the other side of the secret gate into the field, was Julie. She spotted him and waved.

"Michael! Can you come out? Please?"

He threw open the window. "Now?"

"Please."

Heart racing, he closed the window and headed for the stairs. Why was she out there? Would he ever understand her? Would he ever, now, get the chance?

He'd made it as far as the kitchen before he noticed he was only in his socks. He cast around for shoes, afraid she might disappear, but all he could see were the old Crocs he slipped on to take out the bins. Ah well, this was no time to be choosy so stuffing his feet into them, he let himself out into the garden. She was still there.

"Down here, please."

She was fidgeting around, bouncing almost as much as the lambs in the field behind. He headed toward her, feeling a little like a prisoner awaiting a verdict. Funny old courtroom, though. The grass beneath his feet was lush and green, the field beyond was speckled with daisies and dandelions and the low sun was slanting soft light across the whole scene.

"Here?" he asked Julie, pausing before the gate. She nodded. Her skin was flushed and her hair all over the place. She looked beautiful. And still very fidgety.

"Are you OK?" he asked.

"I'm fine, thank you. But I have something to say to you. Well, I have lots of things to say to you, more than I probably even know about, but I'm going to have a crack and, well, I hope at least some of it comes out right. OK?"

"Erm, OK."

"Good. Right." She cleared her throat. "God, I'm crap at this. What I want to say, Michael, is that you are a good man. A good, kind, thoughtful, loving man."

It was a hopeful start, though he feared a "but."

"And I'm a very lucky woman that you agreed to marry me all those years ago."

Still room for a "but." Michael held his breath.

"I used to think I was so good at talking to people, Mike. *Too* good even. I thought I was one of those heart-on-sleeve, take-me-how-you-find-me types, and in some ways maybe I am—like in the 'come in even though my house is a tip' and 'please stay for dinner even though I don't know what we're having yet and it may well involve baked beans' way. But it seems that in other ways I'm not so good at letting people in. Not as good as you are, for example. When Ken died, you just let yourself be sad and let me help you through that sadness, but when it came to my turn, I couldn't do that. I think it might be to do with Mum and how that might all be way more complicated and tangled than I've let myself believe, which is a bit boring and will probably involve therapy or something, but anyway, that's not what I'm trying to say here."

Michael felt his head start to spin and put a hand on the gate to steady himself.

"Sorry," she said. "I'm not doing this very well. Bear with me."

He smiled at her. "What are you trying to say, Julie?"

"Good question. Excellent question. I'll try and, you know, get to the point. I'm nervous. Silly, that, isn't it? How can I be nervous with you? Anyway, listen. What I'm trying to get at is that, quite simply, I should have told you everything—should have let you help, like you let me help you."

"And I should have been there for you to let in," Michael said.

She put up a hand. "Maybe. We can go into all that later, but *I'm* doing self-flagellation for now, OK?"

A little laugh escaped him. "OK."

"Oh, shit, I'm really making a mess of this, aren't I?"

"I'm not sure, Julie—mainly because I'm not sure what 'this' is."

She nodded, suddenly decisive. "Good point. OK, best, I think, if you just come through the gate. I'm sorry it's not as neat as it could be, not as neat as you would do it. Not as clever as your motorbike trick. But I couldn't think of anything as smart as that and I thought, well, I'm a florist after all, so say it with flowers and all that!"

Now he was truly confused, but she was opening the gate and ushering him through and there seemed to be nothing for it but to step into the field and—

He stopped dead. There in front of him, in great big letters made entirely of wildflowers, was the message: *I LOVE YOU*. It was typical Julie—a little scraggly, with the letters totally different sizes, but full of color and life.

"You still love me?" he asked.

"I do. I really do." She stepped up amongst the wildflowers and then suddenly she was on one knee before him. "Michael Marshall, would you do me the very great honor of agreeing to stay married to me? Now and for the rest of our days?"

He beamed.

"Not that we know how many that'll be."

His heart rocked with joy.

"A few, I hope. I mean, a lot. At least another thirty-five, right?"

"Right!" Laughing out loud, he swept forward and lifted her up into his arms, silencing her with a long, deep kiss. When he finally released her, she looked up at him and gave a shy smile.

"Is that a yes?"

He kissed her again. "It's a yes! It's a huge yes. Julie Marshall,

I will stay married to you forever and ever. We'll talk. We'll figure it out. All of it. And above all, we'll love."

"We will?" She twinkled up at him and he crushed her gorgeous body against his.

"Over and over and over."

They just about made it through the gate into their own house, but got nowhere near their bed.

Later, as the sun went down, they dragged their old fire pit out of the shed and built a big fire. Then, sitting snuggled up together, they popped champagne and fed their redundant divorce papers, bit by tiny bit, into the heart of the flames.

"I still remember the first time I saw you," Julie told him, "on that street corner in Budapest. Lord, I thought you were hot standing there in your leathers, leaning on your bike."

"I *was* hot. It was blinking thirty-six degrees and I was desperate to find my campsite and get those damned trousers off. But I could have stood there forever when you came out of that café in those tiny shorts."

"With my big fat legs on show."

"With your beautiful womanly legs on show. I never did get that heroin-chic crap. But it wasn't actually your legs that caught my attention first. Nor your boobs either, before you say it, though I admit they weren't far behind. That red top was exceptionally low-cut. No, first off it was your laugh. You came out of that café and you looked back at Susie—not that I knew she was Susie then—and you laughed, and it was as if an angel had fallen out of heaven."

"An angel?"

"Not a traditional angel. It was far too dirty a laugh for any of the haloed sort, but my idea of an angel. Joyous, that was how you sounded. Absolutely bloody joyous. And then you turned and looked straight at me and I truly did think I was in heaven."

"Is that when you noticed my boobs?"

"Possibly. But it was no one thing. It was just you, Julie—the glorious you-ness of you."

Julie shifted, cuddled closer in to him.

"Clare says I have to just be me more."

"Clare is wiser than I ever gave her credit for. It's all I ask, you know. It's all I want. You. Just you. And nothing you can tell me will change that."

"You're a wonderful man, Michael. I knew that the minute I saw you."

"You knew I was wonderful?"

"I knew you were hot. I knew I had to talk to you. And thank the Lord I did."

*

"I like your bike."

Michael stares at the beautiful girl with the glorious figure and the bell-chime laugh. He checks around to see who she must be talking to and she laughs again.

"You," she says, pointing at him. "It *is* your bike?"

He nods stupidly. "It was my eighteenth birthday present. From my dad."

"Wow. Your dad must be really cool."

"Not as cool as yours, I bet."

"My dad did a runner."

"Oh. Oh, shit, sorry."

She grins wickedly. "It's OK. My mum did a bang-up job by herself, and by all accounts he was a bastard anyway."

"Right. Well then, sorry about that."

"Cheers. So, your bike—what sort is it?" She bends down to peer at the logo, giving him the most delicious view down her top. "A Moto Guzzi? Never heard of it."

"Do you know much about bikes?"

She stands up again, tosses her hair.

266

"A bit." Behind her, her friend laughs and she shoots her a dirty look. "I do! My, er, my neighbor's got a bike."

"Ah. What sort?"

She wrinkles her nose in a way that makes Michael want to lean in and kiss it. Every nerve ending in his body seems to be on fire. He's fancied girls before, of course, but never like this, never with every last bit of himself.

"I think it's a Honda. Is that a type of bike?"

He grins. "It is."

"Phew!" She laughs again. "So—have you ridden this one all the way from home?"

"Yep."

"Who with?"

"No one. Just me and Gertie."

"Gertie?" Her eyes narrow and she looks furiously up and down the street.

"That's what the bike's called. Gertie. Silly really."

"No it's not." She walks around the bike and pats the handlebars. "Hello, Gertie. You're very beautiful."

"So are you," Michael blurts out. He curses his gaucheness, but she just smiles up at him.

"Thank you. And what about you—what are you called?"

"Michael."

"Michael? Cute."

"Is it?"

"Mike with the bike."

He groans. "I never thought of that."

"Probably best you didn't. It's pretty silly."

She looks shy suddenly and her friend steps forward. Michael shifts and rests his weight on Gertie. He's boiling in his leather jacket but there's no way he's taking it off and putting his sweat patches on show.

"Are you at university, Mike with the bike?" Susie asks.

He nods. "I'm in my final year."

She looks him up and down, openly calculating.

"Law," she guesses. He shakes his head. "Science?"

"Nope."

"Medicine!"

"Not that either." He's starting to feel awkward now. "I'm an engineer."

"Ooh!" To his relief, the red-topped girl steps back into the conversation. "That *is* clever. I should probably just marry you right now."

He looks down at her, wanting to grab her hand, hustle her to the nearest church and take her up on the offer. It will, he is already sure, be the best one he ever gets. But now the friend is tugging on her arm.

"We need to get to the shop before it shuts, sweets, or we won't have any dinner. Or any wine!"

"Nightmare!" They both laugh.

Michael tries desperately to think of something to say to keep her here, but nothing springs to mind.

"So, Mike with the bike, see you around."

"I hope so." She grins at him, but her friend is taking her arm now, steering her away. "What's your name?" he calls desperately after her.

"Julie," she shouts back, and then the pair of them turn the corner and he's left alone, instantly cold, and sure he will never see her again.

"There you are!"

A hand taps him on the shoulder and for a weird moment it feels so familiar that he thinks it must be his mother, turned up in Budapest to check he's eating properly. He whirls round to find something far, far better—her, the red-topped girl.

"Julie!"

"You remembered?"

"Of course I did."

"Room for a little one?" She gestures to the circle of random campers around the fire and he leaps eagerly sideways.

"Of course."

"*Two* little ones," an indignant voice says, and her friend appears at her side.

She waves a big bottle of wine and the others are quick to make space. Julie slides in next to Michael, and he feels the softness of her legs against his own. She's still in the red top, though she has a multicolored cardigan thrown loosely over it, and her blonde hair glows in the firelight.

"How did you find me?" he asks.

"Oh, it was almost impossible!" she says happily. "Susie and I have been trekking round Budapest half the night."

"We certainly bloody have," Susie confirms grumpily, but someone has already passed her a hand-rolled cigarette and she's mellowing by the second.

Someone else picks up the inevitable guitar, and the strains of "Hotel California" drift across. Michael has always hated this song—until now. He feels Julie lean in against him and dares to sneak an arm around her waist. The moment his fingers brush against her, she snuggles closer. She's so soft, so pliable, so achingly womanly. And for some wonderful reason she's picked him.

"Was it the bike?" he asks her.

"Was what the bike?"

"Was that how you found me?"

"Oh. Yes. Sort of. The boys had noticed the bike—Moto Guzzi, right?"

"Right."

"But the girls had noticed you."

"They had?"

269

"Course! When I asked for the hot engineer with the ice-blue eyes, they pointed the way immediately."

"Rubbish!"

She giggles. "I'm here, aren't I?"

And she is. She really, truly is. And when, a little time later, she turns to him and says, "So which one's your tent then?" he's on his feet instantly. He's let her get away once today; he's certainly not going to make that mistake again.

*

Julie and Michael looked at each other in the light of another set of flames and smiled at the memories.

"Did we know, do you think?" she asked him softly. "Did we know right then that we'd be sitting here in our own garden thirty-five years later with three grown-up kids and a grandchild in the offing?"

"And that we'd nearly throw it all away because, despite living in the same house, we were less able to tell each other what we wanted than on the first night we met?" He kissed her, and then they drew apart and looked at each other in the firelight. "Thank God for lockdown. I don't think I've ever traveled further than in the last four weeks stuck in here."

"Me neither. And just in time for our thirty-fifth wedding anniversary too."

"About that," Michael said. "I have an idea..."

Chapter Thirty-Four

Day Twenty-Nine

"Turn your video on, Mum."

"What?"

"Your video. Turn it on. It's the button at the top... that's it. Hi!"

Bett beamed. "Michael, hello! Oh, and the rest of you too. Isn't this clever? Sophie—cooee! I hear I'm going to be a great-granny. How wonderful is that? Carol and Liz are so jealous. I'm distilling a special batch of gin. I'm going to call it Baby Bath. Good, hey?"

"Brilliant, Granny," Sophie agreed from her little square, where she was cuddled up with Leo.

"Briony!" Bett went on, apparently working her way across the screen. "How are you, sweetheart? Getting any closer to a vaccine yet? Lord knows we need it. I so want to see you all. Carol and Liz are brilliant but they're not, you know, family."

"We're doing our best, Granny."

"She's working far too hard," Julie said.

"Good," Bett replied robustly. "A brain like that needs to be worked hard." Adam laughed and she swung her laser-like gaze round to him. "I hope you're making productive use of your time in lockdown, young man."

"Not really, Granny, unless you count making TikTok videos."

Bett considered. "I do actually. Very entertaining, some of those are. I'll look up your account and see how you match up."

Adam's eyes visibly goggled and everyone laughed. The last box on the screen opened up and Clare waved self-consciously. Next to her was a handsome Indian man.

"Dharmesh?" Julie hazarded.

"That's me," he agreed, with a matching wave.

"That doesn't look like social distancing, Auntie Clare," Sophie said, but her eyes were twinkling.

"It's not," Clare agreed happily. "But we're a household, so it's fine."

"He's moved in?" Julie gasped. "Sorry, I mean, you've moved in, Dharmesh? With Clare? You're a brave man."

Dharmesh put an arm around Clare and grinned. "There are benefits."

"Yuck!" Adam cried. "You lot are far too old for that sort of thing."

"We are not," Clare and Dharmesh said roundly.

Julie and Michael couldn't resist looking at each other either, and Adam groaned.

"I do not need to know this stuff! You're my mum and dad."

"But we're a couple too," Michael told him.

"Which, in case you'd forgotten," Julie added, "is precisely why we're all here. Sorry we've had to do it this way, but needs must and we promise we'll have a proper party when we're all finally allowed to be together again. But for now, if you don't mind, we wanted to share this with you."

She and Michael stepped back from the computer and faced each other. It was a little odd, a little silly maybe, but it was important. They'd said so much to each other over these last ten days since they burnt the divorce papers, but there was some stuff that needed to be shared.

Julie started, blushing and stuttering slightly but determined: "Michael Marshall, on this our thirty-fifth wedding anniversary, I vow to love you, to respect you and to go out on Gertie with you. I vow to tell you what's going on inside my stupid tangled-up head and I vow, at least once a week, to be still with you. To just *be* with you—because from the moment I first saw you, that's all I've ever really wanted."

Michael bent and kissed her.

"Oi!" Briony protested. "Are you allowed to do that yet?"

Michael waved her away. "We're old—we can do what we want!"

"Hear, hear!" Bett cried.

Michael faced Julie. "Julie Marshall, on this our thirty-fifth wedding anniversary, I vow to love you, to respect you and to visit your beautiful flower shop at least once a week. I vow to listen to all that you tell me and I vow to hold you in my heart forever more, because, without you there, I'm not sure it would even be able to beat."

"That's so lovely," Sophie said, followed swiftly by Adam, crowing, "Sophie's crying!"

"It's the baby," Sophie said, hastily wiping her eyes. "It does that to you."

"It certainly does," Julie agreed. She looked at them all. "Children are a gift."

"Especially when they're as wonderful as us," Adam suggested.

"Especially then, yes. But they don't half get in the way too."

"Oi!"

"Sorry, guys," Michael said. "Your mother's right—though I think we did our fair share of getting in each other's way too."

They looked at each other and kissed.

"But no more!" Julie said. "Now, everyone got a glass?"

"Yep!" came the chorus.

273

"And our own bubbles too this time," Briony said. "All that mock-drinking for Sophie's baby was horribly tantalizing."

"Good. So, if you could raise your glasses..."

"Hang on a minute," Sophie said. "You've got to cut the cake."

"What cake?"

Sophie pulled her camera back, and there in front of them was a beautiful cake, decorated all over with flowers and with a marzipan motorbike on top.

"Oh Sophie, that's amazing!"

"Leo made it," Sophie admitted. "It's carrot."

"Of course it is."

"With a bacon side," Leo laughed, nudging his wife, who happily stuck her tongue out at him.

"Here," she said to the screen, "virtual cut." She held the knife out, and Julie and Michael obligingly made a show of holding it.

"Make a wish!" Leo said.

Julie and Michael looked at each other.

"Greece?" she said.

He nodded. "Greece!"

And together they pushed down their hands as, across electronic space, Sophie made the cut for them.

"And now raise your glasses—"

"Hang on!" Adam had produced a guitar. "I have a song for you."

"No!" Sophie cried. "Don't sing, Adam."

Adam grinned. "It's not just me. Bri?"

And together they launched into a near-perfect rendition of "All You Need Is Love." Julie cried. Michael got something in his eye.

"You must have rehearsed that loads."

"Not loads, Mum. We're just very talented."

"Must be your genes."

"Must be. And *now* we can raise our glasses."

Frothing glasses were lifted to the screen.

"Happy anniversary!" chorused everyone. "Happy thirty-fifth anniversary."

"Best one yet!" Michael told them.

"Best one yet," Julie agreed.

It didn't last long. Zoom parties weren't as sustainable as real ones and all too soon the little squares went blank as the family were locked down again.

"I can't wait to see them all for real," Julie said to Michael.

"Me neither," he agreed, cuddling her close. "But for now, it's not so bad, is it, just the two of us?"

"For now," Julie said, kissing him, "it's perfect."

Reading Group Guide

Discussion Questions

First off, if you're reading *Just the Two of Us* as part of a book group, then a huge *thank you*. I really hope that you all enjoy it. I'm honored to give you an excuse to meet your friends and hope that my novel serves to provoke a few interesting discussions. On that note, here are some things that got me thinking as I was writing *Just the Two of Us*, and might spark some conversation for you, too:

1. Julie and Michael only find a way back to each other once the distractions of modern life are taken away from them. What kind of distractions do you face on a daily or weekly basis? Do you feel that as a society, we fill our days too full?

2. Julie is distressed when lockdown prevents her from going to her beloved flower shop. How much of our identity is connected to our work? To being a parent? And is the amount a good thing?

3. One of the key benchmarks in the decline of Julie and Michael's relationship is when they stop sleeping in the same room. How important is sharing a bed to maintaining

a good marriage? And in what ways— including, but definitely not limited to, the obvious one of sex.

4. Michael finds freedom and peace in his motorbike. What activities offer that to you?

5. It's a big shock to Julie when Adam chooses to stay with his girlfriend's family instead of his own and an even bigger one when he foolishly lets slip that he finds Chelsea's parents both more "normal" and more "fun" than his own. How hard is it when—via friendships, step-relationships, or potential in-laws—children start to have other families to compare to their own? Can it make parents' "quirks" become "oddities"?!

6. *Just the Two of Us* portrays a British experience of lockdown, but COVID-19 was such a global experience. How do you think it has affected the world, both practically and emotionally?

7. One of the things that brings Julie and Michael closer is discovering relics of previous, happier times in their relationship, such as Julie's biker jacket. What tangible reminders of happy times do you cherish?

8. *Just the Two of Us* is written from both Julie's and Michael's points of view. Do you like dual viewpoint novels? What other ones have you enjoyed? And what do you think a dual viewpoint adds to the reader's experience?

9. The family communicates throughout lockdown via Zoom or video chats, with varying success. Do you love video calls or hate them? How important is personal interaction and physical contact?

10. Michael objects to being called a "boomer"—a term often used, especially by the young, in a slightly derogatory

way. Is it right to categorize people by age this way? How can it help us? And what harm can it do?

11. At the end of the novel, Michael and Julie renew their vows. Is that something you would ever consider?

12. Ultimately, Michael and Julie find each other again when they take the time to talk about both the tough stuff they've put each other through and the happy stuff they once shared. How can we all find more time to talk to each other? (Book groups are a great start!)

Acknowledgments

COVID-19 has turned all our worlds upside down, and rarely in happy ways, so I will always be thankful that for me, at least, one good thing came out of it—this novel. The horrors of the virus, of lockdown, and of all that it has meant for us cannot be downplayed but it has also brought great love, patience and kindness to society and, perhaps, as with Julie and Michael's story, some healing as well. Life is lived at such a fast pace these days that the chance to slow down and reflect may have been of benefit to many. I hope that *Just the Two of Us* explores that in a positive way.

All novels are very much a team effort but this one perhaps more so than most and my heartfelt thanks goes to Hannah Wann for her amazingly insightful and incredibly fast editing. Between us, we wrote and polished Julie and Michael's story in 6 weeks; it was an intense and exciting project which I most definitely could not have done without her. Thanks must also go to the fabulous Anna Boatman for her supportive part in the process and the brilliant Jess Gulliver for taking the book forward into the public domain. The team at Piatkus are so enthusiastic, energetic and engaged and I'm honored to be a part of their work.

It's so thrilling to me to now also see *Just the Two of Us* going out to American readers and I owe a huge debt of gratitude to Junessa, Leah, Sabrina, and everyone at Forever for their wonderful work on making the novel US–ready and breathing new life into it for 2022. It's been an honour and a pleasure to work with you all. Thank you.

As always, I owe a huge shout out to my family for backing me all the way. This time, however, I need to offer especial thanks to my team of locked-down kids who took on not just the cooking but the cleaning so I could write more—and did it far better than I ever do too! Thank you Rory, Hannah and Alec. My wonderful husband, Stuart, has also been his usual supportive self—always ready with a listening ear, a wise thought and a small whisky . . . Additional thanks to my lovely Dad and sister for being such speedy and helpful beta readers.

This novel is dedicated to the Hunters—Sarah-Jane, Paul, Ella and Joe. We met this fabulous family on a camping holiday in 2008 when our similarly aged daughters fell out at kids club. Luckily the girls soon became best of friends, as did the families, and we have had so many happy holidays under canvas together since. Here's to many more when we're all allowed out again!

It would be wrong to let this lockdown-based novel pass without a huge shout out to all the amazing key workers who've been keeping this country going under such tough conditions—the doctors and nurses, the care-home workers, the scientists, the delivery drivers, the postmen and women, the rubbish collectors, the emergency services. The list could go on and on and I apologize for any I've missed but you all have my gratitude. Just sitting safely inside writing a book pales into insignificance in comparison to all you've done.

A final thank you to my tireless agent Kate Shaw for her continued work on my behalf and, of course, to all my readers.

I genuinely struggle to understand how anyone could survive the chaos and heartbreak of lockdown—or indeed life generally—without recourse to fiction and am very grateful to anyone who chooses to spend a little of their time in the world of *Just the Two of Us*. Do please get in touch via @jowildeauthor on either Twitter or Facebook. I'd love to hear from you.

About the Author

Jo Wilde considers herself a proud Midlander (despite being told by a university friend that "the Midlands" doesn't exist) and loves living in her Derbyshire village with her two children, two stepchildren, two hamsters, two dogs and—thankfully—one husband. To be fair, with the children now largely grown up, they only live with her intermittently when their own money and supply of booze runs out. Upon retirement, Jo and her husband plan to take off in a mobile home (or, in her mind, a mobile writing office) to see the world.

In the meantime, Jo's very happy with imaginary worlds and has now published a range of fiction, including historical novels as Joanna Courtney and contemporary fiction as Anna Stuart.